"Don't do this, Rosemary," he said.

"Don't punish yourself or me this way. Think about us. Think about this." He reached out a hand. "Put your hand in mine."

"No," she said, a plea in the one word. "I can't."

"Rosemary, God doesn't want you to be alone. He's not cruel that way. Together, with His guidance, we can figure this out."

"No," she said again, her heart breaking. "Let's just leave it the way it is. Go," she whispered. "Before we wake my father."

"I'll wake him," Kirk replied, angry now. "I'll wake this whole town and tell all of them that I care about you and I want to be with you and there's nothing wrong with that."

Hearing him say the words aloud made her realize she felt the same way. But she was still afraid to make good on her feelings. Yet she knew Kirk was right. She had asked God to forgive her, to give her a second chance. Maybe this was that chance.

Slowly she reached out her hand to him. Kirk pressed his hand to hers, his eyes searching her face in the moonlight.

"Tell me you'll pray about this, Rosemary. Promise me you'll ask God to guide us."

"I will," she said, meaning it. "I'm asking Him right this very minute...."

LENORA WORTH

grew up in a small Georgia town and decided in the fourth grade that she wanted to write. But first, she married her high school sweetheart, then moved to Atlanta, Georgia. Taking care of their baby daughter at home while her husband worked at night, Lenora discovered the world of romance novels and knew that's what she wanted to write. And so she began.

A few years later, the family settled in Shreveport, Louisiana, where Lenora continued to write while working as a marketing assistant. After the birth of her second child, a boy, she decided to pursue full time her dream of writing. In 1993, Lenora's hard work and determination finally paid off with that first sale.

"I never gave up, and I believe my faith in God helped get me through the rough times when I doubted myself," Lenora says. "Each time I start a new book, I say a prayer, asking God to give me the strength and direction to put the words to paper. That's why I'm so thrilled to be a part of Steeple Hill's Love Inspired line, where I get to combine my faith in God with my love of romance. It's the best possible combination."

The Wedding Quilt

Lenora Worth

Love Inspired™

Published by Steeple Hill Books™

STEEPLE HILL BOOKS

Steeple Hill™

ISBN 0-373-87012-4

THE WEDDING QUILT

"To everything there is a season, a time for every purpose under heaven."

—*Ecclesiastes* 3:1

To my sister, Glenda, who died from a wreck involving a drunk driver in 1991. We all miss you still.

To Suzannah, a friend who believed in the good in me and taught me so much about courage and dignity.

And especially...to my niece Crystal Howell Smith. Hope this helps to ease your pain.

Chapter One

"To everything there is a season, a time for every purpose under heaven."

Rosemary Brinson read the familiar words of Ecclesiastes and took comfort in the sure knowledge that God was watching over her, and that a new season was on its way.

Today would be different. Today was a new beginning, Rosemary decided as she gazed out her kitchen window, toward the tall spire of the First United Methodist Church of Alba Mountain, Georgia.

Today the steeplejack was coming.

Everyone was talking about Kirk Lawrence, the man Rosemary had personally hired, sight unseen, to come to the little mountain town of Alba to restore the fifty-foot-tall steeple of the one-hundred-and-fifty-year-old church, as well as renovate the church building itself. The small-town gossip mill had cast Kirk Lawrence to heroic proportions. From what Rosemary had found while doing phone interviews and research on-line, the man could leap tall buildings with a single bound, provided he had a good pulley and a strong rope and cable, of course.

In spite of her pragmatic, levelheaded approach to hiring the steeplejack, Rosemary couldn't help feeling the same excitement as the townspeople. She'd last spoken to Kirk Lawrence two days ago, and she still remembered the way his lyrical accent had sent goose bumps up and down her spine.

"I'll be arriving sometime, probably late afternoon, on Monday, Ms. Brinson. I've studied the plans and the photographs you sent me, and I do believe I can have your church looking brand-new in a few weeks. I look forward to taking on the task."

"Please, call me Rosemary," she'd stammered, in spite of trying to sound professional and all-business. "And you're sure you don't need a place to stay?"

"No, I have my trailer. I'll be comfortable there." A slight pause, then, "It's home, after all."

Home. A travel trailer with another trailer full of equipment attached to it. What kind of home was that?

"The kind a wandering soul likes to hang out in," she reminded herself now as she finished her toast and mayhaw jelly. "Apparently, our steeplejack likes to travel light."

She was still amazed that the church board had agreed to let her use such an unusual, yet highly traditional, means of doing the work on the steeple. The old-timers had balked at first, but once Rosemary had convinced them that a steeplejack would be much more thorough and less expensive than cranes and scaffolding, they'd reconsidered and voted to back her.

"We have you to thank, Rosemary," the Reverend Clancy had told her yesterday as she'd closed down the church day care attached to the educational building across from the main sanctuary. "We'da never raised all that money without you in charge of the committee. You sure know how to get things done."

"Only because I wanted this so much, Preacher," she'd replied. "This church means a lot to this town, and to me. We have to preserve it."

This morning, as she stood sipping the last of her coffee before heading off to her job as director of education for the church school, she had to wonder why she'd poured her heart into renovating the old Gothic-designed church.

Maybe it was because she'd been christened there as a baby, as had her older brother, Danny. Maybe it was because Danny had married his high-school sweetheart there, and Reverend Clancy had christened Danny's new daughter, Emily, within the peaceful confines of the spacious sanctuary, illuminated all around by beautiful stained-glass windows. They'd been members of the church all of their lives, after all.

Maybe it was because Rosemary had sat there, through her mother's funeral last year, and somehow, she'd survived a grief so brutal, so consuming, that she wanted the church that had held her in its arms to survive, too.

Or maybe she'd taken on the task of renovating the old church because she needed to stay busy at something tangible, something worth fighting for, something that would bring about hope and rebirth, instead of despair and death.

Pushing away thoughts of the past year's unhappiness, Rosemary turned around to find her father staring at her with the dull, vacant look she'd come to recognize and dread.

"Coffee, Dad?" she asked as she automatically

headed for the cabinet by the sink to get a cup. "Your toast is on the stove. Would you like a scrambled egg with it?"

Clayton Brinson stood just inside the kitchen door, his bloodshot gray eyes wandering over the bright, sunny kitchen as if in search of something, someone. He wore old, worn khaki work pants, left over from his thirty years as a line supervisor at the local manufacturing company, and a once-white ribbed undershirt that stretched across the noticeable paunch hanging over his empty belt loops. His sparse salt-and-pepper hair stood out in stubborn tufts on his receding hairline, its determined stance as stoic and firm as the man who refused to comb it—the man who refused to accept that his wife was dead and gone, the man who refused to even get dressed most mornings, who blamed God and his daughter for the death of his beloved wife, Eunice.

"Toast and coffee, girl," he said in a gruff, early-morning voice. "How many times do I have to tell you, that's all I ever want for breakfast?"

Rosemary didn't reply. She was used to her father's cold nature and curt remarks. It was, after all, part of the punishment, part of the penance she must endure. That she must endure was an unspoken agreement between the shell of the man to whom she'd once been so close and the shell of the woman she'd become.

Clayton had always been a hard, distant man. Strong, hardworking, a good father and husband, he'd never fully understood her mother's devotion to the church. But because he loved Eunice, because she made him smile and laugh, he'd indulged her by dutifully attending services and giving money to the church. The pretense had ended with her death, though. Clayton existed these days on bitterness and loneliness, but

Rosemary refused to give in or give up on Clayton. God would lead him home. She knew this in her heart. This morning, she'd asked for patience to see her father through, and guidance for herself. And she remembered how things once were.

Once, not so very long ago, her father would have bounded into the kitchen with a cheerful smile plastered on his face, to demand his eggs and grits. Once, her mother would have been standing at this window, admiring the spire of her church down the street, thanking God for the new day.

Eunice would have turned to lift a dark eyebrow at her husband. "Hungry this morning, Clayton?"

"Yep, and in a hurry. Got things to do down at the mill. A man's work never ends."

"Nor does a woman's."

Once, Rosemary would have come up on this scene, and she would have smiled at the good-natured bantering between her parents, before she'd gone off to school, or later, after work. Even after she'd moved out of the house to attend college, and then later to live in her own garage apartment just down the street, she could always count on finding her mother in the kitchen with a fresh-baked pie and her father humming and nuzzling her mother's slender neck before he headed off to work.

Once, her father would have greeted her with a smile and a kiss, and a teasing, "Found a fellow yet?"

Once.

As she searched the refrigerator for the raspberry jam her father liked on his toast, she thought about the fellow she'd found and lost, and thought about the life she'd planned with that same fellow, and lost.

"Here's your toast, Dad," she said as she set the plate in front of him. "I'll see you at lunch."

"And don't be late today," he called without looking up. "Twelve noon, girl."

"I won't. I'll be here at five till."

She escaped the house, her breath coming deep and long to take in the fresh air of the coming spring. The nearby foothills were near bursting with it, their greens as fresh as mint, their white dogwood blossoms as delicate as fine lace. A new beginning. A new season.

This morning, this fine new spring morning, Rosemary Brinson looked to God to show her what her purpose was, and asked Him to help her find a new season. She needed a time to heal.

Then she looked up at the towering, ornamental spire of her church and reminded herself—today would be different.

Today, the steeplejack was coming.

In spite of herself, she couldn't wait to meet him.

Kirk Lawrence turned his rig off Highway 441 to follow the Welcome sign to Alba Mountain, Georgia, population ten thousand. He couldn't wait to get started on the renovations for the First United Methodist Church of Alba Mountain. As always, he felt the hum of a challenge, felt the rush of adrenaline a new job always brought, felt the nudge of a new town, with new faces, calling to him.

Alba had called him just as he was finishing work on a two-hundred-year-old church in Maryland. Alba, or Alba Mountain, depending on whom you were talking to, was a small town on the southern edge of the Blue Ridge Mountains, just about seventy-five miles north of Atlanta. Alba, homesite to some of his own

Scotch-Irish ancestors, the highlanders of north Georgia, who'd come from Europe centuries ago to find a new beginning on these rugged foothills and mountains. This would be interesting, to say the least.

Kirk loved to wander around almost as much as he loved his work. The work he could trace back to his great-grandfather, Ian Dempsey, on his mother's side, in his native Ireland. The wanderlust...well, he supposed he'd gotten that from some nomadic ancestor, or from his American father who'd come to Ireland for a vacation more than twenty-five years ago, and stayed to marry a local lass. Or maybe the need to keep moving was all Kirk's alone, since he'd grown up in a small village in county Cork. It really didn't matter. He liked his life and he liked his work, and all was right with his world.

A voice echoed in his head as he searched the street names for Crape Myrtle Avenue.

"And you're sure you don't need a place to stay?"

Rosemary Brinson. Rosemary. Pretty name. It meant unspoiled in Latin, but it could mean several different things in modern society. This particular Rosemary had a slow, soft southern accent that flowed through the telephone like a warm summer rain. Kirk was anxious to put a face to that voice, anxious to meet the woman who'd fought a whole congregation to get him here, because she believed in doing things the right way.

"Well, Rosemary, me darlin', so do I."

That much they had in common. And that would be all, as far as Kirk was concerned. No, Rosemary, he didn't need a place to stay, because no one ever really expected him *to stay*. Kirk had just enough single-minded intent to know that he'd come here with one purpose, and one purpose only. He was a steeplejack.

He repaired steeples, working quickly, accurately and artistically, to make something lasting and beautiful out of wood and mortar and stained glass and stone.

God had given him the talent, and his grandfather had given him the technique, or so his mother still reminded him. He didn't take either for granted.

And he had one very important rule. Never get involved with the townspeople, or their problems or their plans. He wasn't a healer, after all. Just a fixer. He simply liked to restore things to their proper beauty.

To Kirk, that made all the difference.

But then, Kirk had never heard a voice quite like Rosemary Brinson's.

And, he'd never ventured this far south before.

In spite of himself, he couldn't wait to meet her.

Rosemary's voice grew lower with each beat of the favorite children's story she read to the preschoolers. All around the darkened room, small bodies stretched out on colorful mats, their little stockinged feet resting after a morning of running at full throttle on nursery rhymes and building blocks. As Rosemary finished the story, a collective sigh seemed to waft out over the long, cool, colorful nursery.

"I think you've sent them off to dreamland," her aide, Melissa Roberts, whispered softly as she sat down to take over so Rosemary could take a much-needed lunch hour.

Rosemary's own sigh followed that of the steadily breathing children. "Whew, I'm tired! They were in rare form this morning. Must be spring, giving them so much energy."

"Or maybe they've picked up on all the talk," Melissa said, her eyes wide and sincere. "You know...about the steeplejack."

"Could be," Rosemary said, rising quietly to tiptoe to the door. "I've tried to explain exactly what a steeplejack is, but they can't seem to grasp it."

"Just tell them he's a superhero who climbs church steeples," Melissa suggested, laughing as she waved Rosemary out the door. "Go on home and try to rest."

Rosemary wished she could rest, but home wasn't the place for that precious commodity. Bracing herself for her father's cold reception, she started out the door of the educational building, only to be waylaid by the church secretary, Faye Lewis.

"He's here," Faye, a petite, gray-haired woman with big brown eyes, hissed as she hurried toward Rosemary as fast as her sneakers could carry her. "You've got to come and see to him, Rosemary. Reverend Clancy's already gone home for his nap."

"See to who?" Rosemary asked, then her heart stopped. "The steeplejack? Is he here already?"

"Oh, yes," Faye said, her smile slicing through her wrinkled face. "And quite a handsome... devil...excuse the expression."

Rosemary groaned, then looked down the street toward the rambling white house she shared with her father. "Why'd he have to show up just at lunchtime? Dad will be furious if I'm late."

Faye gave Rosemary an exasperated look. "Well, just tell Clayton that you had something important to tend to. Surely the man can fix himself a sandwich this once."

"Yes, but you know he expects me to be there right at noon," Rosemary replied, already headed toward the

main office, which, along with the educational building, was set apart from the original old church.

"Do you want me to call your father and explain?"
Faye asked, a look of understanding moving across her
features.

"Would you?" Rosemary hated having someone run
interference with her father, but Faye was one of the
few people Clayton respected and treated with a fair
amount of decency. "Tell him I'll be a few minutes
late, but I'll be there as soon as I can."

Faye nodded, then shoved Rosemary into the plush
office reception room where a tall, blue-jeans-clad man
stood looking out the wide arched window that faced
the church.

Taking a quiet, calming breath, Rosemary said, "Mr.
Lawrence?"

Kirk Lawrence turned around to find the source of
that soft whispery voice and was at once hit with a
current so strong, he wondered if there was a kinetic
energy moving through the room. He didn't need to
know her name to know this was Rosemary Brinson.

Long swirls of chestnut-hued hair, curly to the point
of being unruly, caught up with twin pearl-encrusted
clips in a sensible yet attractive style, off a face that
was oval in shape. Her face was youthful, yet aged,
touched by the sun, yet fresh and new-blooming, with
eyes that darkened to a deep blue underneath arched
eyebrows the exact color of her hair. Her smile was
demure, while her expression was...hopeful and hesitant all at the same time.

She was lovely.

"You must be Rosemary," he managed to say as he
held out a hand to take the one she offered him.

She wore a bright pink cotton top with a long, flowing floral skirt that swirled around her legs as she stepped forward. A cloud of perfume as delicate as the scent of honeysuckle preceded her touch on his hand.

"That's me," she managed to say through a shy smile. "It's good to finally meet you, Mr. Lawrence."

Rosemary gave him a direct look, all the while thinking that Faye had been right. He was handsome, all right. Dark swirling hair, as close to black as she'd ever seen. When he smiled, his thick eyebrows jutted up like wings, giving him that certain appeal Faye had mentioned. But his eyes, they held Rosemary, causing her to stare at him. Their bright, clear color sharply contrasted with his tanned skin. She couldn't decide if they were green or blue, but whatever color they might be called, his eyes were deep and luminous and…knowing. He had the eyes of an old soul, as her mother used to say.

Realizing that she was staring, Rosemary let go of the warm hand holding hers. "Did you have any trouble finding us?"

"No, none at all," he said, wrapping his arms across his chest in a defensive manner. "I just followed the steeple."

That brought her attention back to the task he'd come here for. "Yes, it's hard to miss, isn't it?"

Together, they both looked out the window, up at the stark brown and gray stone of the rising bell tower that heralded the church from miles around.

"It's beautiful," Kirk said, meaning it. "I can see where you'd want to preserve it—those stones need a bit of cleaning and scrubbing, now, don't they?"

"Yes," she said, glad he understood the job ahead. "They came all the way from Dahlonega—granite with a little fool's gold mixed in."

"A sound combination, no doubt." He grinned over at her. "I've never been to Dahlonega. Hope to see it while I'm here, and I want to climb Alba Mountain, too. I hear Georgia is a lovely state."

She looked away from that intense set of eyes. "Not as pretty as Ireland, though, I'll bet."

"Ireland is a land all its own," he admitted, "but I haven't been there in a long, long time. My parents moved back to the States when I was in high school, and I came with them, thinking to get my college education in America. But I was a bit rebellious, I'm afraid." He looked sheepish, at least. "I went back to Europe, and I wound up in Sheffield, England, at Whirlow College. I got my degree there, mainly because they offered the courses I needed to be a steeplejack. I worked with my grandfather until his death, then I came back to America. I haven't been back to Ireland or England since."

She wanted to ask why, but manners kept her from doing so. "You've traveled all over the place, from what I saw on your résumé."

"I've seen the world." He turned away from the window. "And now, I've come to see Alba. If you'd just show me where to park my trailer—"

"I'm sorry," she said, snapping to attention. "The preacher is at lunch and I was just on my way home for a quick bite. Are you hungry?"

"Are you offering?"

Liking the way he lifted those dark eyebrows with each statement or question, she nodded. "I think I can manage a sandwich, at least. Of course, I need to warn you to save room for supper tonight."

"Oh, are you inviting me then?"

Mmm, that accent was so pleasing to her ears. "Yes,

but we won't be alone. The entire town's turning out for a supper on the grounds, to honor you and to officially begin the renovations on the church, sort of a celebration.''

He followed her out the door, then up the sidewalk. "I've heard about southern hospitality. Now I suppose I get to see it firsthand."

"You won't forget it. You'll go to bed with a full stomach, that's for sure."

Noticing his trailer and attached rig, she pointed to a clump of trees at the back of the church grounds. "You can park there. There are a couple of camper hookups we use for visitors—campers coming through to hike the mountain trails."

"How generous."

"Reverend Clancy figures if we treat them right, they'll stay for one of his sermons."

"Ah, tricky, but effective."

"Yes." She nodded. "Sometimes they stay, sometimes they leave. But they're always welcome."

Kirk eyed the little copse of trees settled at the foot of a rounded upward-sloping hillside. Tall swaying pines and fat, mushrooming oaks made a canopy over the area. It was an inviting spot, complete with a rustic picnic table and just-budding daylilies. It would do nicely for his stay here.

Rosemary watched his expression as he took in his surroundings. Then she touched his arm. "That's my house, over there. C'mon, I'll fix you that sandwich I promised."

Kirk looked up at the whitewashed wooden house standing down the street from the church. He studied the house as they approached. It had that certain charm he associated with the South—long wraparound

porches, a swing hanging from rusty chains, two
cane-back rocking chairs, lush ferns sprouting from
aged clay pots, geraniums in twin white planters—and
shuttered, closed windows.

"It's a beautiful place, Rosemary."

"Yes, it is," she had to agree. "Or at least, it once
was."

She saw him eyeing the shuttered, dark windows,
and she knew exactly what he was thinking.

Why would such a lovely, sunny, open home be
closed up and so sad-looking?

She wasn't ready to tell him why.

She didn't have to. As they stepped up onto the
porch, the front door burst open, and her father's angry
voice told Kirk Lawrence everything he needed to
know.

"Where have you been? It's almost twelve-thirty. A
man could starve to death waiting on you, Rosemary.
How many times have I told you—I like to eat my
lunch at twelve o'clock! Your mother always had it
ready right at twelve noon. Now get in here and get
me some food."

Shocked at the harsh tone the man had used, Kirk
stood with one foot on a step and one on the stone
walkway. Maybe now wasn't the time to get to know
his new employer.

Humiliated, Rosemary turned to Kirk. "I'm sorry."

"You go on. I can wait," he said, not wanting to
intrude. "I'm really not that hungry."

"No, no," she said on a firm but quiet voice. "I
promised you a sandwich, and I intend to deliver on
that promise. Just let me take care of my father first."

Kirk stepped up onto the porch, his gaze on the
woman moving hurriedly before him. He had the feel-

ing that Rosemary Brinson always delivered on her promises, whether she wanted to or not.

Why else would she go into that house and face her father's wrath with such profound determination?

Chapter Two

Kirk watched as Rosemary made ham sandwiches with the efficiency of someone who took care of things with automatic precision. She went about her job with quiet dignity, slicing tomatoes to fall into a pretty pattern on an oval platter, then adding lettuce and pickles to finish off her creation. Then she lifted fat, white slices of bread out of a nearby bin and arranged them on another plate, along with the pink country-cured ham she'd already neatly sliced.

"It's ready," she announced to her father who sat across from Kirk nursing a tall glass of iced tea. "Do you want anything else with your sandwich—chips or some sliced cucumbers maybe?"

The man she had introduced as Clayton Brinson didn't immediately answer his waiting daughter. Instead, he frowned while he pieced together a sandwich on his plate. Then he looked up with harsh, deep-set eyes. "Your mother never slapped a sandwich together. She always had fresh *cooked* vegetables on the table."

"Mother didn't work outside the home either,

Daddy," she reminded him patiently. "I do what I can, but you're right. Tonight at supper, I'll make sure you have your vegetables."

Clayton's look softened to a slight scowl. "Well, some dessert would be nice, too. A peach pie, maybe."

Rosemary sat down with an abrupt swirl of her skirt, then handed Kirk the fixings for his own sandwich. "I'm sorry, Daddy, but I haven't had time to do anything with those canned peaches Joe Mason brought us yesterday. I'll try to get to it later this evening."

"They'll rot before you get to 'em," Clayton proclaimed before clamping his teeth down on his sandwich.

Rosemary looked down at her plate, then in a surprising move, clasped her hands together and said a quick blessing.

Kirk saw the look of disgust on her father's stern face, and said his own silent prayer. He didn't want to slap this man he'd just met, but it was very tempting.

But Rosemary didn't seem to need his help in defending herself. She fixed her own meal, then looked over at her father with compassionate, if not somewhat impatient, eyes. "I'll make you a pie, Daddy. I promise. You know I wouldn't let those peaches go to waste. I love peaches." Turning to Kirk, she gave him a quick smile. "Georgia peaches, just like Georgia tomatoes, are the best in the world, Kirk."

"Then I'll look forward to that pie myself," he replied, glad that she'd smoothed over the awkward rudeness her father didn't try to hide. Kirk chewed a big hunk of sandwich, then nodded. "The tomatoes are very good."

Out of the blue, Clayton spoke directly to Kirk for the first time. "Seems a waste to me—bringing you in special to fix that old steeple. Let the thing crumble, is what I say. A waste of time and money.''

Rosemary shot Kirk an apologetic look. ''Actually, Dad was on the board that voted to renovate the church, but that was a couple of years ago. Now…Dad doesn't support any of our church activities, especially the ones I'm involved in.''

Clayton threw his sandwich down. ''And we both know why, don't we, girl?''

Rosemary's hiss of breath was the only indication that her father's sharp words had gotten to her. She remained perfectly calm, keeping her attention on her plate as she toyed with a slice of tomato to hide the apparent shame her father seemed determined to heap upon her.

Wanting to shield her from any further tirades, Kirk looked across at her father. ''Mr. Brinson, your church is one of the finest historic buildings I've seen, and I've seen a lot of churches and cathedrals both here in America and all across Europe. The people who built your sanctuary did it the right way, it's as solid now as it was the day it was finished. You don't see that kind of craftsmanship much anymore. I've studied the layout from the pictures your daughter sent me, and I'm amazed…each joint and bent is intricately crafted with mortise and tenon joined together without the benefit of nails.'' He paused, then looked thoughtful. ''It's almost as if the church was built on spirit and determination alone. And I intend to make sure that spirit is sound and intact.''

Clayton glared across at the stranger sitting at his table, then huffed a snort. ''Foolishness, pure foolishness, to waste over forty thousand dollars on a face-lift for the church. If it was built to last, then leave it alone!''

"Daddy!'' Embarrassed, Rosemary touched her father on the arm in warning. "Can we talk about something else?''

"I'm through talking,'' Clayton replied, then standing, he yanked up his plate and drink. "I'm going to watch television.'' With that, he stomped out of the room, leaving an awkward silence in his wake.

Kirk realized two things, sitting there at that round little oak table in Rosemary's clean kitchen. One, he was more determined than ever to get his job done and done right, just to prove her father wrong. He was like that; he'd always risen to a challenge, and winning this man over would be a big one. And two, he did not like this man's hateful, hostile attitude toward his lovely, angel-faced daughter. In fact, with just a little encouragement, he would gladly be willing to do something about changing it.

Right now, however, the only thing he could do was try to make Rosemary's beautiful smile return to her pale, drawn face. "Was it something I said?''

She did smile, but it was a self-deprecating tug instead of a real smile, and he didn't miss the raw pain hidden beneath the effort.

"No, it was something *I did*.'' Sending him a pleading look, she added, "He wasn't always this bad. It's just...we lost my mother over a year ago, and he's still not over her death. I do apologize for the way he's treated you.''

"I'm sorry...about your mother, and I understand,'' he said, but really, he didn't understand. Losing a loved one was always painful as he well remembered when he'd lost his grandfather a few years ago, but this anguish seemed to run much deeper than normal grief. Most families turned to each other in times of grief and loss. Rosemary's father obviously hadn't come to terms with losing his wife, but why was he taking it out on his daughter? Kirk had to wonder what had happened between these two to make one so sad and noble, and the other so bitter and harsh.

But, Kirk reminded himself too late, *you can't get involved in whatever is brewing between them. Just do your work, man, then leave.*

When he looked up, Rosemary was watching him with those beautiful blue eyes, her gaze searching for both retribution and condemnation. He gave her neither—her father was doing enough of that. Because Kirk didn't know what was going on, he smiled at her in an effort to comfort her. And somehow he knew, this time it was going to be different. This time, he just might have to get involved.

"Why didn't you simply explain things to him?" Melissa asked Rosemary later after she'd told her friend about the whole episode with her father.

They were sitting on a wooden bench out on the playground, watching the children as they scooted and swayed over the various climbing gyms and swings. Nearby, a tulip tree heralded spring with its bright orange and green flowers. The afternoon lifted out before them with a crisp, welcoming breeze that belied the turmoil boiling in Rosemary's heart.

"I can't get him involved in all that," Rosemary said, shaking her head. "He came here to work on the church, not its floundering members."

"Except your father hasn't set foot in this place in

over a year," Melissa reminded her in a sympathetic voice. "How can you stand it, Rosemary?"

"Living with him, you mean?" Rosemary sat back on the hand-carved bench, then sighed long and hard. "I still love him. And I know he's still grieving. I keep thinking one day I'll wake up and he'll be the father I always knew and loved...before all of this happened. One day..."

Her voice trailed off as she looked up at the towering steeple a few yards away. Amazed, she grabbed Melissa's arm, then held her breath. "Look!"

A lone figure moved up the steep side of the church's wide sloping shingled roofline, loping toward the center of the building.

"The steeplejack," Melissa said on her own breathless whisper. "He sure didn't waste any time."

"No, he didn't," Rosemary replied, her eyes taking in the lean lines of Kirk Lawrence's broad shoulders and athletic body. Not an ounce of fat anywhere on the man. And no wonder. He hopped and jumped over the roof like the superhero Melissa had called him, his long, muscular arms swinging from the rafters, so to speak, as he took his first close-up look at the thing he'd come to wrestle with.

The steeple was a mixture of several different levels and several different foundations. Set at the front of the broad, rectangular, Gothic church building, it started out with an open square belfry, made from the stone they'd discussed earlier, intertwined with sturdy, arched timber-framed beams that shot up to form a tier, like the bottom layer of a wedding cake, over which sat a smaller section with louvered openings surrounded by stained-glass partitions and a smaller version of the same arched wood pattern. That section lifted toward and supported a spire made of thick iron beams that formed the tall shingle-covered cone. This tier was followed by an ornamental rusty iron cross that extended three feet across and four feet up.

The long front of the church was made of the same stone facing as the belfry tower, mixed with the timber framing that the original congregation had made with heavy columns and beams, the arched pattern of the wood crisscrossing throughout the stones, following the same pattern of the tower's beams. The church was intact and sturdy; now it mostly needed scraping, painting, restaining and rustproofing. Which was why Rosemary had hired the steeplejack. He'd do most of it from his boatswain chair, inches at a time if necessary.

Kirk hauled himself up over one of the stone belfry walls, clinging precariously for a moment before lifting over into the open belfry room where an aged brass bell hung from a sturdy iron frame. From his vantage point, he looked out over the town, then down at the playground where Rosemary and Melissa, and now the children, watched him in fascinated wonder.

"Hello there," he called good-naturedly, waving toward them, then holding out both arms as if to say he'd just claimed this spot as his very own. "What a view!"

Rosemary didn't doubt that the view of the surrounding hills and mountains was impressive. She'd never been up in the belfry, but her brother, Danny, had climbed up there many times, and he'd told her he could see the whole town—indeed, the whole county—from there.

"It's Spiderman," a little boy called, jumping up and down in glee. "Miss Ruzmary, Miss Ruzmary, see Spiderman!"

"I see," Rosemary said, smiling up at Kirk before

returning his wave. Why hadn't he simply taken the narrow stone steps just inside the church narthex that led to the bell tower? "That makes me dizzy," she whispered to Melissa. "I've never been one for heights."

"I wouldn't mind getting up there with him," Melissa said, laughing.

"Melissa Roberts, you have a new boyfriend."

"Yes, but we're just good friends—really. And, your steeplejack is sure easy on the eyes. Not at all what we expected."

Rosemary had to agree with her. Kirk Lawrence was intriguing, good-looking and likable. And discreet. They'd talked at length for most of the afternoon, about his purpose here, about their mutual faith in God, about what the congregation expected from him, and he hadn't questioned her once about why her father had treated her in such an ugly way during lunch. For that alone, she appreciated him.

She'd expected a middle-aged, leathery, bowlegged monkey of a man to come and do this job. Instead, she'd gotten Tarzan himself, a man who was at once dangerous because of the profession he'd chosen, and noble for the very reasons he'd chosen this time-honored way of doing things. Knowing he didn't take shortcuts and that he was willing to risk everything for a dying art made her respect him even more.

"He's not *my* steeplejack," she said rather too defensively. "He'll be gone before we know it and all the excitement will die down."

"Then we'd better make the most of his visit," Melissa said, rising to check on a whining toddler.

Rosemary grinned at her blond-haired friend, then looked back up to where Kirk stood surveying the tower and steeple. He was stretched over the short belfry wall, perched with one arm wrapped around a fat stone-and-wood column as he viewed the perilous height of the spire above him. Rosemary wrapped her arms around her chest, fighting the goose bumps that had risen on her skin.

He turned to stare down at her for a long moment, then quickly got back to work, measuring and calculating.

As she just as quickly got back to her own work of watching the children she loved. Only she couldn't help but do some measuring and calculating of her own, from the corner of her eye—but her assessments had little to do with the wood and stone of the old steeple.

A few hours later, Rosemary walked into the living room of her home to find her father sitting in his usual spot in front of the television. Dan Rather was delivering an update of world events, and Clayton Brinson had the volume at full blast, as if he couldn't afford to miss a word of what the broadcaster was saying.

"I'm going to the church dinner now, Dad," she said as loudly as she could. "I left your supper on the stove—plenty of fresh-cooked vegetables to go with your fried ham. And—" she purposely came to stand in front of him now "—I made two peach pies. I'm taking one with me, and I left the other one for you. There's coffee on the stove."

Clayton's only response was a deep-throated grunt. He still wore his khakis and undershirt. He'd barely left this room all day.

Rosemary leaned down to place a small kiss on her father's forehead. "I'll be home early."

Clayton didn't move a muscle. He just sat with his

gaze fixed on the talking head on the television screen. His daughter walked out of the room and gathered her trays from the kitchen, then left.

Not until he'd heard the back door slam did Clayton turn, and then it was only to lower his head and close his eyes tightly shut. When he raised his head seconds later, his eyes were calm and cold again. He sat silent for a minute, then lifted a hand to touch the spot where his daughter had kissed him so tenderly.

"So you couldn't get the old rascal to come on over?" Faye Lewis asked Rosemary much later.

"No, of course not." Rosemary shook out the white cotton tablecloth to cover one of the many portable tables they'd brought out underneath the oaks and pines for a good, old-fashioned dinner on the grounds. "He can hear us from his vantage point—that is, if he turns down that television long enough to listen."

"I'll bet he'll listen," Faye said as she grasped the other end of the cloth to smooth it out. "He's been listening all along, he just can't hear in the same way."

"He's lost all hope, Faye," Rosemary said, her eyes scanning the growing crowd of church members and townspeople who'd turned out to meet the mysterious steeplejack. "And I'm about at the end of my rope."

"Steadfast, Rosemary," Faye reminded her. "Remember, 'for as much as ye know that your labor is not in vain in the Lord.' You're doing the right thing, the only thing you can for your daddy. You're standing firm in your faith. Clayton will see that in time, and he'll come around."

Rosemary appreciated Faye's gentle reminder. "I certainly hope so."

Faye patted the cloth into place then began placing

covered casserole dishes full of hot food on top of it. "Your father is a proud, stubborn man. He can't deal with his grief, but I must say I'm shocked that he'd fight against it this long, and in such an extreme way. Clayton and I were always so close—Eunice was my best friend, after all. I miss her, but my grief is different from your father's."

Rosemary glanced toward her house, then quickly began pulling disposable plates out of a large plastic bag. "No, you didn't turn away from God—or me—when it happened. Poor Dad, he used to be here every time the doors were open. He did it only to please Mother, though. He and Mom, with Danny and me trailing along."

A commotion toward the edge of the crowd caused her to put away painful thoughts of her now-shattered family. She looked up to see Kirk emerging from his little trailer. He wore a clean white button-down shirt, fresh jeans and brown suede laced boots. His dark hair looked damp from a shower. His smile was fresh and enticing. He was working the crowd.

She lifted an eyebrow when the older woman poked her in the ribs and whispered, "Cute, ain't he?"

"Yes. And charming. I've always heard Irishmen are very charming, and probably dangerous."

"Well, the insurance adjuster would agree with you there. I hear the hazards of his work make him expensive to underwrite. The steeplejack's occupation alone makes him dangerous, as far as having to pay out if he falls off that thing."

"He won't fall," Rosemary said, knowing it to be true.

Kirk Lawrence seemed as sure of himself as anyone she'd ever met. He had the grace of an acrobat, and the concentration of a neurosurgeon. She'd watched him working this afternoon, taking measurements, touching the ancient stones and splintered wood, almost cooing to the towering steeple in his efforts to get a handle on his task.

"He might not fall," Faye cautioned, "but I sure hope he doesn't fail. We've got a lot of donations invested in this renovation."

Rosemary playfully slapped her friend on the arm. "Ye of little faith! Just look at the man. He's shaking hands and kissing babies like a politician. Why, he's even got old Mrs. Fitzpatrick's undivided attention."

Faye squinted toward the spot where Kirk had stopped to bend over an aged woman sitting in a wheelchair, her tiny body covered from the waist down in an even more aged quilt. "Sure does. Let's go see what he's saying to her."

"More, what's she saying to him." Unable to stop her curiosity, Rosemary followed Faye across the grounds to where Kirk had stopped in front of the old woman. She watched as white-haired Mrs. Fitzpatrick lifted a bony, wrinkled hand to clasp Kirk's lean, tanned fingers.

"I knowed you was coming when I woke this morning," she said, her wise eyes appraising him with sharp precision. "It was such a strong morning, all bright and crisp. The Lord saves special days like this one for special happenings. I knowed something was a'brewin', but I jist thought it wuz something in the air."

"I got here a little early," he explained.

She wheezed a crusty chuckle. "Yep, and so did spring."

Kirk grinned at that, then waited patiently for her to continue talking.

"I'm the oldest member of the church," the woman told him in a whispery, leathery voice as she held up her tiny bun-crowned head with pride. "Eighty-nine. Emma Fitzpatrick's my name, but they call me Aunt Fitz. You can call me that if you'd like."

"I'd like, indeed," Kirk replied, a twinkle in his eyes. "And I just might need your expert advice on how to go about working on this magnificent church and steeple. I'm sure you have lots of fond memories of this church."

The old woman lifted her chin. "Was christened here, got hitched here, bore seven children, all christened and raised in the Lord's good name here, buried my husband and now two of those children in the cemetery up yonder on that hill. Got twenty-two grandchildren, most of them running around somewhere here tonight." She patted his hand. "Ask me anything you might want to know, son."

"I might need your opinion on the stained glass," Kirk replied. "But not tonight. We'll work on it later."

"Boy, he's good," Faye whispered. "Buttering up old Miss Fitz right off the bat."

Rosemary whispered back, "Well, she did give a thousand-dollar check to the cause."

"Does he know that?"

"Of course not. He's just being kind to an elderly woman. I told you how polite he is."

"Oh, I see," Faye replied, tongue in cheek.

Ignoring her, Rosemary listened to the rest of the conversation. Mrs. Fitzpatrick seemed intent on telling him something.

"You've the look of a hunter," the old woman said,

her rheumy eyes washing over Kirk's features in a bold squint. "Are you searching for something, child?"

Surprised, Kirk laughed. "Not that I know of."

Aunt Fitz moved her head in a shaking nod. "Sometimes we wander around looking, even though we don't realize we've been searching until we've found something to hold on to."

"Oh, here she goes, talking her riddles," Rosemary said beneath her breath. "Kirk will probably get a kick out of that."

Kirk's next words surprised Rosemary. "You might be right, Aunt Fitz. I was born in Ireland, but I know some of my ancestors and kinsmen came to the Appalachians to settle the new land long ago. Maybe I'll find a connection here. I've already fallen in love with the beauty of this place."

His eyes touched on Rosemary then moved back to the old woman still holding his hand. Aunt Fitz, her vision weakened by age and cataracts, still didn't miss the slight shifting of his gaze. She looked hard at Rosemary, then lifted her head back to Kirk.

"The mountains will touch your heart, boy," she said solemnly. "You might leave, but you'll be back here again."

Kirk looked uncomfortable at her prediction, but he quickly covered it by laughing down at her. "Thank you for speaking with me. Are you ready to eat?"

Apparently taking that as a sign that she'd best let go of his hand, Aunt Fitz dropped her hand to her lap to gather her tattered, brightly patterned quilt over her little legs.

"Starving," she said, motioning for her granddaughter to push her to a nearby table. Waving a hand at Kirk, she said, "I'll be seeing you, I 'magine." As she passed Rosemary, she smiled then winked. "A fine choice, Rosemary. Your steeplejack will do us proud."

"Wow," Faye said, glancing over at Rosemary's surprised face. "Praise from Aunt Fitz is like a blessing from above, Rosemary. Quite a coup, your steeplejack."

Rosemary gritted her teeth. "Thanks, but he's not *my* steeplejack."

Kirk came up to her then, his smile soft and shadowed by the coming dusk. "Well, I've heard tales of the folklore in these mountains, and I guess I just encountered some of it firsthand with Mrs. Fitzpatrick."

"She can tell the weather better than any forecaster with fancy computers," Rosemary said by way of explanation.

"And she knows every herb and bush on these hills. We all go to her for advice on everything from making jelly to easing arthritis. She's a dear and we all love her as well as fear her at times."

He looked out over the setting sun clinging to a nearby western hillside like a golden blossom. "She's a real intriguing woman, isn't she? She seems very wise," he observed.

Wanting to make him feel more comfortable, Rosemary shook her head and laughed. "Well, don't pay too much attention to her ramblings. All that nonsense about you coming back—she just wants every tourist and traveler to fall in love with this place the way she has."

Taking her by surprise, he bent low so that his breath tickled the curling hairs along her neck, and his eyes danced and shone like pure water cascading over rocks. "You mean, the mountain isn't going to swallow me up and touch my heart?"

Unable to breathe, she backed away, but didn't back down. She hadn't been out of circulation so long that she didn't know when a man was deliberately flirting with her. Shooting him a challenging look, she said, "Don't be silly—that's just folklore."

He reached out a finger to capture a wayward curl lying across her cheekbone. "It might be," he whispered, his words as gentle as the coo of a dove. "But some say there's always a thread of truth to be found in the old stories, Rosemary Brinson."

Slipping around him and taking her hair with her, Rosemary managed to get her breath back. "Right now I think would be a good time to sample some of Faye Lewis's fried chicken. We can talk folklore and riddles another time."

He ran a hand through his wavy locks and followed her, his eyes moving over the flowing lines of her floral-print sundress. "Another time," he repeated, more to himself than to her. "But not nearly enough time to figure you out, Rosemary."

She heard him, but she kept walking. And reminded herself he'd keep moving too, once he was finished with this job, while she...she was as settled and grounded as the steeple he'd come to mend. She acknowledged the attraction, but knew there was no need to get attached to the man.

No need at all, and...certainly, no hope.

Chapter Three

"Why did you invite him to our family dinner?" Danny asked Rosemary the next night. "You know this is our special time together."

Rosemary stopped buttering bread long enough to give her older brother a stern look. At thirty, Danny was a younger version of her father in looks. Tall, brown-headed with deep brown eyes, he'd taken after the Brinson side of the family, while Rosemary looked exactly like her mother with her light chestnut locks and dark blue eyes.

Those blue eyes were now flashing fire at her stubborn brother. "Oh, please, Danny! The man is living in a trailer just down the street. When I saw him this afternoon, he said he was going home to eat a sandwich. I had to invite him, for manners' sake if nothing else."

Danny leaned back on the polished surface of an ancient cabinet, then picked up a fresh cucumber to nibble while he studied his sister. "You know how Dad feels about him."

Rosemary wiped her hands on a blue dish towel, the echo of those very same words coming from her father not so long ago, ringing in her ears. "Oh, yes, we all know how Daddy feels about the steeplejack, about the church, about me. He tells me often enough."

"Shh!" Danny rolled his eyes and held a finger to her mouth. "Want him to hear you?"

Loud sounds of baby chatter came from the den just off the kitchen. Rosemary had to smile. "I doubt he can hear anything over the shrills of your daughter. Emily takes after her mother—quite a chatterbox."

"Who're you calling a chatterbox?" Nancy Brinson said from the doorway, a mock-stern look on her pretty, round face.

"You, sweetheart," Danny admitted readily, his own dark eyes twinkling. "Did you keep Dad occupied enough so that Rosemary could finish dinner?"

"I didn't have to say a word," Nancy said, tossing her ponytail over her shoulder. "Emily has him on the move."

"She's the only bright spot in his life these days," Rosemary said, quelling the envy she felt for her precious little niece. Clayton had taken to the child from the very first, maybe because in her innocence, Emily couldn't feel the tremendous pain they'd all endured since Eunice's death. Clayton didn't have to put up a front with her.

Nancy was pregnant when Rosemary's mother died. The baby was born two months later.

"I sure wish Mom could see her," Rosemary said to her brother.

"She does," Danny reminded her, his expression darkening with sadness. "I'm sure she's watching Emily from heaven, like a guardian angel."

The room went silent, as if out of respect for their mother's spirit. Nancy came to stand by her husband, one hand automatically going to his shoulder for a gentle, soothing pat. Rosemary turned away to busy herself with finishing dinner, the sight of the love and understanding between her brother and his wife too much to bear. She ached for that kind of bond; she wished for someone to pat her on the shoulder when she was feeling down. Oh, she had the love of all her friends and the congregation, but somehow, something was missing. That something was a husband and her own home. She wanted all the things Danny had—a home to call his own, a spouse who adored him, and a child. She'd come so very close to having her dreams. But, on a cold March night, that illusion had been shattered.

Maybe it wasn't her time yet. Right now, her job was to take care of Clayton, and to try to help him through this rough time. She owed him that much at least, after what had happened. Meanwhile, she'd trust that God would guide her when the time was right for her to find a soul mate.

Nancy took the tray of bread away from Rosemary, startling her out of her frantic motions and punishing musings. "I'll stick this in the oven," her sister-in-law said, her hazel eyes compassionate. "How's the roast coming along?"

Rosemary managed a convincing smile. "Ready. I'm going to slice it in just a minute." Glancing at the clock, she added, "I told Kirk seven. He should be here any minute."

Nancy looked out the back door, toward the church. "Does your father know you invited him?"

"No," Rosemary said in a deliberate tone. "Dad isn't speaking to me very much these days, not that

that's so unusual. But he's even more angry with me for bringing the steeplejack here. Thinks it's frivolous and unnecessary.''

Nancy's smile was indulgent. ''Well, you have to admit it's a bit unusual. I mean, I'd never heard of a steeplejack until you called me all excited about something you'd seen on the Internet, of all places.''

Remembering how she'd sat in Reverend Clancy's office, fascinated with his state-of-the-art computer system, Rosemary had to laugh out loud. ''I got kinda carried away on-line, but hey, I found what I wanted. Which was, someone to do the job right.''

Nancy threw up her hands. ''Whatever you say. You know more about this stuff than I ever will. And I don't care to know. I have enough to occupy me.''

Meaning, little Emily. Rosemary again felt that pang of regret and remorse. Would she ever have children? Or would she have to be content with taking care of other people's?

''Hey,'' Danny said from his perch near the open back door, ''your steeplejack is crossing the street. Better let Dad know he's coming, or he'll make another scene.''

''He's not *my* steeplejack,'' Rosemary said. Even so, her heart started racing and her palms grew damp. Danny was right. Why had she invited Kirk to supper?

Kirk strolled along wondering why he'd agreed to go to dinner at Rosemary Brinson's house. After that fun lunch he'd shared with her father, he'd made a solemn vow to steer clear of Clayton Brinson. Yet here he was, wildflowers in hand, heading for the very spot where he'd been ridiculed and prodded just yesterday.

Had he only been here two days?

This place was so timeless, so quaint and eccentric, that it seemed as if he'd been here forever. Or maybe he'd dreamed about a place like this forever. Quite charming, this Alba Mountain and its eclectic group of inhabitants. Especially one blue-eyed inhabitant.

And that, he told himself with a shrug, was why he was willing to face down Clayton Brinson again. Kirk wanted badly to see Rosemary. Had to see her, in fact. Had to see her up close.

He'd certainly watched her from a distance all day today. Oh, he'd gone about his preliminary work and taken care of what needed to be done. He'd surveyed and measured and analyzed. He'd discussed hiring a local crew with Reverend Clancy—the good reverend was working on that right now. And he'd carefully considered how best to go about renovating and restoring the aging church and its beautiful, inspiring steeple.

All the while, he'd watched the day-care center across the way, hoping to get a glimpse of the angel who'd brought him here. Rosemary. Rosemary with the sweet-smelling, fire-tinged hair. Rosemary with the eyes so blue, they looked like midnight velvet. Rosemary with the guarded looks and the cloak of sorrow. Rosemary with the floral, flowing dresses and the tinkling, musical laughter.

He'd watched her with the children, laughing, singing and smiling. He'd watched her with the townspeople, talking, explaining and sharing. And he'd watched her with her father, hurting, obeying and hoping.

He was intrigued by her. Maybe Aunt Fitz was right. Maybe these mountains did make people long for things they'd never needed to think about before.

And maybe, just maybe, Kirk, old boy, you're getting

caught up in something you have no business being involved in.

He didn't usually accept invitations so readily. Ordinarily, he worked from dawn to dusk, then slumped back to his trailer to grill a hamburger or a steak before falling into bed. Usually. Ordinarily. But then, there was nothing usual or ordinary about Rosemary Brinson. She was like an angel with a broken wing.

And he wanted to heal her.

Bad decision. Bad. Don't do it, man. Turn around and go eat that sandwich you lied to her about. Turn around and forget that you saw her heading out the door, and you purposely made it a point that she see you. Turn around and forget how she smiled up at you and lifted those luminous eyes to you and said, "Come over tonight and meet my brother. You can stay for supper."

Turn around, Kirk.

He knocked on the open door and waited, the sounds of domestication echoing through his wayfarer's logic. A child's laughter. Warm, home-cooked food. Fellowship. Rosemary.

He knocked, and waited, and wondered how he'd ever be able to distance himself from her so he could do his job and move on.

Then he looked up and saw Clayton Brinson's furious expression, and decided it might not be too hard, after all. Not if her overbearing father had anything to do with it.

In order to protect Rosemary from her father's wrath, Kirk decided he would have to force himself to stay away from her.

Somehow.

* * *

"Kirk, come on in," Rosemary said, moving in front of Clayton in an almost protective stance to open the screen door. "Supper is just about ready. In fact, I was just telling Daddy that I'd invited you."

Clayton's scowl deepened. By way of greeting, he grunted then turned to head toward the formal dining room. "Hurry it up, girl. I'm hungry."

Kirk followed Rosemary through the house to the kitchen. He looked around the small room, his gaze falling across the little group of people staring at him. "Hello," he said to Nancy a moment before shoving the wildflowers into Rosemary's hand.

She rewarded him with that little smile, then turned away, clearly flustered in a most becoming way, to put them in water.

"Hi, I'm Nancy Brinson, Rosemary's sister-in-law," Nancy said, taking matters into her own hands. "And this is my husband, Rosemary's brother, Danny. Sorry we missed you at the celebration last night." She patted little Emily on the head. "This one was teething and wasn't up to socializing, so we stayed home to take turns walking the floor with her."

Rosemary regained her composure enough to take one of Emily's fat hands into her own so she could kiss it and squeeze it softly. "This is our Emily, ten months old and full of energy."

Kirk nodded to Nancy, then shook Danny's hand while the other man sized him up. "Nice to meet all of you." He grinned and cooed at Emily.

Spellbound, the baby batted her long lashes and let out a squeal of delight.

"She never meets a stranger," Danny said proudly. "Hey, want a glass of tea?"

"Sure," Kirk said. "I'm learning to like it with ice. You know, my mother taught me to drink it hot."

"Not me," Danny said, grimacing. "I know it's a tradition over where you come from, and up North. But, man, once I was on a business trip in Detroit and ordered tea, and they brought it to me hot and in a cup—"

Nancy interrupted, a teasing smile on her face, "And he was so embarrassed, instead of ordering iced tea, he sat right there and sipped it hot, as if he were at a tea party or something."

Kirk laughed. "I bet you looked extremely dainty."

"I tried," Danny said, guiding Kirk into the dining room. "Have a seat."

Nancy put the baby down in her nearby crib and helped Rosemary carry in the food and drink. Clayton sat stone-silent at the head of the table.

Kirk looked around the long room. It was a lovely setting for a meal, complete with lacy white curtains at the tall windows and a matching lace tablecloth on the spacious mahogany table. Everything gleamed in the rays of the overhanging light fixture, while the scent of something fresh-baked set out on a matching buffet lifted out on the gentle breeze teasing through the open windows.

Noticing the formal settings at the table, he said, "I hope you didn't go to any extra trouble for me."

Before Rosemary could answer, Danny said, "Oh, no. It's a tradition in our house—having all the family together for a meal at least once a week. We usually do it on Sunday nights, but this week Emily was sick, so we put it off a couple of days."

"And used to, your mother would be here," Clayton said in a quiet voice, his stern look intact.

For just a minute, Kirk saw the raw pain and grief in the older man's eyes, and regretted his bad feelings regarding Rosemary's father. He didn't really have any right to judge the man. He'd known grief when he'd lost his beloved grandfather. Still, losing a wife had to be different. And maybe he would never know that kind of loss.

Because you never stay in one spot long enough to get that close to someone.

He glanced up at Rosemary, who stood just inside the wide archway, her gaze searching her father's face, her stance hesitant and unsure. The same pain he'd seen in Clayton's eyes was now reflected in her own.

Danny looked over at his father, then back to Kirk, his expression going soft with memories. "Yeah, Mom went to a lot of trouble. Cooked all afternoon. We'd come back around for leftovers during the week…" His voice trailed off, then he shrugged.

Kirk watched Clayton for signs of eruption, and seeing none, said, "I'm sure you all miss her."

"We do," Rosemary said, sitting down across from Kirk, her gaze still on her father. Clayton stared firmly at his plate.

Kirk watched as she reached for both her father's hand on one side and Danny's on the other. "Let's say grace."

Danny automatically took his sister's hand, then reached for his wife's. Nancy in turn held out a hand to Kirk so they would form a circle. Not knowing what else to do, Kirk followed suit and held out a hand to Clayton. On her side of the table, Rosemary waited for her father to grasp both her hand and Kirk's.

When Clayton refused to take either of their hands, Rosemary didn't bat an eye. She closed her eyes, holding tight to Danny's hand, and said a quick blessing, then let go of her brother's hand to start passing food.

But Kirk didn't miss the hurt, confused look haunting her eyes. She was trying very hard to stay steadfast in the storm of her father's rejection. How could a man do that to his daughter? How could he treat her that way and not know he was being cruel?

Maybe Clayton did know exactly what he was doing, Kirk decided. Maybe he was being deliberate. But why?

"If you don't mind me asking," he began carefully, "how did your mother die?"

Rosemary looked over at her father, then to Danny, panic in her eyes.

Wishing he could take the question back, Kirk added, "If you'd rather not talk about it—"

"She died in a car accident," Danny said quietly. "And, actually, we'd rather not talk about it."

"I'm sorry," Kirk replied, very aware of the undercurrent circling the table with the same fierce intensity with which Rosemary had just graced the meal.

"How'd work go today?" Rosemary said, her smile tight, her eyes shining.

Relieved that she'd given him an opportunity to take his foot out of his mouth, Kirk nodded. "Great. I talked to Reverend Clancy about hiring some of the locals to help with the sanctuary and the outside walls of the church. I'll need an assistant to help hoist me up and to help me from time to time up on the steeple. But for the most part I do all the steeple work myself."

"How did you ever become a steeplejack?" Danny asked between bites of biscuit with rice and gravy.

Kirk grinned. "I get that question a lot. Most people think I'm crazy, but actually, I'm a fourth-generation steeplejack. My mother's grandfather back in Ireland was a steeplejack and he taught my grandfather and my uncle. When I came along, I tagged around behind my grandfather so much, he had no choice but to put me to work, much to my mother's dismay. We traveled all over Ireland and England, repairing and renovating steeples and cathedrals, some of them stretching up a hundred and twenty-five feet.''

Rosemary went pale. "I can't imagine being that high up. I can barely make it up Alba Mountain without getting dizzy."

Kirk gave her a warm look. "Afraid of heights, huh?"

"She sure is," Danny said. "I used to climb up to the belfry at the church all the time when we were little. But she'd get halfway up those old stone steps and turn around and crawl back down."

"I never made it to the top," Rosemary said, "and I don't care who called me chicken." She glared at her brother. "The view from the mountain's good enough for me. I don't need to be on top of that narrow tower to see what I need to see."

Kirk laughed at her stubborn tone, then gave her a hopeful, challenging look. "We might have to change all of that. The view from up there is something else. It's a shame you've never seen it."

Danny patted his sister on the shoulder. "Hey, man, if you can get her up there, you really will be the miracle worker Reverend Clancy says you are."

Everyone laughed at that remark. Everyone except Clayton. He ate his food in silence, motioning to Rosemary when he wanted refills or seconds.

Kirk, determined to win the man over in some form, turned to him at last. "Mr. Brinson, since you've been a member of the church most of your life, I could use your advice. Would you be willing to supervise some of the men on the ground level?''

Clayton's head came up and his eyes fixed on Kirk with a sharp intensity. "No, I would not. I'm not interested in the least. Absolutely not."

Kirk glanced at Rosemary. She looked uncomfortable, but he thought maybe if he could get Clayton involved, it would take some of the heat off her. "I just thought, since you're retired now—"

"You thought wrong," Clayton said, scraping his chair back with a clatter. "Rosemary, bring my cobbler and coffee to the den."

"All right." She rose to do her father's bidding, her eyes centered on Kirk. "I'm sorry," she whispered as she rushed by.

She sure did apologize a lot, when it really wasn't necessary.

"Me, too." He looked over at Danny. "I didn't mean to upset him."

"It's okay," Danny said. "But you have to understand something about my dad. He hasn't been back to church since the day of Mom's funeral. He's turned his back on the world and on God. He can't understand why God would do this to him, after he tried to be faithful and loyal to the church all his life."

Kirk leaned forward, his voice low. "I don't mean to sound insensitive, but hasn't your father missed the point entirely?"

Nancy sighed and leaned in, too. "Yes, he has. But Reverend Clancy says it takes longer for some people than others. We're supposed to be patient and go about loving him no matter how he treats us."

Kirk ran a hand through his tousled locks. "I feel

for all of you, but especially for Rosemary. And I think it'd be best if I go on back to my little trailer."

"Don't," Rosemary said from the kitchen door. "I mean, you haven't had your dessert yet." On a shaky voice, she added, "Now, my blackberry cobbler isn't as good as my mother's was, and granted, these aren't fresh blackberries, but Aunt Fitz herself helped me can them last year and, well..." Her voice trailed off as she brought a hand to her mouth. "Excuse me."

She turned and rushed back out of the room, out of the house. The kitchen door banged after her.

Danny rose out of his chair. "Maybe I should go see about her."

Nancy put a hand on his arm. "No, honey. Let's you and I get these dishes cleaned up." She looked at Kirk.

He was already standing. "I'll go to her," he said, meeting Nancy's gaze head-on. "I enjoyed the meal. Sorry if I dampened the evening."

Danny shook his head, his eyes dull with resignation. "Don't worry, buddy. This isn't the first time something like this has happened."

Well, it would be the last for him, Kirk decided as he stepped out into the cool spring night. The scent of a thousand budding blossoms hit him full force, the tranquillity of the peaceful evening clashing with the turmoil he'd just set off inside that house. Searching the darkness, he spotted Rosemary on the bench inside the church grounds, sitting where she sat every day watching the children.

He wanted to rush to her, but instead, he took his time, wondering what he'd say once he got there. Kirk wasn't used to offering words of wisdom or comfort. He usually dealt in small talk, or technical discussions. Every now and then, he'd get in a heavy philosophical discussion with someone he met, usually involving religion. But for the most part, he steered clear of offering up his opinion on a continuous basis. People didn't like to have their values questioned, and he wasn't one for questioning God's ways.

His mother had taught him simply to accept the daily miracles of life. Kirk firmly believed in God's grace, but he wore his own faith in an unobtrusive fashion, preferring to live and let live. Because he did move around so much, he'd learned to mind his own business.

Yet, his mother, Edana, a wise woman with strong religious convictions, had warned him many times about his nonchalant attitude. "One day, my fine son, you'll come across a situation that will demand more than you're willing to give. You'll learn all about being tested. Then, my lad, you'll start taking life much more seriously. And maybe then, pray God, you'll stop roaming the earth and settle down."

Was this his test then? If he got involved with Rosemary, he would be going against his own rather loosely woven convictions. How could he comfort this woman? Better yet, should he even try?

She looked up as he approached. He heard her loud sniff, saw her hurriedly wiping at her eyes. Oh, that he'd caused her any further pain—it tore at his heart, exposing him to something deep within himself, some strange sensation that tingled to life and pulsed right along with his heartbeat. He'd not let this happen again.

"Rosemary," he said, sitting down beside her to take her hand in his. "I'm so very sorry."

She didn't pull away, but she looked away, and then up, at the steeple looming in the darkness. "We both seem to be doing a lot of apologizing."

"You don't owe me an apology," he said, meaning it. "You've been through a terrible tragedy, and apparently, I've come in the middle of it and made it worse."

She let out a sob, then gripped her fist to her mouth. "People tell you it'll get better," she stated on a tear-drenched voice. "They pat you on the arm and say, 'She's at peace now, dear,' and they keep going. They don't want to see your grief. It makes them uncomfortable, you see.

"During the funeral, everyone was so compassionate and understanding. It was such a shock—it happened so fast. One minute she was there, standing in the kitchen, laughing, talking, making plans for my wedding. Then, the next, she was simply...gone."

She didn't speak for a minute, and he heard her swallow hard. "But then, life goes on, as they say. After a while, you become this robot. You go through the motions, you behave as if everything is back to normal, but you know that something is terribly, terribly wrong. When you see people on the street, you smile and you accept—dread—the sympathy in their eyes, but they don't want you to speak of it."

She stopped, taking a gulp of air, another sob escaping. "But inside, inside you have this silent scream that never, ever goes away, never stops. And you just keep on moving through each minute, each hour, each day. And that scream keeps following you until you think you'll go stark raving mad from hearing it. It...it never ends."

Unable to bear any more, Kirk gathered her into his arms, rocking her gently, whispering soothing words into her ear. Remembering the days when his own mother would try to comfort him, he said something in

Gaelic to her, unaware that he'd even done it. He held her close, letting her sob quietly into the night, letting her purge herself against his strength.

How long had she carried this pain? How long had she been the one to be strong while her brother and her father depended on her to become a surrogate for her mother? How long had she struggled to become that perfect replacement, knowing she could never be the one they all longed for, the one she longed to have back in that little kitchen?

And, what had happened to those wedding plans she said her mother had been working on?

He had so many questions, but he didn't ask for any answers tonight. Tonight, he held her, and with a silent prayer, he asked God to give His strength over to her, and her suffering family. He asked God to give her the comfort he wasn't sure he could bring.

And in the asking, Kirk offered up the only thing he did have to give. He offered up his heart.

"Kirk," she said at last, her voice raw, her words muffled. "What did that mean, what you said to me in that beautiful language?"

He pulled her tight against him. "It means, 'I am here, little one.'" He swallowed the lump in his throat. "I am here."

She leaned her head against his chest, her cheek touching on the steady beat of his heart. "For a little while at least," she whispered.

Chapter Four

Kirk lifted her away so he could see her face in the moonlight. "What's that supposed to mean?"

She sat up, wiping the last of her tears, purposely distancing herself from the warmth of his embrace. "It means...well...you'll be gone in a few weeks. I can't start depending on you. I won't start depending on you. I shouldn't even be talking to you now. I mean, you came here to repair the steeple. You don't need me or my troubles getting in your way."

He turned on the bench to stare at her, wondering if the woman could read his thoughts since that was precisely what he'd been telling himself earlier. "I don't mind hearing your troubles. I just don't know if I can help."

"No, you can't help," she said as she got up to walk to a nearby fence. "And I don't normally go around feeling sorry for myself. According to the Bible, I'm supposed to rejoice, knowing my mother has gone on to a better place. And sometimes, I can do that. Then other times, I can't. I'm selfish because I miss her, but I've accepted my mother's death.''

"Have you?" he had to ask. He got the impression she hadn't really come to grips with any of this. When she didn't answer immediately, he asked, "And have you accepted the way your father treats you?"

She whirled to glare at him. "I don't have much choice there. He's my father and he needs me."

"Why does he talk to you like that? Why do you let him?"

Rosemary swallowed back the urge to spill her guts to this man. She couldn't let him know; she couldn't let him see the pain, the open, festering wound that would never heal, no matter how hard she prayed, no matter how much she tried to forgive herself each and every day. "I...I don't want to talk about this anymore," she said into the wind. "After all, it's really none of your concern."

He lifted off the bench to come and stand beside her. "You're right. It's none of my business, but I think I've provoked this whole situation. Maybe if I knew what happened, I could understand better."

"There's really nothing to understand," she tried to explain. "My father is still grieving, he's still angry because my mother's death was so senseless. I have to hold fast and hope that he'll realize he can't change any of it."

Kirk knew she wasn't telling him the whole story. So her mother was killed in a car accident. That was a tragedy, no doubt. But why would Clayton take out his anger on his daughter? Suddenly, a sad, sickening thought crossed his mind. Well, he'd wondered it since he'd seen Rosemary and her father together that first day, sparring; he had to ask it.

"Does your father blame you somehow—for your mother's death?"

She turned away, her staunch silence shouting at him.

"Rosemary?" He urged her around, then lifted her chin with the pad of his thumb. "Is that what this is all about?"

She faced him squarely, her eyes full of shame and disgust. "Yes," she whispered. "He blames me. And you will, too, if I tell you the truth."

With that, she whirled and ran back toward her house, toward the torture her father would surely inflict on her once she slammed that screen door behind her.

Kirk heard the door slamming shut. It was as if she'd just shut him out of her life.

Over the next few days, Kirk managed to avoid Rosemary as much as possible, considering that she worked at the church, considering that he worked outside, mostly with a bird's-eye view of the comings and goings across the street, considering that he longed to see her again, that he yearned to hold her again, considering that he couldn't get her out of his mind.

He had to remind himself that he didn't want to get involved. He told himself, this way, neither of them would get hurt—especially Rosemary. She didn't need the complication of a short-term relationship added to her already stress-filled life. And short-term it would have to be. He never stayed long enough for anything else. That he was even considering having a relationship with her was enough to make him antsy and restless, and distracted.

Today, frustrated and tired from a day of scraping rust and paint from the gables of the church roof, he decided he'd take a late-afternoon hike up onto Alba Mountain. The trails behind his tiny trailer led straight to the top of the peak, according to Reverend Clancy.

Tomorrow, he'd interview people for the complete crew, then he'd get started on the steeple. That task would occupy his mind enough to keep him in line and away from Rosemary Brinson. Right now, he just needed to escape into nature, to let his mind wander. He needed time to think and regroup. The mountain peak would be the perfect spot.

It should have been.

Except that halfway up the steep, winding path that lifted to the rocky peak, he spotted Rosemary sitting in a field of wildflowers, in what looked like a cemetery.

Aunt Fitz had said she'd buried her husband up on the hill. Was that where Rosemary's mother was buried, too?

He stopped, catching his breath more from the sight of the woman sitting there than from the exercise.

She was wearing one of those soft, flowing dresses she seemed to favor, its colors rivaling the wild yellow roses and delicate pink-and-yellow-tipped lady's slippers bursting to life all around her. Her hair moved in the breeze, lifting away from her face in chaotic shades of deep red and burnished brown. As he watched, she reached one hand out to touch the headstone in front of her, closing her eyes in a silence that only the angels could hear.

He should have kept moving. He was intruding on a private moment, between Rosemary and her mother. Yet he couldn't seem to find the strength to put one hiking boot in front of the other. He couldn't move. He could only stand there, watching her, wanting to go to her.

Like a doe sensing danger, she opened her eyes and looked up, right into his eyes. For a brief time, she didn't move; she just sat there staring up at him, her expression a mixture of surprise and knowing. Then she waved to him and sent him that bittersweet smile he was beginning to need to see.

He forgot about scaling the mountain.

Rosemary saw him through the trees and felt the lurch of her heart against her chest. She'd sensed someone was near, she'd *felt* someone's eyes on her.

And somehow, she'd known it would be Kirk. She'd avoided him since their gut-wrenching encounter the other night. She was embarrassed by her tears, by her confessions, and by her need to have someone hold her. She disliked weakness in anyone else, but especially in herself. She'd avoided him, and she'd thought about him.

She'd thought about him enough in the past few days to conjure him up at any given moment, during work, during prayer, during play with the children. She'd thought about him, and wished she could just get the man out of her mind. She wanted to forget the way he'd held her; she wanted to remember the feeling forever.

Rosemary reminded herself that he was a drifter, a wanderer. His work was important to him, and because of that work, he couldn't stay in one spot for long. In spite of their closeness, she sensed an aloofness in him. Kirk held himself away from people, like a casual observer, watching and analyzing. He had to keep moving. And she had to stay here. Besides, if Kirk knew the real reason Clayton treated her so coldly, he'd turn away from her, too. And she couldn't bear to have him do that.

She told herself these things as he approached her now, looking like an ancient warrior from long ago. He wore hiking boots and jeans, and a torn T-shirt. His unruly hair was having a high old time playing in the wind off the hillside. His eyes, though, oh, his eyes. They held her, making her forget her pragmatic logic, making her forget her own self-disgust and guilt-laden remorse, making her long for something intangible and unreachable.

Automatically, Rosemary gripped the sun-warm gray stone of her mother's headstone, as if asking for counsel. The silence answered her, as it always did when she came up here to visit her mother's grave. Only the wind and the chipmunks and the swallows gave her any conversation. Now, even nature's comforting forces seemed to go silent.

There was an intruder in the woods.

"I didn't mean to intrude," Kirk said as he came up the hillside to the level incline where Alba had buried its dead for two centuries. "I can leave if you'd like."

"No, don't," she said in a rush. As she lifted up, he reached out a hand to help her, causing her to feel the same disruption in her equilibrium as she usually felt when she reached the top of the mountain.

Kirk took her hand in his, then shifted his gaze from her face to the gravestone in front of them. "Your mother?"

She nodded, her gaze falling across the etched roses centered on the stone.

Kirk read the inscription: Eunice Grace Brinson. Born 1942. Died 1996. Beloved Wife and Mother.

"And in heaven, the angels are smiling down on her, watching her sleep."

"That's beautiful, Rosemary," he said, still holding her hand.

"She used to tell us that," she explained, her gaze settling on the inscription. "She'd read to us from the Bible, then she'd say, 'Time for bed. The angels will be smiling down on you now, watching you sleep.'"

Not knowing what to say, Kirk just held her hand. Finally, he asked, "Do you come up here alone a lot?"

"At least once a week," she replied. "When I need to talk, when I need to get away." She looked around at the mountain laurel spreading like a pink-and-white-patterned quilt across the distant hills. "It's always so hushed, so peaceful."

"Would you like me to go?"

"No, I was just about to head back down. I've got to get supper fixed."

Not wanting her to leave just yet, he said, "I was planning on hiking the mountain. Want to come?"

She recoiled instantly, like a blossom settling in for the night. "No. I...I get so dizzy. I'd better go on back home."

"Come with me, Rosemary," he said, his hand tight against hers, his body pulling her toward the peak. "I won't let anything happen to you."

"I know that," she said, believing it to be true. "I'm afraid, is all."

"Afraid of the mountain, or me?"

"Both," she admitted, laughing shakily to hide her discomfort. "I feel so foolish after the way I acted the other night."

"Don't," he said. "You have no reason to feel uncomfortable with me. I don't judge people."

She gave a little huff of a laugh. "You'd be the first not to judge me, then."

That remark caught him off guard. "I can't believe anyone in this town would hold ill thoughts about you. You seem to keep the whole church together."

She laughed again. "I have a hard enough time holding myself together. But you're right. People here are good and strong, supportive. They've helped me through some rough spots, and...they've forgiven me."

"For what? What did they need to forgive?"

She pulled away. "That's private. I...I need to go."

"You tell me the whole town's forgiven you, yet you can't tell me why?"

"I don't want to discuss it," she said, hoping he wouldn't push her. Giving him a pleading look, she said, "It's too painful, Kirk. Please try and understand."

He was trying. And failing. Kirk had made mistakes himself, a lot of them, but he couldn't imagine something so horrible that a whole town would need to send out forgiveness for it. Maybe because he had no life beyond his work. Maybe because he'd been so indifferent to life, never taking it too seriously, that he'd never really experienced the type of pain she obviously had known.

"Come with me up the mountain," he said, taking her hand back in his. "I won't force you to tell me your deep, dark secrets. I just want to walk with you."

She looked up the winding dirt trail, her heart pounding with a new fear that had nothing to do with conquering her vertigo. She couldn't lose her heart to this man. That frightened her more than any mountain ever had.

"Come with me, Rosemary," he said again, his captivating eyes willing her to trust him.

She wanted to trust him, wanted to go with him up the mountain, wanted to talk to him and question him, and get to know the man behind those aged, intense eyes. But, Rosemary reminded herself, she was supposed to be avoiding him.

She thought about what was waiting for her at home, then she thought about the fine spring wind and the smell of new-blooming honeysuckle, and the freedom to just go.

"All right," she said at last. "But we'll have to hurry to make it before sunset."

"We will," he assured her. "There's plenty of light yet."

She moved away for a minute, to stand in front of her mother's grave once again. "Bye, Mom. I'll be back soon."

A gentle breeze kissed her face with a soothing coolness, washing over her to leave her breathless and wondering. Then silence fell back on the hushed hillside.

Rosemary took Kirk's hand, and followed him up the path to the top of Alba Mountain.

Along the way, after getting her breath and calming herself, she stopped to show him the local flora and fauna.

"That's a sourwood tree," she said, pointing off to a jutting hill where a white-tasseled tree shot toward the sky. "Makes good honey."

He watched her expression, thinking her lips would probably taste like honey.

"And over there, growing along that bluff, that's ginseng. Some of the locals still gather it to send to the Orient—they're licensed by the state, though. You've probably heard how potent it is." She blushed, then shot him that endearing smile again.

He decided nothing could be as potent as her charm.

"Look," she said, taking his hand to pull him into the woods. "A rabbit."

Kirk had seen lots of rabbits. "It's lovely," he said, never taking his eyes off her face.

She looked up at him, his gaze warming her like summer rain. "Are you even listening to me?"

"Uh-huh," he said, his gaze moving over her face. "It's all very fascinating."

"Don't look at me like that," she said, moving to pull away.

He gently yanked her right back. "Why? I can't help it if I enjoy looking at you. You're a very attractive woman."

Rosemary's body buzzed with a fine current of electricity. This. This was why she couldn't stay away from him; this was why she should stay away from him. "I've heard about your Blarney stone over in Ireland, Kirk Lawrence. Stop flirting with me."

"I like flirting with you, Rosemary Brinson," he said, grinning when she managed to dart away. "I like watching your skin turn from pale to bright. I like seeing your hair lifting out, curling around your face—"

She interrupted him to put her hair in perspective for him. "Naturally curly and hard to deal with—that's my hair."

"Naturally curly and soft to the touch," he said as he drew near again. Standing apart from her, he reached out a hand to grab a few unruly strands, curling them around his fingers until his hand touched her temple. "There it is again—that becoming blush."

She didn't pull away this time. His hand on her skin

felt too good. "You're mighty tempting," she admitted, her eyes moving over his face. "Handsome, single and apparently carefree. Tell me, Kirk, how many broken hearts have you left behind with each of your newly polished church steeples?"

He had to laugh. "I see, in spite of that innocent blush, you have quite a sting."

"Just being realistic," she replied, her cheek still touching his hand. "Tell me—the truth."

He pulled her into his arms, taking her breath and her resolve away. "There's only one broken heart in my past," he said near her ear. "And it's mine. Caused by a high-school sweetheart who didn't take to my chosen profession. She had her sights set on someone with a little more staying power."

Surprised, Rosemary looked him over to make sure he wasn't making it up. "Really? Did you love her a lot?"

He laughed again. "I thought I did. More like puppy love. She's married now, to a lawyer, I believe. Lives in a fancy house somewhere near New York City."

Fascinated, she asked, "Do you have any regrets?"

"No," he said automatically. "I couldn't give her what she wanted. I decided after that episode, though, I'd better be very sure before I let go of my heart again." Turning the tables, he asked, "What about you, Rosemary? What happened to break your heart?"

She went still in his arms. "We were talking about you, not me."

"And why can't we talk about you? What happened to your wedding plans?"

She wiggled away, then turned to head up the path. "Come on. It's getting late."

"Rosemary," he called. "You can trust me."

She whirled to stare down at him. "Oh, I don't doubt that. I know I can trust you, but I can't depend on you. You said it yourself, Kirk. You've chosen your path. And I...I have to live with mine, right here. There's no point in telling you all the details. It's over, in the past, and I don't want to talk about it with you when soon, you'll be a part of the past, too. I'd rather you didn't remember me that way."

Frustrated, he hiked up to meet her. "Why can't we just enjoy the time we have? I want to understand you, and...I want to remember all of you, good and bad. I could help you, comfort you."

"You already have," she said, taking his hand again. "More than you'll ever know."

He supposed he'd have to settle for that, for now. "Can I at least be your friend, while I'm here?"

"Of course," she said, smiling again. "I could use a friend."

It was a step forward, although why he should feel so gratified and elated was beyond him. They both knew it couldn't last. But then again, friendship wasn't something to be taken lightly.

They rounded the path, hand in hand, each lost in thoughts about the commitment they'd just made. Kirk looked up to find an old log cabin set in the middle of a clearing off the path to the left, its walls shaped and hunched by the various additions and lean-tos that must have been added throughout the years. Several brightly painted gourds in different shapes and patterns hung from its posted porch, while colorful quilts covering rough-hewn benches invited travelers to sit a spell.

"Who lives there?"

"Aunt Fitz," Rosemary replied, glad they'd dropped the subject of their relationship.

"How does she get up and down the mountain in that wheelchair?"

Rosemary had to smile at his joking attitude. "There's a road behind the cabin that leads down to the main road through town. Her children usually drive here to pick her up. She stays in the village with one of her daughters sometimes, but she might be home today. Want to stop in for a quick visit?"

"Why not—or are you stalling to keep from reaching the top of the mountain?"

She shot him a meaningful grin. "You know we need to hurry. Maybe I just feel the need for a chaperon."

"So you don't trust me, after all?"

Rushing on ahead, she called over her shoulder, "No, I think maybe I don't trust myself when I'm around you."

He followed her through the woods. "That's a good sign...I think."

Aunt Fitz was delighted to see them and immediately got them both a Mason jar full of dark, sun-brewed, heavily sweetened iced tea.

Kirk took a long swallow, then licked his lips. "I taste herbs in there. Mint, maybe."

"Scotch mint," Aunt Fitz stated proudly. "And a few other cure-alls."

"Such as?" Kirk asked in a tone full of suspicion.

Aunt Fitz laughed long and hard from her perch on an old bentwood chair on the porch. "A little sang never hurt, son."

Kirk squinted, then looked at his brew. "Sang?"

"Ginseng," Rosemary said, her eyes lifting to his.

"Shaped like a human figure, so the Chinese say it's

good for all over," Aunt Fitz explained. "They believe in plants shaped like organs and such, and since sang looks like a human body, they believe it will cure whatever ails a body."

"How interesting," Kirk said, surprised at her obvious knowledge of the human anatomy.

Rosemary grinned at him from her spot on the porch railing. "Maybe it will give you a boost, Kirk."

Thinking the last thing he needed was a stimulant, he lifted an eyebrow to her. "We might not ever make it back down the mountain."

She laughed good-naturedly at that, but quickly caught herself when she felt the all-knowing intensity of Aunt Fitz's beady eyes on her.

"It's good to see you laughing, gal," the old woman said in a raspy voice. "I knowed one would come along one of these days, to make you laugh again. I seen the signs."

That sobered Rosemary. "Maybe we'd better get going, Kirk."

"In a minute," Kirk said, interested in what else Aunt Fitz had seen. Noticing the basket of bright material by the old woman's chair, he said, "What's this?"

"Quilt remnants," Aunt Fitz explained, her bony fingers grasping a piece of the material to hold it up to the light. "A wedding quilt, maybe." Her smile was serene, while her eyes fell on Rosemary. "A girl needs at least a dozen quilts in her hope chest, you know."

"Time to go," Rosemary said, hopping up to take Kirk's glass out of his hand, her eyes downcast and evasive.

Kirk immediately noticed her agitation, but decided all this talk of weddings was making her nervous, maybe since her own apparently hadn't worked out. "I'm not finished," he protested, enjoying the way Aunt Fitz stared with such all-seeing eyes at Rosemary.

"It will be dark soon," Rosemary said sharply. "Daddy will be furious."

"How is Clayton?" Aunt Fitz asked, rising on wobbly legs to see them down the steps. Finding her cane, she finally managed to stand to her full height of five feet four inches. She refused to use that dadgum wheelchair around the house.

"The same," Rosemary replied. "And he'll be fit to be tied if I'm late for supper."

"He'll survive, I 'magine," the old woman said with a wave of her skinny hand. " 'The Lord hear thee in the day of trouble.' "

Rosemary appreciated the quote from Psalms, but wondered if Aunt Fitz's gentle reminder would help her father. "Daddy isn't listening right now, Aunt Fitz. He's forgotten how to ask for God's mercy and help."

"Have you forgotten, too, child?"

"No, I haven't forgotten," Rosemary answered softly.

"Then know He is with you, Rosemary, and He'll see to Clayton in His own good way. Go to the top of the mountain, girl. Enjoy the view. It's might pretty at sunset."

"And dark quickly afterward," Rosemary said on a warning tone.

"Your hunter there, he'll protect you," Aunt Fitz stated, laughing merrily.

"I don't need protecting." Rosemary was already moving up the path. "Hurry, Kirk."

Kirk had been standing in amazement at the old woman's serene but secure convictions. Aunt Fitz was content to live her days out on this mountain, her roots firmly embedded in the life she had made here. For a brief moment, he wanted to feel that same contentment, that same anchoring of faith. For just an instant, he wanted to stop roaming, searching, traveling.

Aunt Fitz looked at Kirk. "Better chase after her, boy. And let her catch you."

Kirk laughed at her simple solution to a very complex situation. Was that it then? Did he want to be caught? Was that why he was beginning to question his own outlook on life? Unsettled and unsure, he said, "Goodbye, Aunt Fitz."

"I'll be seeing you again, I 'magine."

He imagined she was probably right. That old woman knew too much, he thought as he hurried after Rosemary.

Chapter Five

They made it to the top of the mountain just as the sun was slipping through the Fraser firs covering a distant rock formation. The whole valley below them and the surrounding woods held a blue-green smoky fog that reminded Kirk of some of the faded squares of Aunt Fitz's quilting materials, while the bald where they stood was smooth and almost devoid of trees.

"So this is why they call them the Blue Ridge Mountains," he said, his hand holding tight to Rosemary's.

She stood back, too deathly afraid to come forward on the jutting rocky ridge. "That's it—the fir and spruce trees make the woods seem blue. Beautiful, isn't it?"

He heard the shakiness in her voice. "Are you okay?"

"Oh, I'm great," she said. "Just let go of me so I can sit down, please."

He did, watching as she backed up against a smooth

stone that looked like a nature-made bench. "Is that your particular spot?"

"This is as far as I go," she replied, laughing nervously as she sat back on the rock, gripping the warm gray stone with both hands. "Guess the good Lord put this rock right here to hold me up."

"Maybe He did, at that," Kirk said, his gaze moving over her. She looked radiant in the red-gold light, her hair awash with all the colors of the earth and sun, her face expectant and hesitant, and glowing with the flush of their climb. "But you know, you're missing the best view."

"Maybe, but I can see enough from right here, thank you."

"Come to the edge, Rosemary," he coaxed. "I'll hold on to you."

"No," she said in an emphatic voice. "You take a few minutes to enjoy yourself and I'll take a few to get my breath back." She glanced at her watch, then moaned. "I am so very late."

"We won't linger long." He took a deep breath himself, his eyes moving over the town and countryside below. "I can see the steeple off to the left. Your trail obviously winds all around the mountain."

"It takes a few twists and turns," she said, silently noting that her mundane life was suddenly doing the same thing.

Kirk studied the houses and storefronts below, thinking how picturesque the whole place looked, then strolled over to sit beside her on the rock. Giving her a scrutinizing look, he grew concerned at the pale shade of her skin and the panicked look in her eyes. It just seemed natural to put an arm around her in a protective gesture. "Stop worrying. Surely your father allows you some free time. You are an adult."

She tossed her hair away and tried to smile. "Yes, I'm an adult. I actually used to live on my own, in an apartment down the street from my house. But that changed after Mama died."

"You moved back in with your father then?"

"Yes. I felt...it was the right thing to do at the time. It was supposed to be temporary, but one thing led to another and, well...I'm still there."

"Why can't your brother help out now and then?"

"He does. Or at least, he tries. He offers to take Dad to the doctor, or fishing, stuff like that."

"And?"

She looked out over the valleys and hills that were already filling with the first white dogwood buds, her breath calming down, her pulse almost back to normal again. "And...I usually wind up doing it all, because Danny has a demanding job—logging—and he has a wife and a new baby, and I—"

"And you've given up your life because you feel guilty and obligated."

She lifted her chin, then turned to stare at him. "I didn't give up anything, because...I had nothing to give up. Nothing."

"You mean, because your wedding was called off after your mother's death? Why?"

She would have stood, except that the only way to go was toward the ledge. "I thought you promised not to try and find out my secrets."

"That I did," he said, frustrated that she was so close to telling him about her life, yet still so very afraid to let go. Deciding he'd better make the most of this time with her, he took her hand in his and smiled.

"No more talk. Let's just enjoy the sunset, then I'll take you home."

"Isn't it amazing," she said, her tone hushed and reverent, "that something so beautiful can exist? While we whine and moan and continue to feel sorry for ourselves, this mountain stays intact and solid."

"God put it here for just that reason," Kirk replied. "I think I'm beginning to understand what Aunt Fitz meant when she told me the mountain would touch my heart. It certainly has renewed my faith in God's handiwork."

Rosemary relaxed a little, very much aware of his arm around her, his fingers touching her bare shoulder on one side, and his other hand in hers, settled on the rough fabric of his worn jeans. His nearness made her head spin and she concentrated on the view instead. "It's good to share it with someone who understands."

He concentrated on her. "It's good to be here with someone so centered. And pretty to look at, I might add."

She smiled at that, liking the word *centered* as much as she liked being called pretty. She was centered. In spite of all her worries and fears, she knew that her faith would see her through.

"This land is so old," she said, her words whispered and awe-filled. "Millions and millions of years, at least, and created simply from weather and erosion. The Cherokee lived here before the settlers ever came. Most of what Aunt Fitz knows about cures was passed down from the Cherokee."

He couldn't help it. He had to press his cheek against her hair. "Yep, Aunt Fitz is a very clever woman."

Rosemary felt the tickle of his breath fluttering her hair, but she didn't stop him. She swallowed, lifting her head toward him, letting him bury his nose in the thickness of her wild curls. That little voice in the back of her mind told her that she should not be here, letting him do this. She ignored it for once. Later, when she was alone and lonely, she'd remember this and smile. That wasn't so much to ask for—just a sweet memory, a few stolen moments with a man she found intriguing and unique.

"That's nice," he said, letting go of her hand to pull her around with both arms. "Rosemary?"

"Hmm?"

"May I kiss you?"

Shocked, she drew back, her eyes locking with his as a heated flush moved up her neck. "I...I don't think—"

"Let's not think about it," he said as he lowered his head to hers. Using the only philosophy on life he'd followed up until now, he added, "Let's just enjoy the time we have."

She should have protested, but his mouth falling across hers ended any complaints she might have had. The kiss was gentle and sweet, demanding and dangerous, as untamed as the mountain they'd climbed, and just as beautiful.

Kirk pulled away, his dark eyes filled with a gleam of pure contentment, then pressed his forehead against hers. "I've wanted to do that since I first saw you."

"Oh, really?" she said on a shaky whisper. "I'm afraid Reverend Clancy would have been a little surprised if you had."

"No more than I," he admitted. "You taste so good."

"And that surprises you?"

He grinned. "No, I knew you'd be sweet. What surprises me is the impact—of seeing you, of wanting to get to know you, of wanting to be with you. I've never been jolted quite so hard before.''

She drew back again, her eyes wide and playful. ''I bet you say that to all the church girls.''

He let her go, but not too far since she refused to move from the stone bench. Tracing a finger down the contours of her jawline, he said, ''I've never taken the time to flirt with a church girl before.''

''Kirk Lawrence, you expect me to believe that? Why, you're, you're—''

He grinned. ''What?''

''You know what you are—good-looking—''

He lifted a dark eyebrow. ''Do go on.''

''Charming, interesting, mysterious, confident—''

''All of that, huh?''

''And you know it. I can't believe you haven't left a girl with every steeple.''

He shook his head, laughing. ''That's a new one.''

''Well, I'm sure it's true.''

''You're sure? You think you've got me figured out, right?''

She lowered her eyes. ''Well, no. I'm trying very hard *to* figure you out.'' Then she lifted her gaze to meet his, her eyes widening with sincerity. ''I don't want to be hurt again, Kirk. I…once was enough.''

''Tell me who hurt you.''

She reached up a hand to touch his cheek. ''I can't. Maybe later, but not now. What did you say? Let's just enjoy the time we have.''

Funny, he'd always followed that code before. Now he wasn't so sure it was the best solution for Rosemary and him. He wanted to linger; he wanted more time. But it wasn't fair to let her think they had that luxury.

"So you're okay with the fact that even though I'm highly attracted to you, I can't stay here forever?"

"I never expected you to stay, and I really never expected you to be...highly attracted to me." She stood, and clinging to the stone, turned to start back down the mountain. Then, safe away from the ledge, she said, "And I certainly never expected you to kiss me."

He followed her, taking one last long look at the sprawling vista before them. "Neither did I."

It was late when they got back down to the foot of Alba Mountain. Dusk was long gone, and a new night greeted them, complete with singing crickets and hungry mosquitoes.

Kirk walked her to her porch, where a light was burning brightly. "Should I go in with you?"

"I don't think that's too smart," she said, her eyes darting to the screen door. "I'm used to handling my father. I won't have him browbeating you, too."

"I can take care of myself," he said, moving to go inside with her. Then, belatedly, he remembered he had made a vow to stay away from her, to save her any further grief with her father. "But you're probably right, I'd only make it worse for you."

"Thank you," she said, whirling to head up the steps.

Kirk grabbed her hand, pulling her back down close so he could give her a quick kiss. He wasn't quite ready to relinquish her yet. "I enjoyed the hike."

"Me, too," she said, flustered and thoroughly confused. "Does this mean we're still friends?"

"Always," he said, letting her go with regret because he wanted to keep her near, and with relief because he knew he shouldn't want that. "See you tomorrow."

Kirk watched her go in the house, then turned and strolled to his trailer. It looked sad and forlorn, sitting there underneath the great oak. He'd always adored his little traveling home. Now it seemed lonely. He dreaded going back in there.

He opted to sit outside and enjoy the nice cool evening. He told himself he simply needed to unwind after that long hike. Actually, he needed to think—about Rosemary, about what was happening here, about the devastating kiss they'd shared on the mountain. And he needed to listen. He didn't want to hear any shouting coming from the big white house across the street.

The shouting started almost the minute Rosemary entered the back door.

"Where on earth have you been?"

Not surprised, but saddened all the same, she simply looked at her father, then turned to find Faye Lewis standing in the doorway of the formal dining room.

"Hello, Rosemary," Faye said on a calm voice. "Come on in, honey, and eat. When Clayton called me looking for you, I offered to bring him supper. Stuffed peppers and corn bread, with string beans on the side."

"And a good thing she did." Clayton stomped past Rosemary, headed for his chair in the den. "Or else I'd be sitting here still waiting on you to get home."

Giving Faye a grateful look, Rosemary called to her father. "I went...I went for a walk and ran into Kirk. He asked me to take him up the mountain."

Faye shot her a warning look, but Rosemary refused to sneak around like a coward. After all, she'd done nothing wrong. And she knew from firsthand experience how gossip moved in a small town, with all the accuracy of a homing pigeon. Might as well confess here and now and get it over with, in case someone else had seen them together.

That got Clayton's attention. "I might have known it. You've done took up with that no-account carpenter. You don't even know the man, Rosemary."

The look he gave her only reminded her of her past indiscretions, but this time she wouldn't make the same mistake. "Kirk is a very reputable carpenter, as well as a licensed steeplejack, and I know him well enough to take a walk with him."

"Jesus was a carpenter," Faye said to Clayton, causing both him and Rosemary to stare at her in shock. "Oh, I'm not comparing, or saying Kirk is anything like the Lord. But carpentry and the kind of work Kirk Lawrence does isn't easy. You have to admire the man for taking on the hard jobs. He's been working day and night since he arrived, so I wouldn't exactly classify him as 'no-account.'"

"Well, I don't admire him, not one bit," Clayton said stubbornly, if not somewhat sheepishly. "Not if it means he'll be dragging her out to all hours every night." Glaring hard at his daughter, he held a finger in the air. "We went through this once, girl. Or have you forgotten already?"

Shocked, Rosemary stepped forward, her own eyes flashing fire. "No, Daddy, I haven't forgotten. And I never will, because you'll make sure I'm always reminded, won't you?" Pushing back bitter tears, she said, "Well, this time it's different. Kirk is different. He's a good man and he's just a friend—someone to talk to—someone who's traveled and has interesting stories to tell. And," she added before turning back into the kitchen, "he won't be here forever. So that makes it rather convenient for everybody."

Clayton wasn't through. Stomping after her, he said in a loud, condemning voice, "No, that just makes you even more crazy this time than before. Nothing can come of this, and you know it."

She whirled, the tears falling in spite of all her efforts to stop them. "Yes, I know it. Nothing will come of it. And that should make you very happy."

With that, she turned to go into the kitchen to finish the dishes Faye had obviously started. The silence that followed her was even more hurtful than the shouting that had preceded it.

Faye joined her after a bit. "He's watching television."

"That's what he loves best," Rosemary said, her tears replaced with cold resignation. "I'm sorry, Faye. I should have been here. I appreciate you coming over to be with him, though."

"I didn't mind at all," Faye said, taking up a dish-cloth to dry the pots that wouldn't fit in the dishwasher. "In fact, we managed to have a pleasant evening. He actually opened up a little and really talked to me. You know, your daddy puts on this big front, but deep down inside, he's still a good man."

Rosemary stared at her friend. "You're kidding? He talked to you, in a civil manner?"

"He sure did." Faye smiled, then winked. "I can still turn on the charm, when I need to. Clayton and I had a good long talk."

Surprised, Rosemary couldn't help but laugh. "Oh, Faye, you're priceless. You always make me feel better. I guess I shouldn't have spoken to him like that, but lately, we stay at each other's throats."

."You don't owe me any explanations," Faye said. "He needs someone to be firm with him, especially you. Why, he's got you jumping through hoops, as it is. I know you love him, honey, and I know you respect him as the Bible tells you you should, but sometimes love has to be tough. You stand firm and remember that you've done nothing to deserve the way he's treating you."

"But I have," Rosemary said as she turned on the dishwasher. "And I suppose I'll pay for it the rest of my life."

"You don't need to. God has forgiven you, Rosemary. Maybe it's time for you to forgive yourself."

"I don't think I can," Rosemary admitted. "I didn't tell Daddy, but I went to Mama's grave this afternoon. That's where Kirk found me. I guess I should have come on home, but it was so nice...walking up the mountain with him. He's easy to talk to, and he's been all over the world. Kirk's a fascinating person, and I enjoy his company. But I doubt anything will come of it."

Faye patted her on the shoulder. "I think it's fine, you two becoming friends. You're right about him, he seems to be a good man. Reverend Clancy is real impressed with his knowledge of the Bible, and all the places he's been. They've had some lively discussions, let me tell you. And Clayton and I even talked about Kirk earlier, with not a harsh word mentioned. Clayton just grunted and said he wasn't impressed, but I think he is."

"Oh, really?"

"Yes, really. He told me Kirk had asked him to help with the renovations. Of course, he was all bluster, telling me he had refused in no uncertain terms. But I think he was flattered by Kirk's offer. You remember how Clayton used to be? All bluff, when underneath he was a big, old pushover."

Rosemary looked at Faye, seeing her in a new light, wondering why she'd really come over here tonight. A new hope sparking like a flame in her mind, she said, "Faye, do you...have feelings for my father?"

"Of course I care about him," the other woman said hastily. "He's been a friend for years."

"You know what I mean," Rosemary said, her eyes bright. "Do you care about him, maybe as more than a friend?"

"What if I do? How would you feel about that?"

Rosemary hugged the other woman close, a new happier set of tears misting in her eyes. "I'd feel as if...a prayer has been answered. I think that's wonderful."

Faye patted her on the back, then said, "Now if we can just get the stubborn old dog to realize that I even exist."

"I think that can be arranged," Rosemary said. "But we'll have to be very careful. He's still not over Mom."

"You let me work on it," Faye suggested, smiling. "I don't intend to replace Eunice, but I'm alone and so is he. I think we could make good company for each other. And, he's still got a lot of good in him. I want to help him find it again."

"You have my blessing," Rosemary replied, a warm feeling settling over her in spite of her earlier fight with her father. "I've certainly been praying for him to turn his life back over to God, and you could be a positive influence in that area."

"Keep saying those prayers," Faye reminded her. "If it's meant to happen, it will."

Rosemary wondered if she should use that same logic when dealing with her own growing relationship with Kirk. Alone in the kitchen after Faye left, she lifted a hand to her lips, remembering the way he'd kissed her. She'd been kissed before, of course, but somehow, she didn't remember any of the kisses moving her with such force.

She'd climbed that mountain a hundred times, so many times she couldn't count them. And yes, she'd been afraid to step to the ledge every time. But this afternoon, this time, she'd felt something besides the usual vertigo sitting there on top of that mountain. When Kirk had kissed her, something long dead had stirred inside her, lifting out like a delicate blossom shooting between a jagged crevice in a rock.

She tried to put a name to this new, unfamiliar feeling. Should she dare hope?

And then she knew, that was it. That was the feeling she'd experienced, a feeling she'd hushed and buried for so long now, she'd almost forgotten what it was like. Hope.

Hope. That was the difference, and now that she had accepted it for what it was, she felt renewed and almost at peace. Almost.

Rosemary read from her Bible, as she did each night before going to bed. And there in the aged book she'd received from the church in fourth-grade Sunday school, she read in Psalm 16 the message she had been longing for. "Therefore my heart is glad, and my glory rejoiceth: my flesh also shall rest in hope."

Hope. For a little while at least. Hope. For some cherished moments with a special person. Hope. To enjoy this time she'd been given with Kirk. She'd settle for that, and she'd accept that Clayton's prediction was true.

It couldn't last. But she could make the most of it while she had the chance. Right now, *that* was her only hope.

Later, as she lay in bed, she smiled and remembered that in heaven, the angels would be watching her while she was sleeping.

Then, the next morning all her hope was vanquished as her past came back to remind her she shouldn't hope for things she could never have.

Chapter Six

"**Y**our steeplejack has gone and done it now,"
Danny said to Rosemary after stomping into her office
the next morning, his eyes blazing, his expression grim.

"What?" she asked, surprised to see him here, and
even more surprised by the suppressed anger coloring
his face. "What's going on, Danny?"

"Come here and I'll show you what's going on,"
he said, urging her to the window with a firm grip on
her arm. "Look over there, Rosemary."

She craned her neck to see where he was pointing
and her heart literally stopped beating. "Oh no. It can't
be."

"It is," Danny replied in a dangerous tone. He
clamped a fist against the windowpane so hard, the
glass rattled. "It's him. I didn't think he'd ever have
the nerve to show his face at this church again."

"Does Dad know?" she asked, sick to her stomach
as she watched Kirk giving instructions to another man.

"He was sitting on the front porch, watching the

renovations, until he saw him! Did you know anything about this?''

"No," she said, a hand coming to her dry throat. "Kirk said he was going to hire some locals, but I never dreamed...I can't believe this is happening.''

"Well, it is, and Dad's in a fit. He called me a few minutes ago—caught me heading out the door.''

Her mind filling with dread and worry, she asked, "What did he say?''

Danny snorted, then turned away from the view of the two men across the lot. "Oh, he had plenty to say. Such as, you were out to all hours with Kirk last night, and that you probably knew all about this, had probably suggested it. He's furious, almost as furious as he was the night he found out about the cause of Mom's wreck.''

Rosemary sank into a nearby chair, all her energy draining away with each beat of her heart. "I can't believe he thinks I'd have anything to do with this. He must still think the worst of me, after all.'' This was like a nightmare, a nightmare she'd tried so very hard to forget. "Maybe if I talk to Kirk—''

"Do you think that would help?'' Danny said, his tone calmer now. "I mean, maybe he didn't realize who he was dealing with.''

"I'm sure that's it,'' she said, feeling slightly more balanced. "I'll just explain to him and then he can find someone else to help him.''

"Well, first you'd better run home and explain to Dad. He's threatening all sorts of things.''

Her gaze flew to her brother. "Such as?''

"Oh, you know—taking care of this once and for all, since the law didn't do its job.''

"But they said two years,'' she reminded him.

"They said two years in prison for vehicular homicide. The judge pushed for a speedy trial. He didn't even get out on bond after the accident. How did he get out of prison so soon?"

"That crafty lawyer, probably. You know how he made him look like a choirboy at the trial. He probably got out early for good behavior and the time he'd already served," Danny explained. "There was talk going around at work a while back, about him getting an early release based on letters and pleas from his old college buddies and coaches at his first parole hearing. You know how all the football coaches loved him. But I...I didn't have the heart to warn you, and besides, I didn't think he'd ever come back here again."

Melissa came rushing into the office, her eyes wide with excitement. "Rosemary, have you heard?"

"Yes," Danny said, guessing what Rosemary's assistant was about to tell them. "I just told her."

"Are you all right?" Melissa asked, falling onto her knees in front of Rosemary, her expression full of worry.

"I'll be okay," Rosemary said. "Can you cover for me for a few minutes? I need to go talk to Dad about this."

Melissa bobbed her head. "Sure. Take as long as you need."

Rosemary followed her brother out of the building, hoping against hope that Kirk wouldn't see her crossing the parking lot. After convincing Danny to go on to work, then telling him goodbye, she took a deep breath and steeled herself against her father's sure wrath. Then, with slow, deliberate steps, she headed across the church yard, her head down, her steps choppy and hurried.

She was halfway home when she heard Kirk's voice behind her. "Well, good morning to you, too."

She pretended she didn't hear him. Things would be much easier that way.

"Rosemary?"

She kept walking, willing herself to face forward. If she turned to him now, she'd crumble, and she had to face her father first.

She felt a hand on her arm, but she tugged away and kept walking. "I can't talk right now, Kirk. Something's come up."

"What?" he said, jogging to catch up with her. When she managed to scoot around him, he started walking backward just in front of her, so she couldn't get away.

Kirk took one look at her face and knew this was serious. She was as pale as the gray stone on the steeple facing.

"Rosemary, what is it?" Guessing, he said, "Did you and your father argue...about last night? I'll explain to him. I'll tell him it was my fault. I knew I needed to stay away from you, but I wanted to see you again."

She had been looking down, but now she lifted her head to face him, no longer able to control the turmoil bubbling inside her. They stopped in the driveway of her yard.

"It's not about last night, Kirk," she said, running a shaking hand through her hair to calm her jittery nerves.

"Tell me," he said, reaching out to touch her arm. "Tell me, Rosemary."

The door of the house slammed then, and Clayton came barreling down the steps toward them, his face flushed, his eyes watery and red-rimmed. "Well, don't just stand there, girl. Go ahead, tell the man why you're in such a hurry to cover your steps."

Kirk turned around, his own fury evident in his stance and expression. "This is between Rosemary and me, Mr. Brinson."

"Oh no, son," Clayton said, pointing a finger in Kirk's face. "This ain't just between the two of you. You done went and put your finger into my business now."

"Look," Kirk began, "Rosemary and I did nothing wrong last night. We simply took a walk. I promise it won't happen again, though, if it's going to cause her any more arguments and reprimands from you."

Clayton's hostile glare only deepened. "This ain't about that. This is about you coming here and stirring up trouble—trouble we don't need right now."

"What do you mean?" Kirk asked, holding his hands out palm up. "What could I have possibly done to upset you this way?" He turned to Rosemary, "And what did I do to make you afraid to even speak to me?"

Clayton didn't wait for her to answer. He stepped closer, his finger still jutting out in the air. "I'll tell you what you did. You went and hired on the man who killed my wife!"

Realization warred with shock on Kirk's face. He turned to Rosemary for validation, and saw it clearly in her troubled eyes. "Is that true?" he said, knowing it sounded redundant.

"Oh, yes, it's true," Clayton said, moving closer, his eyes blazing. Then he turned to his daughter. "Satisfied?"

"Daddy, please," Rosemary said, stepping between

the two of them. "Kirk had no way of knowing about...about Eric, and neither did I."

"Eric?" Kirk looked from Clayton to Rosemary. "Eric Thomas?"

Rosemary lowered her head, the pain coursing throughout her body almost too much to bear. She glanced up at Kirk, then over to her father. "Daddy, I didn't know. You have to believe that. I didn't know anything about this, and if you'll just go back in the house, I'll explain to Kirk."

Clayton peered at both of them in disgust. "Oh, you'd better explain. And you'd better keep Eric Thomas away from my yard. I'll kill him with my bare hands if he tries to set foot anywhere near my property." Shoving away from Kirk, he whirled. "And that goes for this one, too. I'm warning you, Rosemary! Keep them both away from me—I don't want you bringing this one home for any more suppers—not at my table, and I don't want to catch you going off to the mountain with him again!"

Rosemary watched her father as he headed back inside, then she looked at Kirk. He appeared to be as angry as Clayton.

"I should have never brought you here," she said on a weak whisper. "I've made another terrible mistake."

He stared at her, seeing the pain in her eyes, seeing the worry marking her face, and wondered what had happened to all the goodness he thought he'd seen in this town. "No, I'm the one who made a mistake. I got involved, too involved, and I broke my own rule." Shaking his head, he added, "But now that I *am* involved, don't you think I have a right to know what's going on?"

"Yes, you do," she said, moving her head in agreement, even while his regret became her own. "But not here."

He grabbed her by the arm. "Then where, Rosemary? Where and when will you tell me the truth? *Did* Eric have something to do with your mother's accident?"

She nodded, then looked around. "Yes. And I...I can't face him—not yet."

"Come with me then." Kirk tugged her to his trailer, pulling her up the steps so he could shut the door firmly behind them.

Rosemary blinked, to adjust her eyes to the dim interior, and to stop the inevitable tears that she refused to shed. Later, she would remember her surroundings—books and CDs, a laptop computer, a cellular phone, economical and minimal—the trailer was consistent with the man who traveled in it.

Right now, however, she could only stare up at Kirk, hoping he could understand what a terrible mistake she had made in bringing him here.

"Talk, Rosemary."

She did. She just blurted the ugly truth right out. "Eric Thomas killed my mother. He was driving drunk and he crossed the centerline and ran her car off the road into a ravine. She died instantly." She looked up, her features twisting in an anguished frown. "He walked away with a few scratches."

Kirk slumped onto the bench that made up his dining area, his elbows coming to rest on the small table where he usually ate his solitary meals. He released a heavy sigh.

They sat silent for a minute, then he asked, "Did he serve any time?"

"He got two years, but apparently he's out after only a year, on probation. That's why we're all so shocked—we didn't expect to see him here."

"And I just hired him as my assistant." He ran a hand through his hair, then looked over at her. "I didn't know, Rosemary. Reverend Clancy told me he'd done some jail time, but didn't say why. I had no way of knowing."

"Of course you didn't," she said, reaching out a hand to him, needing the physical contact to steady her own doubts. "I've caused you so much trouble."

He took her hand, then scoffed at her statement. "I think that's the other way around, sweetheart. I've caused you trouble since I pulled into town."

"No," she said, her eyes holding his. "Last night, for the first time in a very long time, I had a little glimmer of hope, Kirk. And you gave me that." At his confused expression, she held up her other hand. "I don't expect anything more. But I sure did cling to that little bit of...happiness."

He knew what she was telling him. He'd felt it, too. They'd both been so practical, so upfront, telling themselves this couldn't last, couldn't go past friendship. But they'd kissed each other and something had shifted, something had bound them together there on that mountaintop. Kirk knew that no matter where he traveled or who he met after this, he'd never forget Rosemary. And he'd decided that he was fooling himself to even think he could actually leave her without feeling more than a little regret.

Well, he was feeling regret now. He'd hurt her again. "Reverend Clancy came to me," he explained. "He said he had a man who really needed a job, said he'd fallen on hard times and needed a second chance. He had some experience with carpentry, so I told the reverend I'd give him a shot. Eric isn't afraid of heights, like most of the others I've interviewed.''

Rosemary shook her head. "No, Eric never was afraid of anything. He always was a daredevil. And a star quarterback in high school and college.''

"You knew him...before your mother's accident?''

She lowered her head, unable to meet his gaze. "Yes. He lives in the next town, but we met in college.''

Kirk strummed his fingers on the table, impatient to know the whole story. "Reverend Clancy said he wasn't a member of the church, but that he had attended in the past. He really pushed me to consider Eric, he said he could vouch for him.''

Rosemary lifted her head in surprise. "How could Reverend Clancy do that, knowing about Eric? He knows how we all feel about what Eric did. My family is shattered, my life is shattered, because of what happened. I don't understand how my own minister could do this.''

Kirk reached over to stroke her trembling hand. Her fingers were cold, so he rubbed them between his palms. "Maybe he believes Eric needs a second chance, here in the place where he made a mistake.''

She yanked her hand away, then jumped up to glare at him. "A mistake? Is that what you think this is? Just a bad mistake? He took another human being's life, Kirk. And that human being happened to be my mother. It wasn't just a mistake. It was murder!''

Unable to deal with her rage, he stood to take her in his arms. "What do you want me to do?''

She didn't mince words. "I want you to tell him to get lost, to get away from me and my family. My father...well, he might do something we'd all regret if you don't fire Eric.''

"I promised the man at least a month's work, Rosemary.''

"And I've lost my mother forever! I can't bear to watch him working on that church every day, Kirk. It isn't right!''

Kirk stared down at her, wanting to understand her tremendous pain. Now, at least, he understood the rage behind the pain. No wonder Clayton walked around like a zombie, no wonder Danny's laughter was brittle with false cheer, and no wonder Rosemary was trying so very hard to hold them all together. This wasn't just the loss of a loved one. This was much, much more, something so senseless, so wasteful, that none of them could deal with it or accept it. And he'd just brought them all face-to-face with their worst nightmare.

"No, it isn't right,'' he said at last. "This was a senseless act of a very irresponsible person. And two years—no, make that one year serving time—will never be enough to bring your mother back. Maybe that's why Reverend Clancy brought Eric here. Eric can learn a greater lesson having to see you each day. Maybe your minister wants to help all of you accept this, Rosemary.''

She shook her head, her eyes burning with a dark fire. "I can never accept what happened. And Daddy certainly never will. But we were doing okay, until this.''

"Were you really?'' he asked. "Or weren't you just going through the motions? I've seen how your father treats you. I've seen how sad you look sometimes. You haven't even begun to heal, Rosemary.''

"But we had a chance,'' she said, her hands clinging

to his shirt. "We had a chance until Eric came back. Don't take that away from us, Kirk. Don't let this man back into our lives."

Her plea tore through his system. How could he deny her that one simple request. Yet, how could he tell that broken man out there that he didn't deserve a chance, either? Kirk had never faced such a dilemma before. Caught in the middle, he tried to understand both sides. But he did not want to cause Rosemary any more pain.

Tugging her close, he said, "I'll see what can be done. Maybe Reverend Clancy can find him work somewhere else."

"Thank you," she said, her body slumping against his in relief.

Just then a knock shook the small trailer, causing Rosemary to pull away. "I've got to get going," she said. "The children will be asking all sorts of questions."

She moved past him to open the door.

Eric Thomas stood at the bottom of the steps, his gaze meeting hers first in shock, then in shame, then finally in a firm resolve that sickened her all over again.

Rosemary stared down at the man who'd changed her life so dramatically. Eric was slender and good-looking, with thick sandy-blond hair and hazel eyes. Apparently, prison life had changed him somewhat. He was still muscular and had the build of a born athlete, but he seemed calmer, older and more mature. He'd always been so restless and unsettled before. Or maybe, he was just too surprised to move, seeing her in Kirk's trailer.

"Rosemary," he said, moving to let her pass. "I didn't know you were here. I can come back later."

"I was just leaving," she said, her head down as she stepped past him.

"Before you go," Eric said, his hand on her arm, "there are a few things I need to say to you."

She jerked her arm away, recoiling from his touch with a look of disgust and loathing. "We have *nothing* to say to each other, Eric. You have to know how hard this is on my family. I'd appreciate it if you'd have the decency to just leave."

Kirk stepped outside, between them. "Eric, Rosemary told me what happened."

Eric looked from Rosemary to Kirk. "So you're going to fire me before I even get started, aren't you?"

Rosemary glanced over at Kirk. She could see the confusion in his eyes. She knew it wasn't fair to ask this of him, but what else could she do? What else could he do?

Eric shifted his feet, then placed both hands on his hips. "Reverend Clancy promised me a job, and I need the money."

"He had no right to do that," Rosemary said at last. "The money for the renovations came from church members."

"Oh, so I'm not good enough to make an honest living from it?" Eric asked, his tone sarcastic. "I thought you were a Christian, Rosemary. I thought you were supposed to forgive and forget."

"Forgive?" she shouted, throwing a hand in the air. "Forget? Forgive that you killed my mother, forget that you lied to me and everyone else? I don't think so, Eric. You see, I can't forget. I have to live with what you did each and every day of my life."

"So do I, Rosemary," he said on a soft voice, his eyes bright. "So do I."

Kirk pulled Rosemary away from Eric, afraid she'd pounce on him with both fists if he didn't do something.

"Look, Rosemary," he said, his eyes willing her to focus on him, "I've finished the preliminary groundwork. I have to get started on the steeple and Eric is the only one who qualifies for the work we'll be doing. Do you want me to delay the whole operation while I try to find someone else?"

She stared at him, wondering why he couldn't see this the way she did. "I want you to understand how I feel, Kirk. I can't let this happen. You can't let him work here."

"I don't have much choice," he said. "I promised the reverend, and I promised Eric. I'm sure his probation officer will check to see if he's got a job."

"Do you think I care about that?" she asked, pushing him away to glare at Eric. "I can't tolerate seeing him again, Kirk. And especially not here, rebuilding the church. This was my project, my restoration of the church I love. Please, help me."

"I'm not giving up this job," Eric said, his own stance stubborn and determined. "I've served my time and I'm trying to get my life together. Why would you deny me that chance?"

Rosemary whirled on him with all the fury she'd held in check for the past year. "Because you denied me everything, Eric. Everything. You took away my mother, and you...you broke my heart. My whole world has changed because you had to have one more drink for the road. So don't expect me to feel sorry for you, or to welcome you back here with open arms. I can't." She looked back at Kirk, a dark defiance coloring her eyes. "I won't. I'll go to the church board and demand that Kirk fire you."

"Rosemary," Kirk began, trying to reason with her, "listen to me. Let Eric help me until I can find someone else, or the church board will probably call off the restoration altogether. I won't waste my time or the congregation's on this. I've already stalled long enough, as it is."

Her head pounded and her heart wasn't far behind. Why? Why did it have to be Eric of all people? Should she try to be fair and let him stay? No. She couldn't face him, maybe because it meant facing up to her own guilt.

But did she have the right to judge him, in spite of what he'd done? Remembering her own part in the whole thing, in all the events that had led up to her mother's death, she closed her eyes and willed the bitter memories away. Maybe this was part of her punishment, after all. In her heart, she knew it didn't matter how she felt about Eric. They would both have their day of reckoning soon enough. And in the meantime, she could only pray—for both Eric and herself.

"Okay," she said at last. "Do what you have to do. But don't expect me to cheer you on." Then she turned to Eric. "Stay away from my father and my brother. I won't be held responsible for what they might do or say about this."

Then she faced Kirk. "You were right. We...we both made a mistake. Just get your work done and...leave me out of it, please."

Kirk's own heart beat out a frustrated cadence. He couldn't let her go away angry and upset. Yet he couldn't send Eric away, either. But he could keep him busy and out of sight for a while.

"Eric, for now you're still working for me. Right now, I need you to start unloading the equipment from that trailer parked over by the back of the church. You'll need to check the machinery and the cable ropes. Make sure they're all secure and up to standard."

"All right," Eric said, his eyes on Rosemary. He turned to walk away, then looked back at her. "I am sorry, Rosemary," he said. "I know that doesn't mean much to you, or your family. But I am truly sorry about everything."

Rosemary focused on the buds of a fire azalea growing underneath the oak tree. She didn't respond to his apology.

But Eric wasn't through pleading his case. "That's all I wanted to say to you, really. I know there's no chance for us, ever again, but I do want another chance to get my life in order. I only ask that you allow me that chance."

She put her arms across her chest, and kept her head down, her memories acting like a shield against his pleas, against the tender mercy the Bible told her she must issue as a means of forgiveness. She wasn't ready to forgive Eric Thomas. She might not ever be.

After Eric walked away, Kirk forced her head up with a hand on her cheek, his eyes meeting hers. "There's more to this story, isn't there?"

"Yes," she said, thinking it didn't really matter if he knew the truth now. Whatever they'd shared yesterday was gone; vanished, like that spectacular sunset they'd witnessed together. She might as well push the wedge farther between them, and end it once and for all.

"Tell me," he said, his eyes dark with longing.

"I was engaged to Eric," she said simply, softly. At his gasp of surprise, she nodded. "That's right, my fiancé killed my mother." She shot him a wry, bitter smile. "That's why there was no wedding, Kirk. And that's why my father can't stand the sight of me today. Maybe now you can understand why I didn't want Eric here. Seeing him reminds me that my mother's death was all my fault."

Chapter Seven

Rosemary immediately went to find Reverend Clancy. He was in his study preparing to make the rounds of visiting the shut-ins and the church members in the hospital.

"Rosemary," he said as she marched into the cool, paneled room, "I've been expecting you, dear."

"Then you know how I feel about what you've done," she responded, standing over his desk. She couldn't be disrespectful to him. She loved him like a second father and he'd been a source of strength to her in the last few years. But she had to know why. Slumping down in a comfortable wing chair, she said, "Didn't you know what this would cause?"

The reverend placed his plump hands together over his heavily marked calendar pad, his gentle brown eyes never leaving her face. "I knew, Rosemary. I knew this wouldn't be easy, but I've been counseling young Eric in prison for some time now. He is an unofficial member of my flock, and the boy needs a guiding hand.

Should I deny him the nurturing I'd gladly give to any other member of this congregation?''

Rosemary looked down at her hands clutched tightly together in her lap. "No, Preacher, of course not. That's between you and Eric. But to bring him back here and allow him to work on the restoration, of all things! I can't bear to see that.''

"It's not for you to bear, Rosemary,'' the minister replied softly. "Turn it over to the Lord. Let the Lord bear this burden for you. You cannot judge Eric. He's already been judged and condemned, and now he's asking for our prayers and our forgiveness.''

She brought her hands to her face. "I don't think I can do that. I don't think I can find it in my heart.''

"You have to.'' Reverend Clancy got up and shuffled around the massive oak desk, then leaned back on it, his gaze never leaving Rosemary's face. "Think about what you're doing, child. Think about what the Bible tells us. We don't condone what Eric did, but we have to forgive him and give him a chance to prove himself. He's struggling, Rosemary. He's not had a drop of liquor since he went to prison. Now that he's out, the struggle gets even harder. I had to bring him here, because he called me to ask for help. He needs someone to turn to when he feels weak and wants to turn back to the bottle. You know about his family life. He doesn't have any support there, with both parents dead and a brother and sister who've turned their backs on him. Should I really do the same?''

She looked up at him at last. "No. You wouldn't be doing your job if you turned him away.''

Reverend Clancy nodded and pointed a finger. "It's not just my job, Rosemary. It's the entire congregation's. Following God's word sometimes puts us in difficult and uncomfortable situations.''

Reaching out a hand to him, she said, ''Oh, Preacher, this is so hard. Almost as hard as seeing my mother being buried. Will this never end?''

''Only when you let it,'' Reverend Clancy said, patting her hand with both of his. ''You have to remember that at one time you cared deeply for Eric, wanted to make a life with him. And while that can never be the same, you can learn to find that love in your heart again, that Christian love that gives all of us grace. And in that grace, you will find forgiveness. It's the only way to get past all of the pain. Let's pray about it, Rosemary. I'm here to help you, and Eric, too. And I haven't abandoned you. Nor has your Lord. 'I will not leave you comfortless.' He said it and now you must remember it.''

''What about...what about my father?'' she asked, her voice cracking. ''This isn't going to make matters any better for him.''

''Then all the more reason to pray,'' the minister said, closing his eyes as he gripped her hand.

Rosemary bowed her head, her silent tears falling even as she lifted her sorrow to God. She'd pray for Eric, but she would have a hard time forgiving him.

Kirk did something that morning he hadn't done in a while. He called his mother. ''I'm having a hard time dealing with this,'' he explained as the wires carried his voice thousands of miles away to the Wisconsin hideaway where his parents now lived.

''Kirk, Kirk,'' Edana said, her voice soothing and still very much Irish. ''My poor boy. Are you sure this is more than just a conflict with the people who hired you?''

She always did see right through him. He'd only told her of the problem with Eric. Just the facts. But as usual, Edana didn't deal in just the facts. His mother would have made a great Irish cop. She had an instinct for getting to the bottom of a situation.

He sighed long and hard. ''I don't know, Mother. I came here with the usual intent. I was really looking forward to working on this particular church. It's so beautiful, you see. So old and intriguing. And the people here, they're unique and interesting. Now I've gone and caused a ruckus and I don't know how to fix it.''

''Fix it same as you fix your steeples, lad,'' Edana said. ''Slow and steady, with a care for each and every detail.''

''But these are human beings, Mother. That's a little harder—I can't just slap a new coat of primer on them.''

''Might help the lot of them,'' she replied, sending him a throaty laugh. Then turning serious, she said, ''Tell me some more about this Rosemary—sounds like a nice girl.''

''One of the best,'' he admitted, being cautious so his mother wouldn't read too much into his budding relationship with Rosemary. ''She's lovely and so hurt by all of this. She tries so hard to do what's best for everyone, except herself maybe.''

''And you, you encourage her to take care of herself, I suppose?''

''I've talked to her about that very thing, yes.''

''I know the kind of talking you do, boyo. Have you gone and taken that girl's heart away?''

"No, oh no. I'm not after sweeping her off her feet. But I…I do care about her—a lot."

"I see."

Oh boy. Whenever his mother said that, he knew he was in trouble. "Don't go putting too much into this, Mother. Rosemary has been a friend to me, and a champion of my way of doing things. She fought to get me here, you know."

"How impressive."

"And she's still fighting, for her father's love and approval, for forgiveness, which I personally don't think she needs, and…she's sacrificed everything simply because she's that way. She does what's right, what needs to be done. She's amazing, really."

"Quite."

Kirk smiled, then tilted the phone away from his ear. He could just see his mother, her short clipped hair a mixture of salt and pepper, her cup of tea perched at arm's length, her feet up on her favorite stool, her flashing eyes bright with wisdom and a mother's knowing. Ah, he loved his mother, missed her, longed to tell her how he really felt. But he knew he didn't have to. She already knew. As she always did.

"I'll be all right," he finally said. "I just wanted to check on you and Da. How's the fishing?"

"Same as ever. The fish are in the lake and your da is waiting for them to jump on the end of his line."

"Mother, do you ever miss Ireland?"

"What ever kind of question is that? Of course I miss Ireland. Every day. But I'd miss your father more. That's the difference, lad. Why? Are you missing Ireland?"

"Some. But, lately, I guess I'm missing Grandpapa more. I know how Rosemary feels, but at least Papa died in his sleep at a ripe old age. I hope I go that way."

"Ah, Kirk, you're just feeling something you've not yet experienced till now," Edana explained, her voice going soft.

"Oh, and what might that be?"

"Well, you've never had to go through what that young lass has had to bear. But the fact that you're having some sympathy pains for her tells me a great deal—about Rosemary and about my traveling son."

"Oh, all right, what do you mean?"

"I mean, you're maturing into a caring young man. And high time, I'd say. You've always given your best, son. Always done a good, solid job, worked hard with your body and your hands. Only this time you've put your heart into it. And once you put your heart to something, you get so much more back. But you find pain in the giving, and in the getting. And that's something you've avoided in your carefree, free-spirited gypsy life."

"Well, you do make me sound rather shallow, Mother dear."

"Well, you did have this nonchalant attitude about some things, son of mine."

"Not now," he admitted quietly. "Not with Rosemary."

"Will you miss her when you're gone?"

"Aye, I'll miss her a great deal."

"That's the difference, then. You'll have to decide if you'll miss her more than you'll miss the traveling life."

"But it doesn't really matter how I feel—I can't stay here, and I won't hurt her by causing her any more grief with her father. I have to do what I've always done. I have to walk away.''

''Without so much as a good fight?''

Kirk closed his eyes and remembered the feel of Rosemary's soft lips nestled close to his own. He remembered the curl of her hair under his palm. He remembered the bright hope in her eyes when she told him that he'd given her that, for a while at least. Rosemary was a fighter; she was willing to fight off her despair with only a glimmer of hope. She was willing to put her faith into God's promise, sight unseen. Should he do the same?

''Your silence speaks volumes, son,'' Edana said. ''Do your work, Kirk. The rest will follow.''

He gripped the phone, then looked out the tiny side window of his trailer. ''I...don't want to lose my heart, Mum.''

''That, my dear boy, is something you have no say over.''

Kirk finished his conversation then went back outside to start his day all over again. He stood there, looking up at the strong tower and the rising steeple of the church, wishing desperately he could fix Rosemary's hurts in the same way he knew he could fix the aging spires of Alba's antique church.

Then he remembered his mother's words.

Slow and steady, with great care for details.

Should he handle Rosemary in just that way?

He lifted up a silent prayer for guidance and for strength. And if he had to lose his heart, he decided, he wanted Rosemary to be the one to find it.

''This time, Mother, I think I'm willing to stay and fight.'' He just hoped he had the courage to see it through.

* * *

While Rosemary and Kirk both sought counsel on their mutual problems, Faye Lewis searched out Clayton Brinson to see how he was faring with this new development.

"Don't blame Rosemary," Faye said now as she handed him a cup of freshly brewed coffee to go along with the apple bread she'd baked him the night before. "The girl honestly did not know anything about this, Clayton."

Clayton looked over at the woman who'd been a friend to his wife and him for most of their lives. Faye wasn't a pretty woman, but she wasn't unattractive, either. She was petite and slender where Eunice had been tall and voluptuous. Faye's graying hair was styled in a neat, clipped cut that framed her face with spiky curls. Eunice had worn her dark hair neatly piled on top of her head most of the time. Why was he comparing, anyway? he wondered. No one would ever compare to Eunice.

Faye was determined, to say the least. "Clayton, stop staring at me like that and listen."

"I am listening," he said on a snarl. "The bread's good, by the way."

"Thank you. Now, will you please try to be civil to your daughter when she comes home?"

He dropped his fork with a clatter. "How can I be civil to her when she's heading for sure disaster, just like before. That steeplejack ain't much better than that murderer she took up with, and look how that turned out. We're all suffering because of her selfishness."

"Clayton Brinson, you are one stubborn man," Faye said, her eyes blazing. "Rosemary had no control over what happened, no more than you did."

"If she had listened to me, none of this would have taken place. Eunice would still be alive."

Faye glared at him. "You're so sure of that, huh?"

"Very sure."

"And you're so very sure that God decided to pick on you by taking your wife away from you?"

"Yep. God musta had it in for me, and now I've got it in for Him."

"And what do you plan on doing to God—to get even?"

"I plan on sitting right here in this house."

"Oh, your grand boycott of the church? Who do you think that's hurting—God or maybe yourself?"

"I'm not hurting any."

"Baloney." Faye got up to clean away their dessert dishes. "I've watched you this past year, Clayton. We've all been very patient with you, hoping you'd come around, praying you'd stop this nonsense and get back to church. But you just sit in this house, like you're asleep, like you're waiting for Eunice to walk back in that door." Touching him on the arm, she said, "You've got to get on with your life, man. You've got a lovely, caring daughter who's trying very hard to seek your forgiveness, and you've got a son who buries his troubles behind a sad laugh and a hard day's work. And what about that grandbaby? Do you want little Emily to grow up without knowing the love and the faith that sustained you all these years? What kind of example are you setting for that child?"

Clayton slammed both hands down on the table, then stood to tower over her. "I don't recall asking your advice on this, Faye."

"No, you haven't asked my help on anything," she replied tartly. "And you haven't asked me how much I miss my friend, or how much the church misses Eunice, or how much your daughter is hurting. You haven't asked anything of anyone because you're too busy wallowing in your own pity to see that others are hurting, too.''

"Nobody can be hurting the way I am," he said in a voice soft with emotion and hard with bitterness. "You don't know a thing about how I feel."

She placed a hand on her chest and sighed. "Maybe you're right there. But I do know that when my Alton died, I lost my heart. But because I had the strength of this church and God's assurance that we'd be together again one day, I managed to dig myself out of my gloom. Death isn't easy for any of us, Clayton. And blaming others only makes it harder. Isn't it time you stop blaming and start back to praying and thanking God for your blessings?"

"I think you'd better go now," he said, turning away to head into the sheltered darkness of the den. "I don't want to miss 'The Price Is Right.'"

Mad, Faye shouted after him. "Oh, the price is right, all right. And you'll wind up paying a high one if you don't change." When he didn't respond, she mumbled, "Stubborn old man," then left by the back door.

Clayton plopped down in his easy chair, but his mind wasn't on the bright new car the game-show host was trying to give away. For the first time in a long time, Clayton was thinking about something other than his own sorrow. For the first time in over a year, he picked up the worn, dog-eared Bible that had belonged to his wife. He didn't read it, but just held it, his eyes centered blankly on the television.

Rosemary met Faye in the church yard as she was on her way back from making some copies in the office. "Faye, what's going on?"

"Nothing for you to worry about," Faye said. "I just had a nice visit with your father. He's better now."

Rosemary saw the high color in Faye's flushed cheeks. "You don't have to pretend with me. He's furious and he blames me again."

"Don't worry about it," Faye said, taking her by the arm to walk with her back to the educational building. "I gave him a good talking-to, but I don't know if I helped or hindered you. I do know he wants you to stay away from Kirk, though."

"That won't be a problem," Rosemary remarked, her eyes scanning the church. Glad to see that Kirk and Eric had knocked off for lunch, she turned to Faye. "I won't be overtly friendly with the steeplejack anymore. How can I, when he's gone and hired Eric right under my nose?"

Faye craned her neck, then frowned. "Rosemary, you sounded a lot like your daddy just then. It would be a shame to stay mad at Kirk for something he had no control over."

"He could have sent Eric packing once he found out the truth."

"He needed someone to help him, and since he had nothing to do with what happened, I guess he chose Eric based on the facts of his work record and a plea from the reverend."

Rosemary pushed a bouncing curl off her face. "Oh, I know, and Eric fit the bill. This is so complicated. Sometimes I wish I'd never found out about such a thing as a steeplejack."

"The church needed a restoration," Faye reminded

her. Then, turning to pat her on the cheek, she added, "And maybe, sweet lady, so did you."

Over the next few days, Rosemary thought about what Faye had said to her as she attended church and listened to Reverend Clancy's sermon on grace, then started her week watching Kirk going about his work. He was a presence in her life now, good or bad, and she couldn't get him out of her mind or out of her sight.

Oh, but watching him was like watching a ballet in motion, or a song lifting out on the wind. He moved with such grace and such confidence, extended in his tiny chair from heavy cable lines draped over the sturdy steeple columns. He washed and scoured the granite facings, polishing the stones until they shone like precious gems. He lifted away rust spots and fixed leaking corners. He climbed ever higher to nail down loose shingles and replace broken ones. He lovingly washed the stained glass, and good on his word, he walked up the mountain to consult with Aunt Fitz since she had pictures of the church from way back.

Rosemary had heard this last bit of information from Melissa, who'd heard it from Eric. Rosemary didn't want to think about Eric, so she pretended he didn't exist and avoided watching the work when he was involved.

But she couldn't avoid her feelings for Kirk.

Rosemary marveled in the lines of his body, with its sculptured muscles and tanned skin. She appreciated the artistic nature of his work, and the way he took such pains with each detail of his job. He was a beautiful man, a gentle man, who'd been thrust into something beyond his control.

Maybe Faye was right. Maybe she shouldn't blame

Kirk for something she had started. Tonight, as she sat reading her Bible, she prayed as Reverend Clancy had advised her to do. But when she got to the part about asking forgiveness for Eric, her stomach knotted and her head began to pound. She couldn't bring herself to form the words.

Hopping up, she went to the open window of her bedroom to take in the scent of the honeysuckle growing near the back fence. Bugs hissed at the screen, seeking the light from her tiny bedside lamp. The night was sweet and crisp, fresh and enticing. A soft flow of light shone from the tiny trailer parked across the way.

What was he doing in there? Was he reading one of the many books she'd seen stacked here and there in the small space he called home? Was he lying there on that narrow cot, wondering how he'd ever gotten caught up in such a twisted mess? Was he regretting that he'd gotten to know her?

He was lying there, and he was regretting that he couldn't see her, talk to her, kiss her. They'd established a quiet truce since the first of the week, when he'd looked down to find her in the play yard with the children. Each of them went about their work, methodically doing what had to be done, but they no longer laughed or waved or talked between chores. There were no more invitations to lunch, or supper, and no more hikes up the mountain.

Rosemary was punishing him for working with the man who'd killed her mother. Or maybe, she was punishing herself by denying her feelings.

Kirk rose from the cot to throw on a T-shirt and a pair of jeans. He needed some fresh air. He needed to talk to Rosemary. Slamming the trailer door behind him, he walked out underneath the great oak and automatically set his sights on the house across the street.

The image he saw in the window at the rear of the house took his breath away.

Rosemary. Rosemary silhouetted by the light of a single, muted lamp. Rosemary in a white cotton gown that fluffed out over her shoulders with demure ruffles and fell around her curves in pristine folds. She was standing there, bracing her hands on the frame, her head tossed back as she sniffed the night.

Kirk stood staring, his heart pounding a beat that scared him with its intensity. He couldn't move; didn't want to move. He simply waited.

Instinctively, Rosemary brought her head down. Someone was watching her. She knew it. Felt it as a fine chill moved up her spine. She looked over at the trailer and saw him standing there, one hand braced on the pole of his awning-covered side porch.

Kirk.

At first, she started to turn away. After all, she was standing here in her gown and even though it was made of a thick white cotton, it was still her nightgown. And also, she didn't want to see him—that would make her ache even more, longing for something she had no business wanting.

But she didn't turn away. She just stood there, her eyes moving over him, memorizing him, her soul reaching for him, calling to him, until finally he started walking toward her.

"Oh no," she said, turning quickly to grab a floral robe to throw over her gown. Quickly, she tied it tightly around her waist, making sure she was decent. But she didn't put the window down, nor did she run away.

She simply waited.

And he came.

"Rosemary?"

"Hello." Kirk stood eye-level with the window. She couldn't see his face in the shadows, but she could smell the spicy soap-clean scent of him.

"Are you all right?" He couldn't see her face, and that irritated him to no end since he wanted to reach out and touch her sweet-smelling hair.

"I'm okay. How about you?"

"I couldn't sleep."

"Me neither. I was reading the Bible, and trying to pray."

He smiled at the innocent admission. "Did you?"

"Did I what?"

"Did you...were you able to say your prayers?"

Rosemary leaned down, then fell to her knees so her face would be level with his. It was her undoing. Kirk's intense eyes centered on her face, burning her with such a sharp, heated appraisal that she blushed all the way to her feet. "I...I had to give up. I'm just having a hard time with all of this."

"Me, too. I'm so sorry if I caused you any pain."

"I told you—no more apologizing."

"You've been avoiding me."

"Yes. It's for the best, Kirk."

"Why, Rosemary? Why is it for the best? We...we were just getting to know each other."

"You don't need to know me. You don't want to know me," she said on a shaky whisper. "It's for the best."

"Stop saying that," he hissed, his face close to the screen, his eyes flashing fire. "You have nothing to be ashamed of, and I really *want* to know you. I don't care about your past, except to understand it. We shouldn't let this thing with Eric come between us.''

"But it has,'' she said, placing her hands underneath her chin as she gazed at him. ''I'm almost glad, too. Seeing Eric reminded me of all I've done, of how I've hurt my daddy and my brother. I can't do that again, Kirk.''

''So you'll just forget how we feel, because your father doesn't approve of me.''

''No, I'll remember how I felt when my mother died, and know that it's because of me—my own father doesn't love me anymore because of what I did.''

Frustrated, Kirk stomped a foot on the ground. ''How can you blame yourself—simply because you were engaged to Eric? You had no way of knowing he'd have a wreck with your mother.''

She lowered her head for a minute, ashamed to look him in the eye. ''But I knew he had a problem. Kirk, I knew Eric had a drinking problem and I did nothing about it.''

Kirk's heart went out to her. ''What could you have done?''

''I should have broken things off with him, but I thought...I thought I could change him.''

''Why would you want to marry him in the first place?'' From what Kirk had seen of her ex, the man had major problems to begin with, problems he was only now coming to grips with. ''You can do better than that.''

She looked up, laughing bitterly. ''That's exactly what my daddy used to tell me. But I didn't want to listen to him because I thought I loved Eric. I was so sure, so secure in that love, that I was blinded by the truth.''

Suddenly, Kirk realized what he was up against. She wouldn't make the same mistake twice, no matter how attracted she was to him. Because she would deny her feelings, thinking she didn't deserve them, thinking she was wrong to even feel anything for him. Thinking she'd finally win her father's approval and forgiveness if she showed him how strong she could be.

"Don't do this, Rosemary," he said. "Don't punish yourself or me this way. Forget Eric, forget your father. Think about us, think about the mountain. Think about this."

He reached up a hand, touching it to the screen, his eyes touching on her. "Put your hand on mine, Rosemary."

"No," she said, a plea in the one word. "I can't."

"Rosemary," he said, "touch me. God doesn't want you to be alone. He's not cruel that way. Together, with His guidance, we can figure this out."

"No," she said again, her heart breaking. "Let's just leave it the way it is."

"I can't do that," he admitted, slamming his hand against the screen hard enough to rattle it.

"Go," she whispered, glancing back over her shoulder. "Before we wake Daddy."

"I'll wake him," Kirk replied, angry now. "I'll wake this whole town and tell all of them that I care about you and I want to be with you and there's nothing wrong with that."

Hearing him say that made her realize she felt the same way, but she was still afraid to make good on her feelings. She didn't have his nerve, after all.

So she sat there, looking down at the man who'd come into her life and started her heart beating again.

Was this wrong? She didn't have the answers, but

she knew who did. And she knew that Kirk was right. She'd asked God to forgive her, to give her a second chance. Maybe this was that chance.

Slowly, she reached out a hand, stretching her fingers over the thin mesh that separated her from Kirk, touching her palm across the wiry screen.

Kirk placed his hand against hers, and felt the warmth of her skin through the brittle barrier dividing them.

"Tell me you'll pray about this, Rosemary. Promise me you'll ask God to guide us."

"I will," she said, meaning it. "I'm asking Him right this very minute. Please, Lord, show us the way."

"And so will I." He looked up, toward the velvety sky. "We only ask that You show us the right way, the way that was meant to be." Not used to making such appeals, he added, "Whatever happens, we place our lives in Your hands."

"That was beautiful, Kirk," Rosemary said. "Thank you."

Kirk pressed his hand there, near hers, his eyes searching her face in the moonlight, while the heavens watched and the angels listened.

And he prayed someone up there had heard their plea.

Chapter Eight

〜

Things changed between Kirk and Rosemary after that night. They were in a soft truce, both treading lightly toward what they hoped would be a lasting relationship.

Yet the realities of everyday life seemed to get in their way, in spite of their prayers for guidance. Rosemary would find herself watching Kirk work, only to see Eric down on the ground gathering supplies, or worse, climbing the steeple to assist Kirk as the work became more intense and dangerous. At these times, Kirk would look around, his gaze searching her out as if to reassure her.

She tried very hard not to resent Eric, but the pain was still too great. And the bitterness—she wondered if that particular emotion would ever go away entirely.

Today, she was heading up the mountain to a quilting session at Aunt Fitz's cabin, hesitant to get back into quilting since her ill-fated wedding. But Aunt Fitz had asked and Rosemary couldn't say no to the old woman, so now Faye and Melissa joined her just outside the church grounds. It was Saturday, a cloudy, rain-threatening Saturday, but a good day to start the quilt Aunt Fitz was making for one of her granddaughters.

"Why she insisted we come and help, I'll never understand," Melissa said as they started up the winding path. "She knows I failed sewing class."

"You know Aunt Fitz," Faye replied, holding on to Rosemary so she could make a particular curve in the path. "She likes to mix in lessons on life with her quilting. She's probably heard all the latest news and wants to set us straight on how to deal with it."

"Meaning me," Rosemary said, her gaze moving back down the path.

She hadn't seen Kirk this morning. Usually on Saturdays, he went hiking or visiting the shops in the village. Sometimes, though, he just kept on working. Which meant only a couple more weeks and he'd be through. They were aiming for Easter Sunday as the dedication for the restoration.

Thinking of Sundays, Rosemary suddenly realized she'd never seen Kirk in church on Sunday. Where did he go when everyone else was singing hymns and praising God? She'd be sure to invite him to tomorrow's service if she saw him before then.

"Maybe you, since you seem to be struggling with so much these days. This will do you good. Aunt Fitz's advice is usually as sage as her spices and herbs."

"And just as full-strength." Melissa laughed, then tossed her head. "Well, I can tell her I just got rid of that new boyfriend. Things didn't work out. He wanted to play the field, so to speak."

"Melissa, child," Faye exclaimed. "You have the worst luck with men."

"Yes," Melissa agreed. "And I intend to tread lightly from now on."

Rosemary was only half listening to the conversation. Following this path brought back memories of being here with Kirk. True, they'd agreed to slow down and let God guide them in this growing relationship, but she couldn't help being impatient. She felt time slipping away; Kirk would be leaving soon. Then what?

"Frowning causes wrinkles," Melissa teased. "Thinking about your steeplejack?"

"No. Yes." Rosemary had given up on correcting people when they called Kirk "her" steeplejack. Maybe because she was beginning to consider him that herself. "I haven't had a chance to talk to him much this week."

"She's trying to avoid upsetting her father," Faye explained as they reached the cove where the cemetery stood. "I think it's a shame you can't just be with the man. He's so nice, and handsome, to boot. What's the harm in dating him?"

"The same harm as when I dated Eric, I reckon," Rosemary replied. "My father doesn't trust my choices in men, and with good reason."

"So you intend to spend your life as an old maid?" Faye nudged her on the arm. "That would be a shame. You have a lot of love to give and Kirk seems to be willing and able."

Melissa glanced over at Rosemary, then looked up at the darkening sky. "He's different from Eric, isn't he?"

Rosemary had to agree with that. "Yes, he certainly is. He's mature and quiet-natured and rarely ever loses his cool. I believe he has a strong faith."

"Eric—was he a Christian, Rosemary?"

Rosemary looked at Melissa, surprised by the question. "He pretended to be, I think just to impress me, or to fool me maybe. And I fell for it."

"You believed in him," Faye said as they stood to take a breath. "There's a difference."

"Is there?" Rosemary automatically started walking toward her mother's grave. "I believed I could change him. I believed I could make a difference in his life, the same way my mother made a difference with my father. But somehow, I failed."

"Is that what you think?" Faye followed her up the moss-covered stone steps built into the hillside. "You know, Eunice's influence on Clayton was strong, strong enough to get him to church every Sunday. But look at him now. His own faith wasn't firm enough to sustain him. Once your mother passed on, so did Clayton's attempts at being a true Christian. Rosemary, you didn't fail. Eric just didn't have the strength to overcome his obstacles."

Rosemary stood there soaking up what her friend had just said. "You're right. Daddy gave up the pretense once Mama died. But at least he tried, for her sake."

"Eric tried, too, didn't he?" Melissa asked softly.

Rosemary gave her young friend a thoughtful look. "Yes, I guess he did." They were now standing at the foot of Eunice's grave. Rosemary looked down on the clean, pristine stone, then back up out over the mountainside. "I really miss her, especially now. I lie in bed wondering what advice she'd give me about Kirk, about everything. She always knew exactly what to say."

Faye patted Rosemary on the back, while Melissa

stood apart, her own expression grim and thoughtful. The silence was a tribute to the woman they all missed. Rosemary missed having a mother. Faye missed her friend. And Melissa remembered Eunice teaching her in Sunday school, directing the Christmas play each year and baking cookies for Vacation Bible School.

"Your mom was always involved in the church, wasn't she?" Melissa said at last.

"Always. I took that for granted until the day of her funeral. Reverend Clancy read passages from her Bible, passages she'd marked and studied over and over again. I never knew just how devout she really was, because she didn't preach to us. She taught us by her example."

Faye gave a soft chuckle. "That was Eunice. She used to say, 'Teach, don't preach.' And she lived by that code." Placing an arm around Rosemary's shoulders, she said, "Her example will help you through all of this, Rosemary. I do believe she would have approved of Kirk."

Rosemary dropped her head to stare down on her mother's grave, then said, "She tried to approve of Eric. She wasn't sure about him, but she wanted me to be happy. And she didn't want to interfere. She offered her guidance and her opinion, when I asked for her advice. I guess that's one of the things I miss the most."

Unlike her father, Rosemary reflected, who'd disliked Eric on sight and was always insisting she break off the relationship. Then, when the tragedy struck, her father felt proven right—and never missed a chance to remind her.

After a few minutes of silence, Rosemary turned,

ready to continue their journey. "Looks like rain, after all. We might have to wait it out at the cabin."

As they moved back up the path, Melissa said, "Is it hard, seeing Eric again?"

Rosemary didn't look back. "Very. I've had to do a lot of praying to get through these last couple of weeks."

"He seems like a likable person," Melissa stated almost too nonchalantly. "And...he is cute."

Faye shot Rosemary a meaningful look, then they both stared at the young girl.

"So you've talked to him some?" Faye asked, her tone controlled and casual.

"A little, just in passing. He likes to tease me about chasing after the children."

"Eric used to be a big tease," Rosemary said, a sick feeling rolling through her stomach. "And a big talker. Don't let him talk you into anything, Melissa."

Melissa looked shocked. "I won't. I hardly know him. But he does seem nice. And he is trying to change."

They reached the cabin in silence. Rosemary got the distinct feeling that her young friend had been seeking her permission to get to know Eric better. Poor Melissa. Eric was an attractive man, and he didn't mind flirting with a pretty girl. Rosemary certainly knew that first-hand. She hoped he didn't influence Melissa in the same way he'd influenced her. Maybe Melissa would be wiser, knowing about his past. Maybe Melissa wouldn't be taken in by his persuasive promises. She hoped not.

Aunt Fitz was ready with the quilting rack extended and her supplies piled on a nearby chair.

"Come on in, ladies. It's kinda dark in here, what with that rain cloud overhead. Melissa, light that kerosene lantern and bring it close, child."

"Aunt Fitz, you have electricity," Melissa said, her eyes wide. "Want to turn on the overhead light?"

"Yeah, I suppose we could do that, too, though I don't think it will provide much to see by. I still forget that I've got the blasted thing."

They smiled at that. Aunt Fitz's children had insisted she get electricity and a phone after their father died. But that didn't mean she had to like either or use the modern amenities, as she told them often enough.

Rosemary settled down on her patch of the quilt, gathering her threads and needles to get started. Refusing to dwell on the dark memories creeping near in the muted light of the cabin, she said, "Mmm, do I smell bread baking?"

"Of course. We'll have some mint tea and honey and jam with it. And I got a jar of pickled peaches."

"I knew there was a good reason to come," Melissa joked. "Except I'll gain five pounds."

"You could use it," Aunt Fitz told her as she pointed her needle through a colorful piece of paisley fabric. "So, how's life treating the three of you?"

"Good."

"Fine."

"Okay."

Aunt Fitz dropped her needle to stare through her bifocals at the three women sitting in her cabin. "Sounds like we need to talk. I like enthusiasm in my quilting circles."

Outside, a clap of thunder applauded her efforts to cheer up her friends.

"It's been a busy week," Rosemary began. "I

needed to get away. Thanks for inviting me, Aunt Fitz.''

''How's your father, child?''

''He got upset when he found out Eric Thomas would be helping Kirk with the church restoration.''

''So did his daughter,'' Faye reminded her.

''Yes, I was upset,'' Rosemary admitted. ''But Reverend Clancy talked to me and told me to pray about it.''

Aunt Fitz scanned Rosemary's face. ''And have you?''

''I've put forth the effort, but it's not easy. Especially when Daddy still blames me for my part in all of this.''

''No doubt. He still has bitter feelings toward Eric, I'm sure, so he takes that out on you.''

''Very bitter feelings. And…he's even more aggravated with me…because he disapproves of my talking the church into hiring Kirk.''

Faye huffed a breath. ''The man actually accused her of bringing Eric back here to work with Kirk!''

Melissa sat up, her eyes wide. ''But you didn't, right?''

Shocked, Rosemary stared across at the blonde. ''Of course not. I never wanted to see Eric again. But Daddy thinks I still care about him.''

Aunt Fitz yanked a strong cord of thread through her square. ''Now, that's downright unreasonable. You broke off your wedding with the man. That Clayton always was a stubborn, proud man. Your ma, she knew how to calm him down and make him see things in a better light.''

''I don't seem to have that capability,'' Rosemary replied, her eyes centered on the floral square she was tacking across the heavy quilt backing. The design was part of a favorite quilt pattern, the variable star. She couldn't help but remember other designs, other patterns from her own wedding quilt—packed away now, but not forgotten.

Aunt Fitz listened, all the while watching her helpers closely to make sure they did their assigned task correctly. "Remember, Rosemary, ten stitches to the inch." Then, "You have your mother in you, girl. 'Haps that's why Clayton finds it hard to look upon you. Keep trusting in the Lord, and fight the good fight, Rosemary. And in the meantime, redo that stitch right yonder on the end, child. It's puckering."

Rosemary smiled, a genuine full-faced smile. Aunt Fitz had seen her discomfort, and as usual, had forced her mind back to the task at hand. "I love you, Aunt Fitz."

"I love you, too, honey."

The rain came, drenching the green woods in a clean shower that perked up the lush ferns sprouting at random from the coves and balds. A fresh-smelling mist settled over the mountain as Aunt Fitz declared it break time because her old eyes were starting to "draw up" and because the bread was officially ready to cut.

"Better be careful going back down, children. Don't anybody slip up and break a bone."

"We'll hold on to each other," Faye said before biting into a fluffy slice of white bread dripping with honey and butter. "That was a quick shower, but we sure needed it."

Melissa came to sit on a stool by Rosemary, her blue eyes bright and eager. "So...how do you feel about Eric now?"

Rosemary thought the girl didn't possess very much tact, but she answered the question anyway. "Honestly, Melissa, I feel nothing for Eric Thomas. Absolutely nothing." Placing her cup of tea down carefully, she gazed across at her friend. "Be careful with him. I hope, I really, truly hope that he has turned his life around. But I'd hate to see you get hurt in the same way I did."

"We're just friends," Melissa said on a defensive rush. "I didn't want you to think—"

"It doesn't matter what I think," Rosemary interrupted. "I care about you, though. I can't interfere, but I can offer you my opinion."

"I appreciate your concern," Melissa said, her smile tight and controlled. Then she touched Rosemary on the arm. "You are a lot like your mother, you know. And I understand why it's hard for you to see Eric in a different way."

No, you don't, Rosemary thought, touched by Melissa's comparison of her to her mother, yet worried by the girl's impressionable nature. Melissa was young, several years younger than Rosemary. And Eric was clever and manipulative, and very convincing. She'd said she wouldn't interfere, but she wouldn't stand by and let him get away with it again, that was for sure.

A knock rattled the screen door of the cabin, then a deep voice called out, "Hello, Aunt Fitz. Got a cup of hot tea for a wet and chilled soul lost on the mountain?"

"Kirk?" Aunt Fitz lifted up with a spurt of energy, her old eyes twinkling with the sure knowledge that things were about to perk up around here. "Come on in, boy. You look like a drowned rat."

Actually, Rosemary thought as her heart hit the pit

of her stomach, he looked wonderful. His dark hair was drenched, but he had tugged it back, slicking it down across his head to reveal the broad lines of his forehead. He wore a flannel shirt and torn jeans, and his hiking boots.

When he looked up to find the room full of women, his eyes stopped on Rosemary as if she were the only occupant of the suddenly tiny room. Without blinking or taking his eyes away, he said, "Good afternoon, ladies. Did I interrupt some secret meeting?"

Aunt Fitz went along with his assumption. "Oh, yes. A highly clandestine meeting of the minds. No men allowed."

Kirk laughed nervously. "Maybe I'd be better off out in the rain."

Aunt Fitz chuckled, then urged him into the room. "Sit yourself down, son. We're jest stitching a quilt for my granddaughter's wedding."

At the reference to a wedding, Rosemary lowered her head. Kirk didn't miss the gentle action.

Faye handed him a dish towel to dry his face. "What brings you up the mountain?"

"I took a hike," he said, his gaze holding Rosemary's when she looked back his way. "There's this one particular spot I've fallen in love with."

Aunt Fitz nodded her understanding. "Sit a spell with us, then. We're taking a little break from our work."

Kirk did sit, his eyes shifting to the colorful quilt across the room. "A wedding on the mountain, then? That will be a blessed event."

Aunt Fitz gave him a direct look. "Weddings are always blessed events. How come you ain't never hitched yourself up with a good woman, Kirk?"

"Never found the right one, I suppose," he replied as he took a long sip of the strong tea Aunt Fitz had slid in front of him, his eyes still on Rosemary.

The direct intensity of his eyes heated her, making her shift uncomfortably on her stool. Faye and Melissa both sat mesmerized by the silent courting ritual going on between the two of them, but Aunt Fitz worked the room like a pro.

"A good partner is sure hard to find," she said as she placed a hunk of buttered bread before him. "I sure had me a good match. My Samuel, now that was a fine man. Came up the mountain a'courting, went down the hill to his own wedding. Never knew what hit him."

Kirk finally tore his gaze away from Rosemary. "I guess you set him straight right away, Aunt Fitz."

She chuckled again, the movement causing the wide ruffle on her rickrack-edged apron to shake. "I laid down the law first thing. I told him I was a God-fearing, Christian woman and I wouldn't cotton to no drinking, smoking or cussing in my home. Then I told him I wanted lots of children and enough land to plant a good garden."

Kirk chewed his bread, then sat back to give her a broad grin. "Obviously he agreed to your stipulations."

"Oh, he agreed all right. Stuck around for over fifty years, until the good Lord called him home."

"Fifty years." Kirk looked over at Rosemary again. "I've never stayed in one place longer than a few months."

"You had a home once, didn't you, though?" Melissa asked, surprising everyone.

"Aye, county Cork in Ireland was my home growing up. But once we moved back to the States, I got the wandering spirit. I never could get settled here for some reason.''

"Maybe you didn't want to leave Ireland," Faye said quietly.

"I never bothered to give it much thought," he admitted. "I was young though, and resented having to leave my friends, even though I'd heard so much about America. I think that's why I took off—I wanted to see what everyone was talking about.''

"And have you seen enough yet?" Aunt Fitz asked.

"I'm beginning to think it's time to slow down a bit," he said, his gaze once again seeking out Rosemary. "My mother would be thrilled to hear that. She wants me to give her grandchildren before they cart her off to the old folks' home.''

Aunt Fitz clapped her wrinkled hands in approval. "Children are a blessing. Best handled with great care.''

Rosemary jumped up off her stool. She was warm, too warm, in the close confines of the room, with all this talk of weddings and babies and with Kirk's eyes watching her every move. "I...I think I'll step out onto the porch. I do love to watch the rain." Smiling at Aunt Fitz, she added, "Don't worry. I won't shirk my quilting duties. I've just about got that star stitched.''

"It's a lovely star, too," Aunt Fitz said after her retreating back. "A corner star—solid and tightly stitched.''

"Why, thank you," Rosemary said over her shoulder.

Faye and Melissa watched Kirk as he watched Rosemary. Aunt Fitz winked over at them from her spot by the stove.

It took all of two seconds for Kirk to stand up to

follow Rosemary. "I enjoyed the tea and bread, Aunt Fitz. I think I'll go out and look over your gourd collection before I leave."

"Suit yourself," the old woman replied, bowing her head to him. "My gourds are mighty pretty."

"Yes, she is—I mean, yes, they are." Embarrassed, Kirk made a beeline for the door.

The remaining women grinned silently as they went back to their stitching.

"He's got it bad," Aunt Fitz whispered.

He did have it bad. Nervous and unsure, Kirk pulled up to the railing beside Rosemary, needing to talk to her, wanting to be with her, and all the while thinking fifty years was a long time to stay with one person. Then she looked up at him with that endearing, innocent, hesitant smile and he realized fifty years might not be nearly long enough to spend with her.

As if sensing his doubts, Rosemary tried to smooth things over. "Aunt Fitz prides herself on her matchmaking skills. No wonder she's always making a new quilt for yet another wedding."

Kirk relaxed a little at her pragmatic observation. "Poor Samuel. The man probably stayed on a very tight leash."

Frowning, Rosemary replied, "Not a leash, Kirk. More like a tight bond, a connection that joined them together. He wanted to be with her. And he was so attached to her, so very caring and solicitous of her feelings. They were a special couple."

He sighed, then stepped closer. "I meant no disrespect. Actually, I'm in awe of the whole thing. And it's made me take a good, hard look at my own philosophy on life."

Taking this opportunity to find out more and get her mind off her own failure as a bride, Rosemary asked, "And just what is your philosophy on life?"

He snorted. "Just that. Just a philosophy, never applied. Up until now, my whole attitude was one of shallowness and a definite stance against any form of commitment other than my work, at least according to my dear mother."

Intrigued, she said, "And...was your mother right?"

"I'm afraid so." His gaze moved over her features. "But I'm working hard on changing all of that. You talked about how I'd given you hope, remember?"

She remembered. Nodding, she matched his gaze with one of her own, her breath holding against her ribs as she waited for his next words.

"Well, Rosemary, you've given me something I'd neglected to nurture in my solitary existence."

"Oh, and what's that?"

"You've given me back my faith, and my ability to trust in God's plan for my life."

Surprised, she frowned. "But your faith seems so solid to me."

He touched a hand to her hair. "Oh, it's solid. But it was much like your precious church building. Built on a firm base, built to last, but it needed rejuvenating."

Touching her nose with a finger, he added, "I guess I needed to see that life isn't an easy road. Before, I could simply pack up and move on. Now I'm starting to realize that in order to be strong in our faith, sometimes we have to face tough obstacles. I teased you about being afraid of heights. Well, I'm just as afraid, but it's a different kind of fear."

"So even though you're able to leap tall buildings, you're unable to take a leap of faith?"

"Exactly. Or I was before. That's changed now, though. Because of Reverend Clancy, and Aunt Fitz, but mostly because of you, I'm beginning to see that in order to win what we want, in order to achieve our goals, we have to depend on a source beyond our control."

Rosemary swallowed back the dryness in her throat. As his finger drifted down the line of her cheek, she ignored the little tingling sensations cresting in the pit of her stomach, to ask, "And what exactly has changed, as far as your goals in life?"

"Only one thing," he said honestly, his eyes meeting hers. "Now I want to share my journey with someone else, that special someone who makes it all worthwhile and complete. I think I want to stick it out, for fifty years or longer at least."

She closed her eyes as he lowered his head to kiss her, then quickly opened them again to glance sideways, concerned about being seen.

"Don't worry," he whispered. "We have three very capable chaperons and—don't look now—but they're all watching us through the kitchen window. I won't do anything to embarrass you."

Glad to know he was aware of her feelings and their audience, she concentrated on the question burning a hole in her brain. She had to ask, had to hear him say it. "Who is this special someone, Kirk?"

He kissed her then, a quick, feathery touch that left her breathless and wanting.

Then he nudged her chin so she could see into his eyes. "You," he whispered. "Only you."

Rosemary forgot all about the three women watching

them from inside. She let him kiss her again, and she kissed him back, meaning it with all of her heart, wanting it with all of her being.

Inside, Aunt Fitz shooed away the nosy observers, her smile gentle, her eyes watery as she ordered her charges to get back to stitching. "Soon as we're finished here, I think it's time to pull out that quilt we made for Rosemary." She motioned toward the couple out on her porch. "And I do so hope this time, she gets to use it."

Unaware of her friend's hopeful words, Rosemary rested against Kirk's broad chest, watching as the rain began to fall again in a gentle rendering, its water washing over the hills to clean away the residue of winter, bringing with it the sure promise of spring.

Chapter Nine

"Those two are certainly becoming mighty friendly," Faye said a few days later as she stood at the window watching Melissa and Eric laughing and talking out in the prayer garden.

"Yes," Rosemary agreed, keeping her eyes purposely averted. "And I can't stomach it."

Faye turned back to helping Rosemary divvy out cookies and fruit juice for the children's morning snack. "Have you tried talking to her?"

"I warned her straight off," Rosemary said. She counted the cookies to make sure each child had the same amount. "But it's not my place to tell her how to live her life. She'd only think I was doing it because of my resentment toward Eric."

"That's probably true." Faye finished pouring the juice, then placed the container back in the large refrigerator located in the church social hall. "Maybe I should talk to her. Poor girl. Her parents don't come to church with her. I wonder if they even know she flutters from one boy to the next."

Putting away the cookie container, Rosemary shook her head. "I doubt it. I don't think they've given her a very solid foundation. From what she tells me, they fight all the time and generally make her own life miserable. She took this job to pay for her night courses at college because they don't have the money to finance her education, or the inclination to encourage her."

"That's a shame. She's a sweet girl."

"Which Eric will take full advantage of."

Faye leaned into the counter to study Rosemary's frowning expression. "Is that what happened with you?"

Rosemary looked off into the long, dark hall filled with tables and chairs for the Wednesday-night supper meeting. "No. I mean, maybe. But I take responsibility for my failures with Eric. I knew he had problems, I just didn't want to admit it."

"And now that's why you're being so cautious with Kirk?"

"Yes. Although there is no comparison between the two."

Faye lifted the tray full of juice cups. "No, not at all. So don't be unfair to Kirk. Honey, the way that man looks at you—you'd be an idiot to let him get away."

After Faye left with the juice, Rosemary stayed behind to make a fresh batch for the afternoon break. Naturally, her thoughts shifted to Kirk. In spite of her growing feelings for him, she still didn't have the answers to their particular problems.

First, there was her father, of course. She'd managed to keep him calm and consistent in his indifference by avoiding any mention of Kirk or the work on the church and steeple. And she didn't dare stop and talk to Kirk outside the church, where her father might see them together.

In fact, the only time she managed with Kirk was during one of their chance meetings, such as up at Aunt Fitz's cabin the other day. That particular meeting still lingered like a sweet dream in her consciousness, making her hum with joy and happiness. Chance meetings were one thing, but despite Kirk's sweet admission, a lasting relationship still seemed impossible. In order to have that with any man, she had to win back her father's approval and love.

And mostly, his blessings.

Then of course, she knew Kirk would be moving on soon. And he knew it, too, even though neither of them had talked about it the last time they'd been together. Yet it was there between them, and needed to be discussed. Would Kirk pledge his heart to her, then simply pack up and leave?

Would he ask her to go with him?

In her heart, she wanted to go. But in her mind, she knew it would be impossible. She had to stay here for now, near her father. She had made a pledge to see him through this horrible time, to help him find his faith again.

She wouldn't abandon him, even for the man she...loved.

A small gasp escaped from Rosemary's parted lips as the realization hit her full force. Shocked and embarrassed, she glanced around the empty hall to make sure no one was watching her, as if her true feelings had just been teletyped across her forehead.

She loved Kirk. Maybe she'd loved him from the first time she'd heard his voice, or seen him standing there with the church in the background. It didn't matter; what did matter was the new responsibilities that came with that love. She'd have to be very sure this time. She'd gone against her father's wishes once before, and it had only brought her family tragedy.

She turned to take the second tray out to the room across the catwalk where the children were finishing up their alphabet lessons, only to find Eric standing there staring at her.

"Oh, you startled me," she said, anxious to get away from him, and afraid he'd be able to read her thoughts.

But when she tried to move past, he reached out a hand to stop her. "You could be civil, at least, Rosemary."

Gripping the heavy plastic tray so tightly her knuckles turned white, she lifted her chin in defiance. "I don't have to be civil to you, Eric. Now let me by. I have work to do."

"Ah yes. Taking care of the children, such a sweet and noble profession. But then, you always were sweet and noble. And so sanctimonious. Does it even matter to you that I'm trying very hard to make a new beginning?"

"Yes, it matters," she said in a tight, controlled tone. "I'm glad you're making a fresh start, but I can't be a part of it."

He folded his arms over his chest, then leaned back against the doorjamb. "That's because you think you're so much better than me. You always did, didn't you? You went on and on about the church and your beliefs, hoping some of that holier-than-thou junk would rub off on me, didn't you?"

"Yes," she said, angry that he'd make fun of her

convictions. "But obviously I failed at trying to save you, Eric. And it looks like you still haven't learned anything from what you've done."

"Oh, I've learned," he said, coming close so his face was near hers. "I've learned that I never want to go back to prison. I've learned how it feels to know I've killed another human being. And...I've learned what it's like to be turned away from the very people who wanted to turn me into a decent Christian man. I've learned I can't trust any of you, because you all spout out one thing when you really mean another."

Shaking now, Rosemary tried to move past him. "Eric, I don't want to discuss this with you. I'm trying so hard, so very hard, to find it in my heart to forgive you."

"Don't do me any favors," he said, the words ringing loudly in the empty hall. "I don't want your forgiveness. I only wanted your love—that's all I ever wanted."

"And you know I can't give that anymore," she said, tears brimming in her eyes. "Now, let me go."

He stepped forward, but a strong arm from behind stopped him from touching Rosemary. Shocked, Eric turned to find Kirk glaring at him from the open entry doors.

"You heard the woman," Kirk said, his eyes almost black with rage. "Now, if you want to keep working for me, you'd better get back out there and finish putting that weatherproofer on the roof beams."

Eric rolled his eyes, then lifted a hand. "Fine. I just came in to get a drink of water. I didn't mean any harm."

"I'll keep that in mind," Kirk replied, his gaze moving to Rosemary. "From now on, I'll set a watercooler outside so you won't have any reason to venture inside the educational building.''

"That's very thoughtful," Eric said in a sarcastic tone.

Kirk watched Eric walk past, then said, "This will be your final warning, Thomas. I hired you in good faith. I expect you to do your job and stay away from Rosemary.''

Eric snorted. "Right, so you can have her? I've heard all about you two—pretty hot and heavy, huh?''

In a blur of motion, Kirk pounced on the smaller man and sent him crashing back up against a concrete wall. Rosemary screamed and dropped the tray of cookies, her heart pumping with fear, humiliation coloring her face.

Kirk pressed Eric close to the wall, one hand firmly gripping his throat. "I'm not going to waste my energy on hitting you, Eric. And out of respect for Rosemary and this church, I'm not going to cause a scene. Now, get back to work, or you will be out of a job come nightfall.'' Lifting Eric away from the wall, he added, "Oh, and before you go, I think you owe Rosemary an apology.''

Eric immediately looked sheepish. After a long, controlled sigh, he turned to Rosemary. "I'm sorry. I really am. And I am trying, Rosemary. You have to believe me. It's just hard being back here. Almost worse than being in prison, but I can't lose this job.''

"Then stop losing your cool," Kirk suggested, his own temper simmering. "Now go.''

He watched to make sure Eric went back out to the yard, then turned to find Rosemary on her knees picking up broken butter cookies. He didn't need to see her trembling body to know that she was shaking uncontrollably.

"Come here," he said, dropping onto the floor beside her.

She pushed him away. "I...I have to pick the cookies up and get more. The children are waiting."

"Rosemary, let them wait." He took both her hands in his, stopping her frantic efforts. "Rosemary, look at me."

She faced him then, her eyes red-rimmed and wet, her hair falling in soft waves around her damp, flushed face.

"Oh, Kirk." She fell into his arms like a drowning woman seeking a lifesaver. "Oh, Kirk."

"Shh," he said, kissing her hair as he sat on the floor and held her close to rock her gently against him. "It's okay. It's okay. Don't think about him. Think about us, instead."

About that time, Faye came in. "All right. The natives are getting restless—" Seeing Kirk and Rosemary huddled together on the floor, she stopped. "What happened?"

"I'll explain later," Kirk said. "Will you take the cookies to the children. Rosemary is too upset right now to face them."

"Of course." Faye hurriedly grabbed the white plastic container from the refrigerator, then, skirting around them, headed out of the building again.

"Thank you," Rosemary managed to murmur against his chest. "I'm sorry I lost it like that."

"Silly," he said, running a hand over her wet face. "You had every right to lose control. Eric has a long way to go in the grace department."

"He's as bitter as my father, and he has no right to feel bitter. He's the one who messed up."

"Yes, and he's just feeling his own guilt. Believe me, I've had quite a few talks with him and he's fighting this every step of the way. He thinks he can justify his actions by making excuses, but there is no excuse for what he did. If it weren't for my promise to Reverend Clancy, I'd fire him today."

Rosemary lifted her head to stare up at him with open, luminous eyes. "How can you do that?"

"Do what?"

"How can *you* be so gracious to him, after what just happened? I wish I could be more like that."

Kirk adjusted her to a more comfortable position in his arms. "I can afford to be gracious. He didn't kill my mother. You, on the other hand, have a lot to work through before you can extend your hand to him in forgiveness."

"I don't think I can do it."

"I'm willing to help," he said as he lifted her onto her feet. "Can we go somewhere and talk?"

She shook her head. "I have to get back to the children."

"When, then? I want you to tell me everything. I want to help you through this, Rosemary."

She wanted that, too. She wanted to unload this tremendous burden once and for all. And if she really was going to have a strong relationship with Kirk, she needed to be honest with him from the very beginning.

Straightening her mussed hair, she thought for a minute, then said, "We could...we could go up the mountain after work this afternoon."

Amazed that she'd agreed to open up to him, Kirk smiled. "I'd like that. I'd like that very much."

"Me, too," she said. "But right now, I've got to go back to work." She wiped her eyes. "Do...do I look together enough?"

He kissed her quickly, then held her away for a careful inspection. With the tail of his cotton shirt, he wiped the rest of the moisture off her face, then smiled. "You look lovely."

She started to leave, then saw the broken cookies all over the floor. "Oh, I've got to clean this up."

Kirk stilled her. "I'll do it. You go, take care of your children. I'll see you this afternoon."

Rosemary hurried away, wanting to cry all over again. But not because she was upset. This time, the tears were for Kirk's kindness. It had been a long time since any man besides Reverend Clancy had offered her any form of kindness, no less such tender concern. She accepted it and wore it like a shield as she went on with her day.

From his work station, Eric watched her walk by. Rosemary glanced up in time to see the regret in his eyes. That regret didn't soothe her one bit. It only made her more determined to get past all of this, no matter how much it hurt.

The Wednesday-night suppers were a tradition at the church. Different groups took turns cooking or furnishing the meal, and the rest of the congregation paid a small fee to help cover the expense. After the meal, everyone went inside the church to listen to a short sermon and sing a few hymns. Reverend Clancy said these services and the fellowship made the middle of the week go by better.

Rosemary usually attended, but she'd missed the last

couple of weeks. Tonight, she planned on inviting Kirk to go with her after their hike up the mountain.

Looking at her watch, she decided she'd better hurry. It was four o'clock. Melissa would see that the rest of the remaining children at the church school got home all right. She usually stayed late, along with another aide, so that the teachers could go home to their own families.

Rosemary buzzed out of her office, intent on getting home to fix her father's meal—a meat loaf she'd already cooked at lunch, and some potatoes and corn—before taking her walk to meet Kirk. That would give Kirk and her at least two good hours before the church supper and service.

Faye met her as she was leaving. "Feeling better, honey?"

Rosemary smiled at the older woman. "Much better. I'm going to check on Daddy and get his dinner, then I'm going for a walk up the trail."

"With Kirk?"

"Yes." Stopping to grab Faye's arm, she asked, "Is it wrong of me to go without telling Daddy?"

Faye put a finger to her cheek. "Hmm. You said you were going for a walk. You can't help it if Kirk's planning on doing the same thing."

"I don't like being deceptive, though."

Faye took her by the arm and started walking down the catwalk with her. "I can't blame you there, but you're not exactly being deceptive. Clayton told you to keep Kirk out of his yard. And you've done that."

"But he also told me to stop meeting Kirk on the mountain."

Faye lifted her gaze, then shrugged. "Like I said, if you both happen to be going the same way..."

"I like your logic," Rosemary said. "I just need to talk to Kirk, to explain all of this once and for all. Then I'll talk to Daddy when I get back."

"I think that's a good idea after that stunt Eric tried this morning," Faye said. "And don't worry about Clayton. I was planning on going by to see him anyway, to ask if he'd walk over to the supper with me."

"Good luck," Rosemary replied, waving a hand.

"You, too."

Faye turned to find Melissa standing in the gated door of the toddler room. She walked over to the girl. "How's it going?"

"You tell me," Melissa said in a hushed voice. "Something happened between Rosemary and Eric today, but he won't tell me anything about it. Are those two getting close again?"

"I hardly think so," Faye said, keeping a cheerful smile on her face for the benefit of the children. "They had an argument, I believe. But Rosemary's okay now."

Melissa tossed back her hair. "Well, if you ask me, she's not being fair to Eric. He only wants her to give him a chance."

"Was it fair of him to fill himself with liquor then get behind the wheel of a car and cause her mother's death?" Faye countered, her tone firm and full of fire.

"Of course not. That was a tragedy, but we're all supposed to be Christians," Melissa said. "Shouldn't we treat Eric a little better now that he's turned his life around?"

Faye thought about that, then said, "We're giving Eric all the support we can, under the circumstances. And you're right. We owe him the benefit of the doubt."

"Including Rosemary?"

"I wouldn't worry about Rosemary," Faye told the young girl. "She's happy, for the first time in a long time, and Eric would do best to just let her be." With that, Faye waved and started toward her own office. "See you tonight at supper."

"Yeah, see you."

Bored, Melissa looked toward Kirk's trailer. Kirk emerged and started walking up the trail that led to the top of the mountain. About thirty minutes later, she saw Rosemary come down her back porch and hurry in the same direction.

"Now, that's interesting," Melissa said to herself.

Rosemary fluffed the flowing denim skirt she was wearing, then put her hands in her pockets as she approached the halfway point up the mountain. Right above her stood the cemetery. Deciding to visit her mother's grave while she waited for Kirk, she lifted her skirt to climb the stone steps. When she reached her mother's grave, she found a bundle of colorful fresh-cut flowers lying there.

Looking around, she wondered if Kirk had placed them on the grave. When she heard footsteps from a nearby ledge, she whirled to find him climbing down.

"Oh, there you are." She motioned to the flowers. "Did you do this?"

Kirk hopped over the last of the rocks, then looked down at the flowers. "No, it wasn't me. I was up on the ledge watching for you." He sent her a compassionate look. "Your father left those, Rosemary."

She looked around, afraid Clayton might still be near. "That explains why he wasn't home when I got there. I couldn't imagine where he might be since he rarely leaves the house, except to drive into town for household supplies when I remind him. But his truck was still in the shed.''

''He walked up here, kneeled down for a few minutes, then left the flowers,'' Kirk explained. ''Does he do that often?''

Tears pricked at Rosemary's eyes as she looked down on the black-eyed Susans mixed with pink phlox, white daisies and fresh red clover. ''He's...he's never done this before. I've tried to get him to come up here with me, but it's always been too much for him.'' She reached down to touch a velvety soft cluster of phlox. ''Why now?''

Kirk bent down beside her. ''Maybe all of this with Eric has made him miss her even more.''

Rosemary lifted her head. ''Yes, that could be it. Or it might have something to do with Faye. She cares for him, but she's been holding back out of respect for my mother. Lately, though, she has been spending more time with him.''

Kirk sat back to study her, thinking how gorgeous and natural she looked in her white cotton blouse, thinking no one wore their feelings more beautifully than Rosemary. Or more openly. ''Does it bother you, to think your father might find happiness with another woman, maybe get married again?''

She waved a hand. ''Oh no. Especially not when it might be Faye. She's a good friend, and she'd take care of Dad. She and my mother were close, so she knows how my father is—she can deal with him, I think.''

''Then why the frown?''

She lifted her mouth in a smile then. ''I was just thinking how I wish I could have been here with Daddy. Did he look...okay?''

Kirk hesitated a minute, then decided to be truthful with her. "He was crying, Rosemary." When she gasped, he added, "But...that might be a good sign. That might be the first step toward acceptance."

Rosemary sank onto her knees to begin automatically pulling away weeds. "You're right. I just can't stand to see him in so much pain."

Kirk stopped her weeding with a steady hand. "Wouldn't you rather see him in this kind of pain, rather than so cold and distant that no one can reach him? I mean, that has to be the worst kind of suffering."

She looked over at him, amazed that he'd managed to calm her worries and assure her that her father was on the mend. Taking his hand in hers, she said, "Mama, I'd like you to meet Kirk. He's a good man. Very compassionate and understanding. And patient, real patient with the likes of your daughter."

Kirk laughed softly. "I could say the same about your daughter, Mrs. Brinson."

"Say a prayer with me," Rosemary told him. "For my father, and for my mother."

"And for us," he replied, his gaze holding hers.

"And for us," she agreed. "For all of us."

A little while later, they reached the peak of Alba Mountain. Rosemary found her rock and sat down to get her breath, her eyes scanning the distant peaks and valleys while Kirk strolled around to get a closer look. Off in the distance, a white spark of lightning flashed through the sky.

"Oh, looks like rain again," Rosemary said, trying hard to still the spinning in her head. If she just sat here long enough, she'd be able to enjoy this without too much vertigo. "We'd better hurry."

Kirk walked up to take a seat beside her. "Oh no. Not so fast. You promised me you'd tell me everything. Do I have to hold you up here against your will to make you do that?"

"No," she said, shaking her head. "I want to tell you the whole story, Kirk. I'm just afraid—"

He touched a hand to her hair, something he'd wanted to do since he'd spotted her coming up the trail. "Afraid that I'll turn away, like your father did?"

"You might be disgusted with me."

"I can't imagine that. Rosemary, why don't we apply some of the teachings of Jesus to this situation. One, you don't have to carry your burden alone. Jesus carried all of our burdens when He carried the cross. And two, there is no sin so great that it can't be forgiven. That's why He died for us."

Awestruck, she stared up at him, seeing the sincerity in his face, hearing the conviction in his words, fascinated by the simple truth he'd just spoken. "You really know your stuff, don't you?"

He grinned then. "Aye. My mother certainly raised me in the best Christian tradition. I'd just forgotten my stuff until I met you."

She leaned against him, thankful that he felt the same as she did. "You don't know how much that means to me, that you believe in the same way as I do. That's important to me, you know."

"I do know. And I also know that you need to talk to someone, get this off your chest. I want to listen, I'm willing to listen, and I won't condemn you, or judge you. Indeed, I have not the right to do either."

"Okay, then," she said, taking a deep breath to

brace herself. "You know most of it—the worst of it. But it's important that you know the rest, so that you'll know me better, and my father, and so that you'll understand why I need to see him through this—no matter how long it takes."

Kirk didn't like the tone of that, but he pushed the uneasy thoughts to the back of his mind. For now, she was here in his arms and they didn't have to hurry. They had a little time to be together. That alone was a blessing.

In spite of the threatening rain clouds hovering off in the distance.

Chapter Ten

⌒

"I met Eric in college," Rosemary began, her gaze moving over the blue-green, flower-sprigged hills and valleys before them. "I was so in awe of him. I guess I fell for him right off. He was funny and carefree, a star football player, and I was shy and awkward, the studious straight-A student. He captivated me."

Kirk could imagine only too well how Eric might be capable of doing just that. And, knowing Rosemary the way he did now, he could see her being demure and endearing, and completely vulnerable. "He swept you off your feet?"

"Yes, he did. And I let him," she continued, her fingers laced with Kirk's. "When I came home and told my folks, at first they were happy for me. Then when Eric started coming for visits, my daddy noticed something right away—Eric seemed too animated at times, too wound up. Daddy suspected he was drinking, but at first he didn't say anything."

"Did you know?"

"No, not at first. I was so naive, I didn't have a clue.

And Eric was very careful, very secretive about what he was doing. He didn't want me to find out because he knew how I felt about such things. I told him from the first that I was a Christian. I'm not ashamed of my beliefs. My only mistake was in thinking Eric was the same. He did pretend, for my sake." She shook her head, causing her fiery hair to spill all around her face. "And to his credit, I think he wanted to be like me, wanted to change for me. But...he was already in too deep with the drinking. All of his friends did it, so it was hard for him to just give it up."

Kirk nodded his understanding. "It's hard to resist when you're hanging around with the wrong crowd." At her questioning look, he said, "I went through a partying phase myself, until my grandpapa got a hold of me and set me straight. He said, 'Lad, how can ye be dangling off one-hundred-foot buildings if your head's not on straight. Liquor and steeplejacking don't mix, and your poor mother will kill me if I let anything happen to you.' He gave me an ultimatum that probably saved my life."

"You were wise enough to listen," she said. "Eric wasn't listening to anything or anybody. He thought he could lead a double existence, I suppose."

"Only it caught up with him?"

"Yes." She jumped as another fierce streak of lightning flashed in the distance. After a moment, she relaxed again. "People started dropping hints to me about Eric being seen drunk at places without me. At first, I passed it off, telling myself he was entitled to some time with his friends, that surely if he did take a drink, it was in moderation. Then when my brother came home telling me some people he worked with had seen Eric very drunk at a local bar, I had to listen.

Of course, Danny wasted little time telling our parents. He thought he was doing what was best for me, but things got pretty ugly after that.''

"He wanted to protect his baby sister," Kirk reasoned. "Understandable.''

"Yes, but not to me at the time. I got so mad at him. Then when Dad tried to reason with me, I told him I loved Eric and that I would talk to him and try to make him give up the drinking.''

"How did that go?"

"Not very well. We fought and broke up, mainly because Eric said he was hurt that I couldn't trust him." Her voice became still for a minute as she remembered. "I was so heartbroken. I'd been sheltered and protected and Eric was my first love, and my first rejection. I thought I'd never get over him.''

Kirk gave her a grim look. "Well, obviously, you got back together.''

"Yes, we did. Eric promised me he'd change. And for a while, he did try. He started coming to church with me. We had meals with my family. He gained my trust, but he also charmed my parents just enough to convince them he had dropped the drinking. Then he asked me to marry him.''

"And you agreed.''

"Oh, yes. I loved him, or so I thought. Mom was happy for me, but hesitant. Yet she didn't try to interfere, except to offer advice here and there. Daddy, though, did not want me to marry Eric. It caused a rift between us, the first we'd ever had. When I stood up to him and told him there was nothing he could do to stop me, I think I broke his heart. But I was young and so caught up in wanting to have a marriage and a family, I didn't see what my actions were doing to my parents.''

Seeing the pain in her eyes, Kirk urged her on. ''What happened next?''

Rosemary swallowed, then took a deep breath. Kirk felt the tightening of her fingers around his and waited for her to find the right words to finish her story.

''It happened a few nights after my shower—an engagement party and combined shower at the home of one of Aunt Fitz's daughters in the next town. Eric and I had attended the shower together. Daddy stayed home, angry and hurt. Danny didn't come, either—he had to work late—but his wife, Nancy, did. She was seven months pregnant with Emily, but she wanted to be there with me on my big night. The party was great—a buffet with all the trimmings, a beautiful cake, and so many gifts, so many lovely, homey things to get Eric and me off to the right start in our marriage. Aunt Fitz had made a beautiful wedding quilt for us. She presented it to me at the party, but needed to add a few finishing touches. So, a few days later, my mother went back to Aunt Fitz's daughter's house to pick it up.''

She stopped, her breath leaving her body with a great trembling sigh. ''Sometimes I think back on that night and wonder if I dreamed the whole thing. I can still see Mama standing there in our dining room surrounded by shower gifts, her eyes misty with tears, happy for me in spite of her misgivings, loving and caring. Her faith sustained her—she prayed for Eric and me to be happy, and then she turned it over to the Lord.''

Rosemary's voice caught, but she went on in a rush. ''I can still remember waving goodbye to her. We'd had supper with them, Eric and me, and he was giving me a ride back to my apartment. She said, 'You two go on, honey. You spend some time with your intended.' She kissed me, and she smiled and said, 'I'm gonna run over to Linda's house to get your wedding quilt so we can display it with the rest of your things.' Mom and Aunt Fitz and several other women from the church had worked on it together. It had a creamy-white background, with flowers and ribbons embroidered on it in mint green and rose colors. It was so beautiful. I can still remember Mom's smile, so peaceful, so serene.''

Kirk wrapped an arm around her as she hung her head. ''Go on, Rosemary,'' he coaxed.

''That was the last time I saw her. She never reached Linda's house,'' she said, the anguish in her broken words echoing over the still mountaintop. ''Eric took me back to my apartment. We talked for a while, but he...he seemed restless. I thought he was just nervous about the wedding, so I kissed him good-night...and he left.''

Kirk's own heart began to beat a swift tempo. He knew what she was about to tell him, yet he didn't want to hear it. He also knew how very much it was costing her to tell this tragic tale. Taking her face in his hands, he held her, touching his fingers across her moist cheeks, his eyes centered on hers. ''Tell me, Rosemary.''

Rosemary gulped back the tears, then steadied herself, leaning into his hands, his touch, clinging to the solid strength he offered. ''About an hour later, I got a call from Danny.'' She stopped, her own hands gripping Kirk's shoulders. ''Oh, Kirk. I don't think I can—''

"Hold on tight and tell me," he said, his eyes watering up in spite of his tightly clenched jaws. "I'm here, right here."

She moaned, much like a hurt animal, then looked up at him, her eyes pleading and pain-filled. "Danny was crying. I'd never heard him cry like that. He told me to come home right then. Something...something had happened to Mama." Her eyes held a faraway look then, as the horrible memories rushed through her. "I ran all the way down the street to Daddy's house. I could hear him screaming, screaming. He kept saying, 'No, no. Oh, God, please, no.' When I was finally able to get to him, I tried to take him in my arms. I kept asking what had happened. Danny looked at me, this strange kind of look on his face. Nancy took me by the shoulders and pulled me away from my father."

She shuddered, a lone sob racking her entire body. "Then my daddy...he looked up at me. I can't get that look out of my mind—I'd never seen him like that before. I'll never forget what he said.

"He lifted a finger to me and he...he said, 'Your mother is dead. Dead, Rosemary.'

"I remember crumbling, I remember Danny and Nancy catching me, holding me. Then I whispered, 'How?'

"Daddy jumped up, coming at me...and Danny held me away. Daddy said, 'It was him, the one you had to have. It was Eric Thomas. He was driving drunk and he ran her car off the road. He killed your mother.'"

She quieted then, her eyes brimming with tears, her hands so tight on Kirk's shoulders he could feel her fingers digging into his shoulder blades. And still, he held her, kept her steady, murmured softly against her skin.

Finally, she spoke again, her voice weak, hoarse. "I think I must have fainted then. Danny and Nancy led me to the couch, but Daddy...he just stood there staring at me with this awful vacant look in his eyes. Danny told me that...that Eric had apparently met my mother on one of the winding roads, at the spot we call the S-curve. He veered his truck over the centerline and...ran my mother's car off the road. It crashed into a ravine. They told us she died instantly."

Kirk moaned, then pulled her into his arms, rocking her much in the same way he'd done earlier that day. He felt drained, washed away, numb. Now he understood completely. Now he knew why Clayton held such denial and resentment. Now he saw how Rosemary had survived, had been sustained only by the threads of her faith. How else could anybody endure this kind of pain? No wonder she'd held it all inside for so long. It was much too unbearable to talk about.

But now that the floodgates had been opened, she did talk, softly and huskily and in a quiet, calm tone. "They took us to the scene and...I thought I would die. I wanted to die right there with my mother. It was awful, Kirk. The black night, the woods, the mountain on one side of us and that dark, deep hole on the other. And we saw, knew that was where they'd found her car, shattered and burned, broken.

"It was so awful to imagine her trapped down there, all alone in the dark. They wouldn't let us see her, not then. They wouldn't let *me* see her."

Kirk hushed her then, unable to picture the grim scene she must be reliving. After a minute, he asked, "So...there was no hope?"

She moved her head against his chest, frantically, hurriedly. "No hope. No hope. Dead on impact." Then she moaned again and wrapped herself against the shelter of his arms. "Eric had called the authorities from a nearby house. He walked away! Walked away after his truck skidded to a stop a few feet from a pull-off—a place where people stop to enjoy the view."

Without realizing it, she lifted away from Kirk, then started beating her fists against his chest. "I hate that view. I get sick to my stomach if I even have to drive that way. I hate that view because each time I go there I can still see the shape of the car down in that ravine. I can see them handcuffing Eric and I can hear him calling to me, telling me how sorry he was, telling me he didn't know it was her. He didn't know he'd killed my mother until we arrived at the scene.

"And my father—I remember him trying to...to climb down the side of the mountain to get to her, and Danny holding him back, both of them crying. Oh, Kirk, my father kept calling her name over and over."

The raw pain in her eyes sliced through Kirk. Stopping her almost hysterical movements, he took both her hands in his, stilling her. "Hush, hush. Rosemary, look at me, love. I'm here and I do not blame you. Do you understand what I'm saying to you? Do you?"

Rosemary stared up at him, her gaze searching his face for condemnation. She saw none. Instead, she saw compassion, sorrow, pain and...absolution. "How can you touch me?" she asked, disgusted with herself. "How can you forgive me, when...when I can't forget what I caused, when I can't look at myself in the mirror without wanting to be sick."

"I don't need to forgive you," he said. "God already has. And for you to turn away from that forgiveness, that unconditional love, is a sin in itself."

Her features sharpened in surprise. "How can I expect God to forgive me, Kirk? My father can't. My brother pretends to, but I know, I know that deep down he resents me because of what happened. I was so intent on getting married I became selfish. I ignored all the warnings. I knew Eric wasn't so sure about the marriage, but I was determined to make it work. He couldn't deal with the pressure so he drank even more. I pushed him to this, Kirk. It's all my fault, so you see I don't deserve your forgiveness. I don't deserve their forgiveness or their love. I don't deserve yours, either.''

"No,'' he shouted, the echo of the one word crashing against the distant mountains and vibrating back to them. "No, Rosemary, I won't let you continue to do this. I won't let you go on punishing yourself for something you had no control over. It was Eric's responsibility to stop drinking, not yours.''

The lightning clashed, closer now, threatening them with its white-hot intensity. A clap of thunder followed a few seconds later.

"We need to go,'' she said, pulling away from him, suddenly unable to face him after her full and complete confession.

"No, not yet. You have to see—you can't go on living this way.'' He held her even as the first drops of rain splattered across their skin. "Rosemary, you have to forgive yourself or…or everything you believe will only be a sham.''

"Let me go,'' she said, gripping the rock to find her footing. "I didn't tell you all of this to ask for forgiveness. I don't know why I told you. I'm…I'm so ashamed, so ashamed. I want to go home now.''

But Kirk refused to let her run away. "No, Rosemary,'' he said. "We're not finished yet.''

The rain started pouring harder now. She looked up at him, letting the rain wash over her, hoping that God's glorious power would wash all her sins and doubts and fears away. But she knew it wouldn't be easy. As strong as her faith had always been, she'd fought against using it to heal herself. Because she didn't believe she deserved to be healed. Better to bear the scars as a reminder of her mistakes.

Indeed, she'd been fighting against absolution since the moment she'd seen the twisted wreckage of her mother's car. Afraid now, she said, "We need to go, Kirk."

Kirk lifted his face to the cool rain. The fresh wetness hit his fevered skin, sending a refreshing, awakening chill over his body. Then he looked back down at Rosemary, and knew in his heart that he wanted, needed, to be here with her, rain or shine, good or bad.

Pulling her into his arms, he shouted over the rain's increasing fury. "Rosemary, I...I can't let you go. I love you. Do you understand me? I love you."

She heard his words coming through the storm. Her heart lurched, bumped against her being, moved beyond a mere beating. It pumped with new life, new joy, through her battered system. "How can you say that?" she asked, amazed that he could even stand to be near her.

Kirk reached out a hand to touch her wet face. "Because it's true. It's true. I love you and I don't care how much you fight me. I can't change it, and neither can you."

They stood there, inches separating them, the only contact his fingers touching her face. Then he wrapped his hand through her hair and urged her to him, kissing her hungrily as the wind and rain moved over them and washed them and purged them.

Fighting for breath, fighting for control, Rosemary lifted her body away from his, her eyes wide with wonder and fear. She wanted to tell him that she loved him, too. But she was so afraid of saying it, afraid that she'd be struck down. She didn't deserve his love. And she wasn't sure she could give him the kind of love he needed. So she stood there, her screams still silent, her secret pain still safe.

Kirk saw the need in her eyes, saw the love she wasn't yet ready to give him, and realized she'd fight against it with all her being.

Well, he intended to fight, too. To win her over.

He kissed her again, wordlessly telegraphing an affirmation of his commitment, his awakening, his ability to love and be loved. But when he lifted his mouth from hers, her next words stopped him cold.

"Don't waste your love on me," she said, shouting into the wind, "because there's nothing you can do about it. There's no hope for us, Kirk. No hope. And you might as well accept that now, before we go any further."

"I don't think we can make it down," Kirk said minutes later as the rain ran in rivers and rivulets around them to form a muddy, treacherous path down the mountain.

Worried, Rosemary gripped his hand as he guided her along, the blinding rain and heavy wind making their descent almost impossible. "Aunt Fitz's cabin," she called. "It's just ahead. We can wait it out there."

She'd be in trouble. They were already late and Faye was the only person who knew where she was. Clayton would be so angry, and she deserved that anger, she decided. She'd deliberately gone off to meet a man her father had told her to stay away from. It was as if the nightmare of being with Eric was happening all over again.

Except this time, the man she'd fallen in love with was a good, decent human being. And this love, ah, this love was twice as powerful as anything she'd ever thought she'd felt for Eric. This was real, and abiding, and secure. And unconditional.

But she couldn't acknowledge this love; she couldn't follow her heart with Kirk without destroying what little love her father had left for her. This was her punishment for being so determined to find happiness.

And from the looks of this storm, even the heavens weren't pleased with her tonight.

"Come on," Kirk said, leading her to the slippery plank steps of the cabin. The porch looked dark and gloomy in spite of Aunt Fitz's cheerful, colorful gourds. "I don't think she's here," he said to Rosemary as they trailed water up onto the porch.

"Oh, she's probably down at the church dinner," Rosemary explained. "I know where she keeps the key. She won't mind if we go in to get out of the storm."

She lifted a nondescript gourd, then fished inside. "It's not there," she said, stretching to make sure she hadn't missed the heavy key to the planked front door. Sinking back onto her wet loafers, she looked at Kirk, worry evident in her words. "Guess we'll have to stay out here on the porch."

Kirk took matters into his own hands when he saw her shivering. Grabbing several dry quilts from a large wooden rack on the wall, he urged Rosemary to the bench settled back well away from the driving rain. "Here. Sit down and I'll wrap us in this. We can wait for the storm to pass and then decide what to do."

"She has a phone," Rosemary said, thinking the statement was redundant. "Only it's locked inside. They'll be worried."

"Meaning, your father?" Kirk arranged her against his chest, then pulled a bright comforter over them. "Speaking of your father, we didn't get to finish our conversation, did we?"

Rosemary purposely avoided looking at him. Instead, she watched the rain as it fell in sheets across the heavy mountain foliage. They'd said a lot of things up on the mountain. But reality would be back soon enough. Especially when she had to face her father.

"Rosemary, we need to talk," Kirk whispered against her wet hair. "I meant what I said, love."

She shifted her head then, to see his face. "So did I, Kirk. You have to understand, no matter how strong my feelings for you are, I can't act on those feelings."

"Because of your father?"

"Yes. I made a vow to stay by him until he's over this. However long it takes."

"So you won't be able to just pack up and leave with me?"

"No. Not that I ever expected you to take me with you. I...I was willing to settle for what little time we have while you're here."

"Well, I'm not willing to settle," Kirk replied tersely. "Oh, I was at first, I'll admit that. But it's just not that simple anymore. I want more. I want you with me. I don't think I can leave you here, Rosemary."

She held on to him, willing him to understand. "I can't go, Kirk. I abandoned my father once, turned away from him, and you just heard the horrible consequences of what I did. I won't do it again.''

''Aye, and you're setting yourself up as some sort of martyr. Do you think your dear mother would want you to waste away like that, out of some sort of obligation?''

Rosemary knew the answer to that. ''No, she'd want me to be happy. But she'd expect me to do what was right, too. And that means helping my father, staying near him, until he's better.''

Frustrated, Kirk turned her in his arms. ''Or until he forgives you, right?''

She buried her face against Kirk's chest. ''I need his forgiveness, Kirk. I have to have it before I can go on with my life.''

''And what about love, what about how we feel for each other?''

She sat up, her features going soft with yearning. ''I...I don't have an answer for that.''

He had a question for her, though. ''Do you compare your feelings for me with the way you felt about Eric? Are you thinking you'll be making the same mistake again?''

''No,'' she said simply. ''No mistakes this time. What I feel for you is completely different from the infatuation I felt for Eric. But I do have to be sure. I can't take any more regrets.''

With fierce determination, he kissed her again, then held back, his eyes searching hers. ''You love me. I can see it in your eyes, but you think you might regret loving me, don't you, Rosemary? Is that the way of it, then?'' His Irish accent became more pronounced with each question, a sure sign he was as frazzled and frustrated as she felt.

Wanting, needing to soothe him, Rosemary leaned forward to place her hands on his face. "I could never regret loving you, Kirk. You've saved me, helped me to heal and to realize that I need love, I need forgiveness."

"But you think you don't need me in your life?" Trying to make her see reason, he pulled her close. "Don't turn your back on us, Rosemary. Don't turn away from something God wants for you."

"Does He want this?" she had to ask. "I was so sure with Eric, so sure I was doing the right thing. I intended to make him a good wife, and I intended to change him into a better human being. What went wrong?"

Kirk pushed heavy strands of wet hair away from her face. "I surely don't have all the answers you need, but I think I can tell you what went wrong between Eric and you. You had the best of intentions, but you forgot one important element in your relationship with Eric."

"What's that?"

"You forgot to turn the changing and the intending over to God. You should know, Rosemary, my love, that you can't change another human being. That has to come from above. And in Eric's case, the changing had to come from within. It didn't happen, through no fault of yours, but because Eric wasn't willing to open his heart and *receive* the change willingly. God gave us free will. It's certainly up to us to use it for its best purpose."

Sitting there, all wet and shivering, and listening to his lyrical, inspiring voice, Rosemary felt a strange sense of peace settling over her soul. Was Kirk right? If she had left the changing up to the Lord and Eric, between the two of them, would things have been different?

She didn't have any answers, true. But she felt immensely better, after hearing Kirk's compelling reasoning.

"You're right," she said at last. "I've certainly learned that lesson well. I won't meddle with the Lord's work anymore, or more specifically, I will learn to accept the things I can't change, and pray about the rest. But where does that leave us, Kirk?"

"Together, I hope," he said. Then he tugged her into his arms and kissed her with all the love and warmth flowing through his heart. "But only if you use the same logic with your father. You can't change him, Rosemary. Oh, you can stand by him, pray for him, show him your example by loving him in spite of how he treats you—that's exactly what your mother did, isn't it? But any change in your da will have to come from his own heart. It will have to come from within. Please, keep that in mind before you shut me out of your life."

"I will," she promised. "Starting tomorrow. I'm going to be completely honest with Daddy. I think it's time my father and I had a long talk."

The rain gentled, slowing to a soft tinkling. The night darkened around them, and in spite of the wet and the cold and the worry, they fell asleep, huddled there together underneath Aunt Fitz's warm quilt.

It was the best sleep Rosemary had had in a good while.

It would also probably be the last she'd have for some time to come.

Because with the morning came the sun—and the hour of reckoning with her father. Somehow, in spite of his sure wrath, Rosemary had to convince him that this time, things would turn out differently. And she had to ask him to forgive her so she could go on with her life.

Until then, she couldn't make any promises to Kirk.

Chapter Eleven

A search party met them about halfway up the mountain, with Rosemary's brother Danny at the head of the pack.

"Rosemary," he called, waving to her as he rushed to greet them. Giving Kirk a level look, he asked, "Are you all right?"

Rosemary nodded to her brother, then lifted wild curls away from her face. "I'm fine, Danny." She and Kirk waved to the other men with him. "We got caught in the storm and couldn't make it back down. We stayed on Aunt Fitz's porch all night."

Danny looked skeptical, but didn't question her in front of the others. "Daddy is fit to be tied, I might as well tell you."

"I'm sure he is," Kirk interjected. "And I take full responsibility. I'll explain things to him."

Danny shook his head. "I don't think that'd be too wise, buddy. My father doesn't want you around Rosemary, and this didn't exactly endear you to him."

Rosemary touched Danny's arm. "We don't need to

go into that right now. I'll talk to Daddy. He and I need to talk. We've been avoiding it for too long."

Danny called to the other four men. "Go on back down, fellows. They're okay. Thanks for your help."

After Rosemary shouted her own thanks to the departing men, Danny turned back to her. "Oh, he's ready to talk, all right," he said, turning to lead them down the still-slippery path. "In fact, if Faye hadn't been there with him last night, I think he would have tore off up here to find you."

"Faye stayed with him?" Rosemary asked, glad to hear her friend had been there to spend time with her father.

"Yeah, till around midnight," Danny said, shooting her a questioning look. "What's that all about anyway? I've noticed she's been coming around a lot more lately."

Rosemary glanced over at Kirk, then back to her brother. She'd wanted to approach Danny about this, but had purposely put it off. She didn't think he'd accept Faye as readily as she had. "She cares about Dad, Danny. She's a good friend."

Danny didn't miss the evasiveness in her words. "I don't think I like the tone of this, sister. Are you telling me our father has...a girlfriend?"

"A friend," Rosemary corrected. "Someone to share time with, a companion. It's a healthy sign, if you ask me."

"I didn't ask you," Danny snapped. "But I bet you had something to do with this. Rosemary, how could you condone something like this so soon after Mama's death?"

Hurt that he didn't seem to be thinking of her father's best interest, and that he immediately wanted to blame her, Rosemary stopped walking to stare across at him. "Mama's been dead over a year now, Danny. And I think Daddy needs to get on with his life. I can't stand to see him so lonely and cooped up in that house. If Faye can make him smile again, yes, I am all for it."

"That figures," her brother said on a hushed whisper, so the men farther down the path ahead of them wouldn't hear. "I guess you think if you can keep Daddy distracted with Faye, you'll have more time to pull stunts like this one. Rosemary, haven't you learned anything?"

Kirk saw the humiliation on Rosemary's face, and wanting to shield her from any further unjustified attacks, moved toward Danny, his face inches from Rosemary's brother's. "You've got it all wrong, Danny. Rosemary cares about her father, and Faye is a good woman. And your sister didn't try to distract your father. I asked her to walk up the mountain with me. I needed some answers, and Rosemary poured out her heart to me. I know all about what happened, everything. And I think it's time both you and your father stopped blaming Rosemary for your mother's death."

Temper flared in Danny's eyes. "Man, you don't know a thing about me or my family. And I suggest you just stay out of it before you do any more damage. I'm telling you, my daddy is furious."

"Why?" Kirk asked, his own temper matching anything Danny could throw at him. "Because Rosemary wasn't at her appointed spot in the kitchen when he got home? Because people will talk? Is he angry because he was worried about his daughter, or because his daughter didn't check with him first before she took a walk? Does he even care that she's hurting as much as any of you?''

Danny stepped close, but Kirk refused to back down. "I don't want a fight with you, Danny. But someone has to make both you and Clayton see that Rosemary has suffered enough.''

Danny scowled. "Oh, and I suppose you're the one who's going to set all of us straight. Thinking you can fix us, patch us up like you're doing to that old church? Well, pal, this family will be a lot harder to work with than rocks and wood, let me tell you.''

"I don't want to fix anything," Kirk replied. "I just want to have a chance to get to know your sister. And she deserves that same chance. You're happily married, with a child. Doesn't your sister deserve some happiness, too?''

That question stopped Danny in his tracks. Confusion warring with pride and anger in his eyes, he turned to Rosemary as if looking at her for the first time. Kirk watched as Rosemary stared up at her brother, her eyes brimming with hope and pain.

Rosemary lifted her chin, daring her brother to say anything more. She certainly wasn't ashamed of being with Kirk. They'd done nothing wrong, and now he was defending her honor like a knight of the realm. She'd never had anyone do that for her before. It only reinforced her feelings for him, and her determination to face her father with the same courage she was showing her overprotective brother.

Danny spoke at last. "I'm sorry, sister. I guess I've been so caught up in my own bitterness I never stopped to think what all of this has cost you. Rosemary, you know I don't blame you, don't you?''

Rosemary swallowed the lump in her throat, then

said, "We've never really talked about how you feel, Danny. Oh, I know you've never said a harsh word to me, but sometimes I see you looking at me with that strange expression and I wonder if you're remembering that night, too. And I have to believe you do blame me. You've been a good brother, but I miss the closeness we had before...before Mom died. I love you, Danny."

Danny tugged her into his arms. "I love you, too. You have to know that. And I don't blame you." When she lifted her head, he added, "Okay, at first I was upset and resentful, but that passed. Nancy helped me work through all that. And I've prayed, and talked to Reverend Clancy about it. I hope I haven't made you feel that way, Rosemary."

"You just always seem to take Dad's side," she tried to explain. "And when I ask you for help with him, you always have a ready excuse, something to do. I can't do it alone, Danny. He needs both of us."

Danny looked down at the muddy path. "I know, I know. It's just...it's hard for me to be around him. I can't sit there and take it the way you do. I can't stand to see him like this...like he's half-dead or something. It's hard, Rosemary."

"Tell me about it," she retorted, but with a gentle smile. "Danny, you don't have a clue how hard it is to face him each day, or how hard it is to live in that house with him. You've got Nancy and Emily and your friends at work. Me, I have a good, satisfying job and my friends from church, but I always have to go home to face him each and every day. Until Kirk came along, I didn't have any hope of ever finding my own happiness again."

Danny looked at Kirk then, a sheepish expression

falling across his face. "I'm sorry, Kirk. I guess Rose-mary turned to you for help because I didn't offer her any." Extending a hand, he shook the one Kirk offered him. "Thank you, for listening to her, for helping her, for making her happy again." Then he gave Kirk a mock punch on the arm. "But did you have to take her off in a storm?"

Kirk shrugged. "Sorry. I can't predict nature. But I'm glad you didn't belt me one when you saw me."

Danny ran a hand through his short, thick hair. "I was just worried. In spite of my acting like a stubborn mule, I do love my sister."

Rosemary smiled at her brother. "Do you mean that, Danny?"

He grinned. "Yes, even though I haven't slept all night from worrying about you, I do mean it. I want you to be happy. And from now on, I'll sure try to be more open and sensitive, as my pretty wife would sug-gest—if that's possible for someone as bullheaded as I am—and I'll try to come around and spend more time with Dad."

"Thank you," Rosemary said, reaching up to give him a kiss on the cheek. "And thank you for coming to look for us."

Danny frowned then. "I had to, to keep Dad from charging up here." Then he took his sister's hand. "Come on. You've got to face him sometime. Might as well get it over with."

"You'll go with me?" she asked, surprised.

"I'll go with you," he said. "And this time, I'll stand up to him. I don't like taking sides, but I'm will-ing to try and make him listen." Then he halted. "Only if you promise you won't sneak off like this again."

"I won't," she said, glancing over at Kirk. "From

now on, I'm going to be up front with Daddy. It can't make things any worse than they already are.''

''Might make them better,'' Kirk said, wishing that for this family with all his heart. Of course, he had his own selfish reasons for wanting peace in the Brinson household. He wanted Rosemary to love him, completely, and without any regrets.

''I sure hope so,'' Danny replied. ''I hate missing a good night's sleep.''

A crowd of curious townspeople greeted them at the foot of the mountain, everyone whispering and speculating about what had happened.

Faye waved, tearing away from the crowd to come forward. ''Oh, you're all right. We were so worried. That was some storm and we had a bit of flash flooding during the night.''

''I know,'' Rosemary said, patting her friend's hand. ''That's why we couldn't make it back down the mountain. The path was a river of water.'' Looking down at her rumpled clothes, she added, ''And I'm a mess. The rain caught us on top of the mountain and we had to sit it out on Aunt Fitz's front porch. I'm really sorry I had everybody in such a state.''

Faye glanced at Kirk, then back to Rosemary. ''Aunt Fitz spent the night with one of her daughters. She said she hoped you'd try to stop at her place, but she worried because she forgot to put the key in the gourd.''

''We found that out quick enough,'' Rosemary said, glancing around. ''Where's Daddy?''

''Where do you think?'' Faye said on a snort. ''In that house, pouting and fuming.'' Touching Rosemary on the arm, she added, ''Be careful, honey. He's not too happy and he hasn't slept at all.''

"Did he eat supper at the church?" Rosemary asked on a hopeful note.

Faye lifted her eyes. "I had him just about talked into it, but he wanted to wait for you. When the storm hit and you didn't come back, he told me to forget it."

Rosemary moaned. "Oh, why didn't I just tell him where I was going!"

"Too late to worry about that now," Faye said. "And I encouraged you, so it's partly my fault."

"I've got to go talk to him," Rosemary said. Turning to where Kirk stood making polite conversation with several people about the storm, she told him, "Danny and I are going to see Daddy. Then I'm going to get cleaned up and get to work."

"That'd be good, if you feel up to it," Faye called. "Melissa isn't here yet."

"Neither is my help," Kirk said, his eyes searching the grounds for Eric. Then he said to Rosemary, "I'll see you later—unless you want me to go with you now."

She shook her head, very aware that the crowd gathered around to make sure they were safe was also making sure they hadn't done anything scandalous while up on that mountain. "No. There'll be talk enough without you and my father having a fistfight."

"I'm not afraid to face him," Kirk said, his gaze holding hers. "And I'm not worried about what people say. Remember what I told you, Rosemary."

Several people nearby leaned in to see if they could hear exactly what he had told her.

Rosemary shot him a meaningful look, then turned to leave. Gossip. Just one more thing for her to worry about.

Deciding she'd deal with that later, she hurried to confront her father.

Clayton sat in the dark kitchen, nursing a lukewarm cup of coffee, his eyes bloodshot from lack of sleep, his mind numbed by the fear that he'd lost his daughter for good.

Rosemary. His lovely little girl, so afraid to face him that she'd run off up the mountain into a storm. How had they come to this? he wondered as he glanced around the clean, empty kitchen. If it hadn't been for Faye, encouraging him, comforting him, telling him Rosemary was a sensible, smart girl, he'd have gone crazy. Again.

He'd been up on that mountain mere minutes before his daughter, he reckoned. They must have just missed each other. His first time to go there, and now this.

He'd gone because of the dream. Eunice. He'd dreamed about Eunice. And in the dream, she had spoken to him in that soft, quiet voice. "Clayton, be kind to her. Clayton, show her how much you love her. Clayton, remember God's promise. We will be together again."

So he took flowers up to her grave, for the first time since her funeral. Having survived that painful experience, he decided he'd have a talk with Rosemary. Just a few civil words, just an opening, a beginning. He couldn't promise anything beyond that, even to Eunice.

Only, Rosemary hadn't come home. Faye came and told him Rosemary had gone for a walk with the steeplejack, told him not to worry.

But he had worried. He'd had all night to think about how he'd treated his daughter this past year. A long night, an angry, storm-tossed night that only reminded

him of another horrible night. Had he really slept any
since then? Had he really lived at all in the past year?

No. He'd been too busy punishing his daughter, too
busy blaming God for taking his wife away from him.

And now he had Faye to contend with. That woman
didn't mince words, or beat around the bush. But a lot
of what she said made sense.

"You need to get out of this bleak house, Clayton.
Come on over to the church supper. I fried some of my
famous buttermilk chicken."

"I'd rather stay here, if you don't mind."

"Well, I do mind. You can't go on like this. Why,
you're wasting away, and you're hurting Rosemary.
Don't you care about her? Don't you see what you've
done? Is it really your place to sit in judgment of your
own daughter?"

He'd come so close to making it across the street to
that lovable old church. So close.

Then the storm had hit, and Faye, worried enough
herself about Rosemary, had told him where his daughter had gone.

Lost in the storm. Lost and alone and frightened and
searching. Lost with a man he didn't want to like,
didn't want to respect, didn't want to admire. Lost with
Kirk Lawrence.

Clayton told himself he wouldn't be angry, if she'd
just come home safely. He told himself he wouldn't
shout or nag, or condemn her. He only wanted another
chance.

He told himself these things as he sat there, afraid
someone would come in and tell him it was too late,
afraid that once again God would take away someone
he loved.

But when the back door opened and both his children walked in, safe and sound, all he could do was glare up at his daughter. He didn't have the courage to face her, or to ask for her forgiveness, so he just sat there, staring, the echo of his dead wife's words still fresh in his mind, along with Faye's warning.

"Good morning, Daddy," Rosemary said, coming to sit down in the chair across from him, her nostrils flaring at the scent of fresh-brewed coffee. "You made coffee?"

"Had to, now, didn't I?" Clayton retorted hotly, all graciousness gone now and hidden away like her mother's pictures. "Do you know what a bother you caused everybody, girl?"

Rosemary slumped her shoulders for a second, then sat up straight. "Yes, I do, Daddy. And from now on, I'm going to tell you exactly what I'm doing and who I'm doing it with, whether you like hearing it or not."

"Defiant as always." He glared up at Danny, waiting for his son to confirm what he'd just said.

Danny, however, didn't react as his father had expected. Instead, he went to the cupboard and got two cups, then he poured coffee for Rosemary and himself.

Coming to stand between them, he told Clayton, "She's had a long night, Daddy, and she's tired. But she's also right. Rosemary and Kirk didn't do anything wrong last night. They just got caught in the storm. With the flash flooding, they had no choice but to sit it out on Aunt Fitz's porch."

"That's where you were all night?" Clayton asked, thankful in his heart, but firm in his anger.

"Yes," Rosemary replied, nodding her head. "And I don't mean to sound defiant." She paused, hoping she wouldn't lose her courage. "But...I'm a grown woman, and I won't do anything to disgrace you any,

Daddy. I've purposely avoided even dating anybody since Mom's death, but I...I like Kirk. And I think it's time we get everything out in the open, between you and me. I can't keep going on, hoping you'll change, hoping you'll...start loving me again.''

Clayton started, his hand reaching out in the air, but then he let it drop on the table before he touched her. ''Then why do you continue to do things that only cause all of us pain, Rosemary? Why did you go off with Kirk Lawrence?''

Steeling herself against his rejection, she said, ''Because Kirk needed to hear the truth, from me. I told him the whole ugly story, Daddy. I had to tell him before I could let things go any further between us.''

Regaining some of his righteous anger, Clayton slammed his hand down on the table. ''And just how far did things go last night, daughter?''

Rosemary gasped and jumped up as if he'd slapped her. ''How can you even ask me that? You and Mama taught me to have principles and morals, and to do what is right. I'm asking you to please trust me, and all you can do is accuse me of something immoral and shameful?'' Shame surfaced, old and worn and waiting, but this time, this time, she refused to wear it. ''Kirk and I sat and talked on Aunt Fitz's porch, then we fell asleep, sitting straight up, with all of our wet clothes on, with a pile of quilts on us to keep us warm until morning. That's all that happened.''

Clayton looked down at the dregs of his coffee.

Danny shot Rosemary an encouraging look, then touched a hand to his father's shirtsleeve. ''Daddy, are you more concerned about appearances than about what's really going on in this family?''

Clayton snorted and pushed his son's hand away.

"Oh, I see she's got you convinced now, huh? I guess you've decided to condone her wild ways."

Danny stomped to the sink to pour out the remains of his coffee. "Rosemary has never been wild, and I'm not condoning anything, except her right to have a life of her own and her right to some happiness." Pivoting to face his shocked father, he added, "There's been too little happiness around here in the last year."

Then he lifted a finger to point to the church across the way. "We've attended church all our lives, we've read the Bible, we've heard the Lord's teachings, yet somehow, we've conveniently forgotten to apply those very teachings to ourselves and our own situation. So do we turn away from everything we've held dear just because God decided it was time to call Mama home? Do we, Dad? And will that bring her back? Will that really make anything any better?"

"You're out of line, boy," Clayton said as he rose. "I don't need to sit here and listen to this kind of talk."

Danny was right by his father's side. "Oh, yes, Daddy, you do need to sit here and listen. We need to talk, really talk about how we feel—we've hardly talked about Mama's death at all because you refused to let us even mention her name."

Proud of her brother, Rosemary said, "He's right. Mother was a wonderful, warm person, but she's gone. Instead of shutting that out, we need to accept it and...celebrate her life, instead of being bitter over her death."

"There is nothing to celebrate," Clayton said, his jaw clenched, his face white with rage. "I will not listen to any more of this." Waving a hand at Rosemary, he added, "You go where you want, do what you need to do. You find that happiness you want so much, girl. But don't expect me to be happy along with you. I lost my happiness the night I saw your mother lying dead in that ravine.''

Crushed, Rosemary reached out to him. ''Daddy, please, can't you just try to...to start over? Can't you try to forgive me?''

Clayton heard the pain in her voice, saw the anguish in her eyes, but pride held him back from taking her in his arms to comfort her. Pride born of his own pain, stubborn, hateful pride that wouldn't let him give in or give up. After all, his pride was the only thing holding him together. If he let go of that, he'd crumble completely. So he used that pride as a shield, and he used his anger as a sword. And with that sword, he slashed at his daughter's defenses.

''There's nothing to forgive, Rosemary. You only did what you wanted to do. Same as now. Well, go ahead and be with Kirk Lawrence. Go ahead and shame me again. Go ahead and live your life. Just leave me alone.''

Before he could push past her, Faye came through the screen door, her face white, her hands trembling. ''There's been an accident,'' she said on a breathless, worried voice. ''Eric—''

At the mention of that name, all heads came up. Clayton halted his tirade, stilling as he waited for Faye to continue. Rosemary sank into her chair, too weak, too afraid of the horrible images playing in her head, to ask Faye what had happened. Danny clutched the counter, his eyes darting from Rosemary to his father, then back to Faye.

''Eric had another wreck,'' Faye explained. ''And, Rosemary...well, Melissa was in the car with him.''

Chapter Twelve

The county hospital buzzed and hummed with all the efficiency of a well-honed machine, its doctors and nurses hurrying by with purposeful steps and set gazes while the four occupants of the tiny waiting room lifted their own faces each time a swinging door flapped open.

"Why won't they tell us something?" Rosemary said, worry evident in her question. Faye sat beside her on a blue vinyl divan, while Reverend Clancy and Kirk sat across from them on an identical one.

"They're busy, Rosemary," the reverend said gently. "When they have all the details, we'll be the first to know."

"I'm glad we all came," Faye said. "Especially since we couldn't get in touch with Melissa's parents."

"And poor Eric," Reverend Clancy added. "His brother didn't even seem concerned when I finally got him on the phone. At least I got a chance to speak with Eric myself for a few minutes."

Rosemary stayed silent, her gaze locking with

Kirk's. He'd insisted on coming, not only for her sake, but because Eric worked for him. And she was glad to have him here. She was having an extremely hard time feeling sorry for "poor Eric."

After they heard the news, Danny had gone on to work, asking for an update later. And Clayton, well, he'd gone back into the dark den to watch a talk show, his cold shroud firmly intact.

Before Faye interrupted them, Rosemary had sensed a change in her father though. She couldn't put her finger on it, but somehow he had seemed different this morning. Not as cold, not as condemning. And the way he'd looked at her—had she seen a flash of compassion and concern in her father's eyes?

No. She was probably only hoping to see something that could never be there. His clenched jaw and tight fists told her how he felt about hearing Eric was involved in another accident, and whatever he'd been about to say ended when Faye came with this latest news. Now Rosemary felt the same as she had the day Eric had come back—sick to her stomach and so afraid. How many tragedies would it take before Eric reached inside himself to make a change?

Kirk got up to come and kneel in front of her. "Want something to drink?"

"No. I'm fine."

"You need to eat. You didn't have breakfast."

She smiled at the sweet concern in his eyes, savoring the surge of joy his attention brought, in spite of their reason for being here. "I'll eat later. I'm too keyed up now."

"And probably exhausted," he said. "We didn't get much sleep."

While Faye talked quietly to Reverend Clancy,

Rosemary looked down at Kirk, studying his face with bliss-filled intensity.

"What?" he asked, clearly intrigued by her direct look.

"I was just remembering how we talked last night. I haven't stayed up late to talk to anyone like that in years. I feel as if we've known each other for a very long time."

He grinned, then touched his forehead to hers. "That's the way it's supposed to be between two people who love and care about each other."

Rosemary closed her eyes for a moment to soak up his words. "I haven't had anyone to love and care about for some time now. And this time, I don't intend to take it for granted."

He gave her a hopeful look. "Is that your way of admitting you're madly in love with me?"

She wanted to say yes to that question, but fear still held her in a solid grip. "That's my way of saying thank you for helping me through this."

Kirk lifted her face with a finger underneath her chin. "You've grown up a lot since Eric, Rosemary. And I'm not the same as him. We'll work through all of this, together."

She looked around as a doctor came out of the room where they had taken Melissa. Kirk stood, taking her by the arm as she lifted up off the couch to hear what the doctor had to say.

"Hello, folks," the young, redheaded Dr. Harris began, shaking hands as he prepared to give them the news. "Sorry you had to wait, but we wanted to be sure. Melissa will be all right."

After the collective sigh that came from the group, he paused then continued. "She's badly bruised, though. Her head hit the windshield, so she has a slight concussion. I'm afraid she's going to be sore for a while, but things could have been much worse. She was wearing her seat belt, so that prevented her from getting hurt more seriously. We'll keep her overnight just to make sure we've covered everything.''

"And what about Eric?" Reverend Clancy asked.

"A couple of cracked ribs," the doctor said. "And a cut to his left cheek. We stitched that up, but his eye will be black-and-blue for some time to come. He can go home today, though."

"I'll call his brother to come and pick him up," the reverend said, shaking the doctor's hand again. "Thank you, Doctor."

Rosemary turned to Faye. "So, he walks away again while Melissa has to stay here. Honestly, I don't think I can face him."

"Why don't we go in to see Melissa?" Kirk suggested. "That way you won't have to deal with Eric."

But it was too late to avoid him. He walked out into the hall just as they were making their way to Melissa's room. Rosemary had to admit, he looked scared and worried. As well he should, under the circumstances.

His gaze searching Rosemary's face, Eric asked, "Is Melissa all right? They won't tell me anything."

Rosemary wanted to lash out at him, but Kirk's firm grip on her arm helped her to quell that particular desire. "She's going to be okay. But they're keeping her overnight. She has a concussion."

Eric closed his eyes in relief. "It was the storm. I couldn't see, the car swerved." When he opened his eyes, he focused on Rosemary's skeptical expression. "Why are you looking at me like that?"

Rosemary couldn't speak. The anger, the resentment, boiling up inside her was too raw, too strong.

Eric leaned back against the wall, his face going pale. "You think...you think I was drinking, don't you?"

Kirk put a protective arm around Rosemary, then turned to Eric. "Were you?"

Eric threw his hands in the air. "Why do I even bother? Why should I have to answer that question? You've all already decided, haven't you? You've already judged me and condemned me and now you're wondering how I managed to survive one more time, right?" When neither Rosemary nor Kirk responded, he shouted, "Right, Rosemary?"

The nurses looked up from their work at a nearby station, then Dr. Harris finished signing Eric's release forms at the desk and turned on his heel to stomp toward them, his stern look centered on Eric.

"What's the problem, Mr. Thomas?"

"Tell them, Doc," Eric said, his eyes wide, his face red with rage. "Tell them I wasn't drinking when I had that wreck last night. The police checked me out, they can tell you."

The doctor stared long and hard at Eric, then pivoted to face Rosemary and Kirk. "I don't know what's going on here, but there was no sign of alcohol in Mr. Thomas's bloodstream, folks. The police did a routine check because of his being on probation, but he had not been drinking. Just a case of bad weather and slippery roads."

"You see," Eric said, his gaze moving over Rosemary's face. "Bad weather—same as you and him." He pointed a finger to Kirk. "You got stuck in the weather—Reverend Clancy told me all about it—and nobody jumped to conclusions about what you were doing. I had an *accident,* Rosemary. But it's different with me, isn't it? I've been condemned for life.''

Rosemary couldn't speak. Her breath seemed to be stuck in her throat. All she could do was cling to Kirk and watch Eric's face, her emotions churning from fear and frustration to guilt and remorse.

''I want to see Melissa,'' Eric said. Then he turned to head toward the room to which a nurse pointed.

Reverend Clancy came back, shaking his head. ''Eric's brother refuses to come and get the boy. I'll take him back to the parsonage and see that he gets a good breakfast.''

For the first time since her mother's death, Rosemary felt a spark of sympathy for Eric. But it was short-lived and weak, and gone as soon as she reminded herself that because of Eric, she'd been condemned, too.

Still, on the way back home, she was quiet and contemplative. She had been quick to judge Eric this morning. Maybe, just maybe, he really was trying to make a change this time. She hadn't questioned Melissa about Eric, or why she'd been with him in the car. Melissa had been too weak to do anything more than whisper, yet Rosemary had glimpsed the defiance in the girl's eyes. Then Melissa's parents had shown up before Rosemary could ask her too many questions, so she couldn't say much about her concerns for the girl.

Kirk sensed her withdrawal and reached across the seat of her car to touch a hand to her arm. ''Are you all right?''

''Just worried,'' she admitted as she steered her economy car around the looping mountain roads. ''Melissa seemed so quiet, I know she's in a lot of pain.''

"She'll be okay," he reminded her. "She's very lucky, that's for sure."

"But why was she with Eric in the first place?"

Kirk studied her face for a minute, then sighed. "Rosemary, they both have a right to see each other. In spite of how you and I feel about Eric, Melissa is a very headstrong young lady. I have a feeling she's attracted to the danger she senses in Eric."

Shocked, Rosemary glanced over at him for a split second before returning her focus to the road. "That's silly. Why would any woman be attracted to a man who's committed vehicular homicide—murder? And especially when she knows all about what he did?"

"That doesn't matter to some people," he tried to explain. "Melissa is sorry for what happened to your mother, but she's interested in Eric anyway. From everything you've told me about the girl, and from watching her each day, I'd say she's looking for love in all the wrong places."

Rosemary shook her head. "Then the song's true, huh?"

"In some cases, yes," he replied, nodding. "Think about her home life, Rosemary. No guidance, no good examples to follow. No wonder the girl is attracted to Eric. He represents the type of freedom she craves, the excitement she can't find at home."

Putting his theory to the test, she said, "Then explain why *I* was attracted to him? I had a good home life, and I didn't crave excitement." She grew quiet then, remembering how in awe she'd been of Eric. And how exciting it had been to be noticed by someone she didn't know everything about, someone who was a bit mysterious. That realization brought her current motives into sharp focus. Was that why she was attracted to Kirk, too?

Kirk shrugged, but didn't miss the added anxiety her thoughts had brought. "I don't know. Maybe because you were so sheltered, so structured in your upbringing, you turned to Eric because *he* showed an interest in you?"

She scoffed. "You make it sound as if I was needy or something, Kirk. I had boyfriends before Eric."

He had to smile at that. He could only imagine Rosemary as a beautiful teenager, tempting all boys, both good and bad. "But did you feel the same about any of them?"

"No." She watched the road, a frown marring her face. "He was like a breath of fresh air, so different from anybody else I'd ever known." She shrugged. "Okay, maybe I was attracted to him for all the wrong reasons myself."

"And that's how it is with Melissa, except the difference is, you didn't know about his dark side, and she does."

Starting to understand, she glanced back at him. "So, I was interested in Eric's good side, while Melissa is attracted to his dark side?"

"Exactly. Because you have strong moral fiber, based on your upbringing, you could only see his good, and try to change the part of him that you didn't like. Melissa, on the other hand, hasn't had the same solid upbringing as you, so she's tempted by a man who should be forbidden. She doesn't necessarily want to change him."

"And I sure did. Melissa won't do that, will she?"

"Not at first. But the newness will wear off soon enough. Only, we can't make her see that now. I have a feeling if we try, she'll just run right into his arms.'' Then, taking a different stance, he added, "Of course, because she doesn't judge him the same way you did, Melissa could be the one to help Eric turn around. And in doing so, she just might settle down herself.''

Rosemary didn't like the tone of that. Had she been too judgmental of Eric? She had demanded perfection from him, but only because she'd cared about him. "So you're telling me to stay out of their relationship?''

Kirk waited until she had stopped the car in her driveway, his own dark thoughts swirling like the left-over rain clouds passing by in the sky. "I'm not telling you anything. I'm asking you to concentrate on *us,* and let Melissa and Eric work this out between them. Unless, of course—''

"What?'' she interrupted, not liking the serious look on his face.

He had to voice the one fear he'd held since Rosemary had told him the whole story about her mother's death and her own sudden breakup with Eric. "Unless you're still attracted to Eric.''

Amazed that he'd even dare to voice that, she stared at him, her hands tightly gripping the steering wheel. "How can you think that, Kirk?'' Her voice softened, while her eyes held his. "Especially after last night?''

Kirk lowered his head, then glanced out at the tall pines swaying in the morning breeze. "I had to ask, Rosemary. You seem so defensive whenever we talk about Eric. And you're sure set against Melissa seeing him.''

Angry now, she opened the car door. "I'm defensive because the man ruined my life. And I'm trying to protect Melissa—I won't let the same thing happen to her.''

Kirk got out, too, then came around the car to stand in front of her. "Are you sure that's all it is? Or do you have unresolved feelings for him? I have to know, Rosemary."

Hurt, she wondered how she could make Kirk see that she was so in love with him, no other man could ever compare in her mind. Of course, Kirk himself had just alerted her to the danger of falling for someone she didn't know very well. Her first instinct was to lash out at him, but then she stopped to remind herself that she'd learned something from her talks with Kirk. She'd tried to change Eric, and that had backfired. Was she still trying to change him in her own roundabout way? And would she wind up trying to do the same with Kirk?

"Maybe you're right," she said at last. "But not about how I feel about Eric. I do not feel anything for Eric anymore. And that's the truth. I care about you, I care about what happens between us now, Kirk." Wanting to be honest, she told him, "But...I still have a lot to work through. I can't make any promises, but I do know that what I feel for you is very real."

He reached out a hand to touch her cheek. "I want to believe that, but we both know if I were to leave tomorrow, you wouldn't be going with me, now, would you?"

She took a minute to let that soak in. "No, but not because of Eric. Because of my father. I can't leave him yet, Kirk." *And if I try to make you stay, I'll be repeating the same pattern.*

"I know that's what you're telling yourself, but...Rosemary, you can't change your father any more than you can change Eric. All you can do at this point is pray for both of them."

"I am, I have," she said, her temper flaring again. "I've prayed for my father every day and night since my mother died."

"And what about Eric?"

"I'm trying, Kirk. Really, I am."

He dropped his hand away, then stood watching her. "How can you pray for someone you say you have no feelings for?"

"It's not easy," she admitted. What she couldn't admit was that her prayers hadn't been nearly sincere enough to be heard. They were feeble at best, but that was because she still had so much anger and bitterness inside.

Kirk brushed his hair off his forehead with one hand, then looked down at her, his eyes full of longing and compassion. "Rosemary, until you find it in your heart to forgive Eric, we won't be able to make a full commitment to each other. You have to resolve your feelings for him before you can move on with your life."

"That's crazy," she said, turning to stalk away. "I don't have any unresolved feelings for Eric. I told you, I don't have any feelings for him, period."

"My point exactly," he called after her.

She kept walking toward the church.

"Rosemary, you loved the man once and…that love ended so suddenly. Have you even stopped to think about it?"

"No," she called back. "I don't want to think about Eric Thomas. Ever again."

Kirk watched her hurry to the educational building. She'd pour herself into her work with the children to keep from thinking about what he'd said. But she would have to face it sooner or later. And until she did, things would be at a standstill between them. He wouldn't allow her to pretend she was okay, when she was still hurting over Eric.

And, he told himself as he headed to his own work, he wouldn't let her settle for loving him to replace what she had lost with Eric. She'd said she wanted to be sure this time.

Well, so did he. Kirk knew he was in deep, so deep that he wouldn't be able to walk away so easily. He was willing to fight for Rosemary, but only if she was willing to fight for herself. She wouldn't be completely free until she resolved everything with her father and with Eric. And that meant letting go.

That also meant forgiving.

Rosemary wasn't sure how she made it through the rest of the day. Tired and restless, she went home after making sure all the children were safely on their way, only to find a mess waiting for her in the kitchen.

Digging in with all her might, she began putting dirty dishes into the dishwasher with absentminded concentration. Maybe Kirk was right. Maybe deep down inside, she was denying her true feelings.

Did she still feel something for Eric?

Thinking about how much she had loved him once, she recalled their good times, and couldn't help comparing them to her few precious minutes with Kirk.

There was no comparison. True, she'd loved Eric once. But that love had stopped suddenly, swiftly, the night her mother died. In fact, she had only spoken to Eric briefly that night, to say they would talk later.

Only, later never came.

Her family was so distraught, she couldn't bring herself to see Eric again. So there were never any final goodbyes, no spoken words, between them in the following weeks. Eric was in jail, unable to make bail. Then his trial came up a few weeks later, and she'd attended, determined to make sure he got what he deserved.

His pleading looks, his sorrowful words, had gone unheard. Out of respect for her grieving father, and because of her own raw pain, Rosemary had refused to listen to him.

Stopping now, she looked out over the yard, her eyes automatically searching for the church steeple across the way. "Was I wrong, Lord, to refuse to talk to Eric? Was I wrong to turn away from him so suddenly?"

He killed her mother. What else could she do?

The echo of Kirk's words came back to her, loud and clear. "How can you pray for someone you have no feelings for?"

"How can I, Lord?" she asked out loud.

As she gazed at the steeple, she saw Kirk scaling one side of the tall tower. So, he was working late to make up for lost time. Or maybe like her, he needed to stay busy to keep his mind off everything else. Maybe he was wishing he'd never fallen in love with such a mixed-up person.

"But I'm not mixed-up," she told herself. "I know where I can find my strength. And I know God will show me the way."

She watched, fascinated, as Kirk went about his work. He hung suspended by a cable wire, his body held inside his little wooden chair, his tools dangling from his belt. Kirk worked with meticulous care. Today, he was washing the stained-glass windows that sparkled with such brilliance each time the sun hit them.

The windows were beautiful. Kirk would clean them,

nurture them, make them shine all the more for God's glory. Because of his care, they would be better. But he wouldn't change them.

He wouldn't change them.

The brilliance from the windows shot through Rosemary at about the same time realization flowed through her, sharp and clear, and sure.

She couldn't change Eric, or her father, by simply praying for them to turn their lives around. She could only change others by changing herself, and by changing *how* she prayed.

"I've been doing it all wrong," she said, a rush of joy sweeping over her. "I've been asking for the wrong things."

About that time, Clayton came into the room. "Talking to yourself, girl?"

Rosemary turned, a fresh smile on her face. Why, she never really smiled at her father anymore. She was always pious and quiet, trying so hard to respect his grief. Today, though, she really smiled at him, the kind of smile she used to give to him whenever she'd see him walk into a room.

"No, Daddy," she said as she approached him with a purposeful intent. "I was talking to God."

"Hmmph." Then, "How's Melissa?"

"She's going to be all right." She waited, then looked up at her father. "And...we found out Eric wasn't drinking. The weather was bad, he lost control of the car."

Clayton stood there, so silent, so still, she wished she hadn't mentioned the accident. He started to turn away, but Rosemary reached out to touch him, startling both of them. They rarely touched each other anymore.

"Daddy?"

"What?"

She saw the hesitation in his eyes, but she couldn't stop herself. Rosemary hugged her father. Hugged him hard, hugged him tightly to her. Patted him on the back. "I love you, Daddy."

Clayton stood rigid for a minute, then to her amazement, he awkwardly patted her on the back before pulling away. He didn't say a word, just stared down at her for a long time.

Then he whirled and shifted away. But he didn't head for the dark den as she had expected. Instead, he went out onto the porch to sit in one of the rocking chairs. Then he said, "Call me when supper's done. I'm going to watch your steeplejack."

Rosemary could have squealed with joy. This, *this* sounded like the father she had always remembered.

She took him a glass of tea, then stood there to stare down at him. Finally, she asked, "Daddy, why did you go to Mama's grave yesterday?"

Clearly surprised that she knew, Clayton refused to look at her. "A man has a right to visit his wife's grave, doesn't he?"

It wasn't the answer she needed or wanted, but it would do for now. "Yes, a man has every right," she said quietly.

Then she went back into the house to fix his supper.

That night, Rosemary didn't ask God to make Eric a better person, or to make her father love her again.

That night, Rosemary asked God to help her instead.

"Help me to forgive," she prayed. "Help me to heal. Help me to feel something for Eric, so that I can learn to forgive him."

When she finished her prayers, she automatically went to the window to see if Kirk was still up. She saw him standing there in the moonlight, watching and waiting.

And she knew she loved him completely. This was a different kind of love from what she'd felt for Eric. Kirk was a different man from Eric. Mysterious, yes. But willing to tell her all his secrets. Refreshing, very. But not in a dangerous way. Changeable? Maybe, but not to the point that he'd resent her trying to mold or shape him, and she didn't feel the strong need to mold or shape him the way she had with Eric. Kirk was willing to compromise and to commit in order to have a life with her. Just when and where that life would be was a question they had yet to answer.

But, unlike with Eric, Rosemary wouldn't have to make all the decisions alone this time. There would be no ultimatums, no one-sided set of values, no showdown. This time, she and Kirk would decide their future together, through open and honest communication, and through prayer.

She loved him completely. She loved him for all the *right* reasons. She'd prove that love, somehow.

And one day soon, she'd be able to tell him exactly how much she loved him.

Chapter Thirteen

Melissa came back to work a few days later, but she was sullen and withdrawn. Worried about the girl's state of mind as well as her physical health, Rosemary tried to talk to her. They were having lunch in the prayer garden while another aide watched over the children who were napping inside.

"Isn't it a beautiful day?" Rosemary said, her eyes centered on her friend, her smile full of contentment.

"Great," Melissa said, purposely avoiding glancing up at Rosemary. Instead, she pulled little bits of wheat bread from her ham sandwich to toss to the squirrels roaming in the nearby oak trees.

"Melissa, aren't you hungry?"

"Not really."

Rosemary stayed silent for a while, then tried again. "How have you been feeling?"

"I'm well, completely well," Melissa snapped, her head still down.

Concerned, Rosemary leaned forward on the stone picnic table. "Have I done something to upset you?"

Melissa looked up then. Rosemary recoiled from the malice in the girl's blue eyes.

"Obviously I have upset you," she said. "Talk to me, Melissa. Tell me what's bothering you."

"As if you didn't know," Melissa said, her gaze sweeping the church yard. "You had Eric fired, didn't you?"

"What?" Shocked, Rosemary glanced around. "I haven't seen Eric since the accident. As far as I know, he's still working for Kirk."

"Then why hasn't he been back?"

"I honestly don't know," Rosemary replied, hoping the girl would believe her. "I assumed he was still recovering from his injuries. Have you heard from him?"

"No, and I doubt I ever will again," Melissa said, throwing down the remains of her half-eaten sandwich. "Why did you have to interfere, Rosemary?"

Angry now, Rosemary took a deep breath to hold her temper. "Melissa, I haven't interfered. I don't know what you're implying, but I'm telling you—I don't know where Eric has been for the last few days. As I told you, I haven't seen him since the hospital."

Thinking back, she realized he hadn't shown up for work Friday. She'd chalked that up to his cracked ribs.

But why was Melissa treating her like an enemy? "So you think I've driven Eric away? Is that it?"

Melissa shot her a hostile look. "Well, you did accuse him of drinking the other night. And he wasn't!"

"I know that now," Rosemary said. "And I'm sorry I jumped to the wrong assumption. But I was only concerned—for both of you."

"I don't need you mothering me, Rosemary," Melissa retorted, her eyes flashing. "I have enough nagging from my parents, when they even notice I'm around.''

Taking that into consideration, Rosemary cooled her own anger at the girl. "Okay, I won't mother you. But you do work for me, and I'm entitled to worry about you because we used to be friends. Are we still friends, Melissa?''

The girl looked away then, but when she finally faced Rosemary again, her eyes held a cloudburst of emotion. "I'm in love with Eric, but he's still pining over you, Rosemary. Why do you lead him on when you know you don't want him?''

"Lead him on?'' Surprised, Rosemary could only stare at Melissa with an open mouth. "I haven't done that. Just the opposite. I've tried to avoid Eric since he came to work here.''

"He claims you flirt with him to make Kirk notice you,'' Melissa admitted, a despondent sob leaving her body. "Is that true?''

Her own appetite gone, Rosemary put down the shiny red plum she'd been about to bite into. "No, that's not true. Not at all.'' Wording her explanation carefully, she said, "I talked to Eric a few days ago, in the fellowship hall. We had an argument—''

"I know,'' Melissa interrupted. "He wouldn't tell me everything, but he did say you were angry with him for talking to me.''

"That's not exactly what happened,'' Rosemary replied, her lips set in a grim line. "We didn't talk about you at all, Melissa. Eric...was bitter and defensive, and he accused me of being holier-than-thou.''

"Well, aren't you?'' the girl questioned, her eyes bright. "You can't seem to forgive him.''

"No, I can't. I'm having a really hard time dealing

with his being released so early, but I'm trying to cope. I only asked him to stay away from me, and Kirk backed me up on that.''

"So you did provoke him to get Kirk's attention?"

"No! Kirk came in and found us arguing. Look, Melissa, Eric and I will always have trouble being around each other. I'm not out to make anyone jealous, or get anyone's attention. And...I no longer have the same feelings for Eric that I once did.'' Frustrated and hurt that Melissa would even think such things of her, she stood up to go back inside her office. "And as far as you and Eric go, I promise I will not interfere. I can pray for both of you, though. And I certainly intend to do just that.''

"How very gracious of you," Melissa said, her voice cracking. "Well, go ahead and pretend you're so good. The whole town's talking about what went on between you and Kirk up on that mountain.''

That stopped Rosemary in her tracks. Whirling, she stared across the breezeway at the mixed-up girl sitting there watching her. "Kirk and I have nothing to be ashamed of, Melissa. And I believe you realize that. Eric is the one trying to cause trouble here, but I guess I'll have to let you find that out for yourself. Just be careful.''

"You really hurt him, you know," Melissa called after her. "You let him go to jail without ever hearing his side of the story. How can you live with yourself?''

Rosemary had to grip a steel pole supporting the catwalk, to keep from lashing out at Melissa. What did the girl know about *her* suffering, anyway? Calming herself, she turned one last time. "I have to live every day with the knowledge that my fiancé was driving drunk and killed my mother," she said through a clenched jaw. "Isn't that enough?"

Melissa looked embarrassed and, thankfully, remained silent. Rosemary went into her office and collapsed into her chair, her hands shaking.

Kirk found her there, the cluster of wildflowers he'd picked for her forgotten. "I can see I missed lunch. What's the matter?"

She lifted her head, glad to see a friendly face, glad it was his face, and glad for the fresh-smelling honeysuckles and Cherokee roses he'd picked for her. "Melissa and I just had a nasty confrontation. Eric has her thinking I'm some sort of evil person." Shaking her head, she said, "How did things get so twisted?"

"He's just grasping at straws, Rosemary," Kirk said as he came around the desk to drop on his knees beside her chair. Handing her the bundle of fragrant flowers, he told her, "Eric is so confused, so full of guilt, he has to say things like that in order to live with himself."

"But hasn't he caused us enough suffering? Haven't we all suffered enough?" She reached out a hand to touch his face. "I just want to get on with my life. I want to be happy again, Kirk."

He took her hand then kissed it, his lips warm and firm on her clammy skin. "I want to make you happy again. As far as Eric—you haven't seen him around here because he's too banged up to be much good to me, and the toughest part of my work's finished anyway, so I told him...I told him I no longer needed him."

Relieved that Eric wouldn't be hanging around anymore, Rosemary was also worried about Melissa's warped accusations. "Well, Melissa thinks I had him fired."

He shook his head. "If Eric hadn't gotten hurt, he'd still be working here. But I didn't see any point in letting him come back. In fact, his injury was a perfect excuse to get rid of him. We've only got a week or so to go, anyway."

That brought her head up. "You'll be leaving soon."

"Yes," he said, the one word soft-spoken and hesitant, his dark eyes full of questions. "And we need to talk about that, but first, I want you to do something for me."

She laid the flowers on her desk, the tone in his voice alerting her, warning her. "What's that?"

"I want you to go see Eric."

"What? I...I can't."

"Yes, you can. You have to face him, Rosemary. Really face him and get it all out of your system. That's the only way to stop these rumors he and Melissa are spreading, and that's the only way to really get on with your life."

She lifted her eyebrows, her expression skeptical. "You're not making this easy."

"This isn't supposed to be easy," he said. "I should know that better than anyone. I'm still fighting—as much as I want to be with you—I'm still terrified of making that final commitment. But I'm willing to try. I wouldn't ask this of you if I didn't believe it's really important."

"You didn't come to church Sunday," she said, glad to turn the tables for a while. "You've never attended a service, Kirk? Why not?"

Kirk lifted up to lean on her desk. "That goes back to my carefree philosophy, I suppose. I always had this unspoken rule—work on the church but don't become a part of the congregation. It was just less messy that way.''

"And now? Have I made your life too messy?"

He grinned, then crossed his arms over his chest, giving her a good view of his large biceps and muscular shoulders. "Let's just say you've messed up my *way of life.*"

"But you still aren't ready to be a part of the church?"

"I can't be a part of the church," he admitted. "To do so would mean I've taken that final step."

"Which means—you're not really as committed to me as I thought?"

"No, I'm committed to *you,* but if I give in and become a part of the congregation, it will be like I'm putting down roots. And I can't afford to do that. My job requires that I travel—a lot."

"Then we're right back at an impasse," she said. "I can't go with you, you can't stay here with me."

"I'm hoping after you talk with Eric, you'll be ready to move on," he said, his gaze gentle and coaxing.

"And what about my father?"

"He's a grown man, with friends who care about him. I think he'll be all right."

"I can't leave him, Kirk."

Kirk moved away from the desk and headed for the door. "Just go and talk to Eric. It's a start. We'll worry about your father after you sort through all your feelings for Eric."

She rose, both hands pressed on her desk pad. "I told you, I have no feelings for Eric."

"Talk to him, Rosemary." With that, he turned to leave. Then before she could form a retort, he stomped back into the room to pull her into his arms. After giving her a thorough kiss that left her longing and aching for more, he stood back with a hand on each of her arms. "I won't settle for being a replacement for something you lost, Rosemary. I'm willing to bend, I'm willing to meet you halfway, but I won't be second-best."

"Is that what you think?" she asked, her breath leaving her body in a soft whisper. "That I'm trying to…to get back what I lost, by falling for you?"

"I have to be sure," he said. Unable to stop himself, he reached up a hand to pull his fingers through her curly hair, then held her head against the weight of his hand. His gaze moved over her lips, then across her face, his eyes filled with longing. "I'm treading new waters here. When I look at you, when I touch you, I know I want to be around you for a very long time. It's when I'm away from you that I start doubting. So, just like you, I have to be very sure."

Shocked, she asked, "Do you think I love you for all the wrong reasons, Kirk?"

"Oh, I hope not," he whispered, his fingers pulling through her hair. "Not when it feels so right between us."

With him looking at her with such intensity, with him touching her, holding her like this, as if he could never let her go, it certainly felt right. But was it wrong? Well, she'd wondered the same thing herself, and she'd been working hard to convince herself that this time, *this love*, was good and right. She wouldn't blame him for wondering the same thing. She was embarrassed that he could read her so well, though.

Kirk pulled her close to kiss her temple, then her forehead, his touch soft and confident, gentle and disturbing. "I want you to love me for all the right reasons, truly I do. I pray that you can see it in your heart to do so without any doubts or fears."

"How can you *doubt* me?" she asked on a breathless whisper, her eyes closing as his lips skimmed over her jawline.

He reluctantly lifted his mouth away from her creamy-sweet skin. "Because I know that you doubt yourself. I can see it in your eyes, Rosemary." At her guilty look, he let out a deep sigh. "Your fear of loving me is just as strong as your fear of heights. I want to conquer both, but it's not up to me. You have to conquer your own fears, if we are to have a true and abiding relationship."

Rosemary fell against him, holding him to her, clinging to his strength, his wisdom, his spirituality. "I hate it when you make sense."

"Aye, and I hate to see that doubt and pain in your lovely eyes."

She lifted her gaze to his. "Tell me again, Kirk. Tell me in that beautiful Gaelic language what you told me the first night you held me."

Touched, and even more determined to make her his own, he crushed her close, then pressed his mouth to her ear and spoke the timeless language of his ancestors. Then he repeated the phrase in her language. "I am here, little one. I am here."

Kirk held her for a few minutes longer, then he backed away, his parting words coming on a low, hopeful growl. "Go and see Eric, Rosemary. Then please...come back to me."

Rosemary took comfort in Kirk's words and touch even after he was no longer there in the room with her.

How would she survive when he was no longer there at all?

Praying for strength, she decided she would begin the process Kirk had suggested. She would try to conquer her fears; she would prove her love for him was strong, and right, and good.

And so, with that thought in mind, that afternoon after work, she got in her car and drove to Eric's house.

She would begin by conquering her bitterness and her anger. It was time she said some things to Eric that needed to be said. She couldn't change him, but she could shift her own attitude.

It was time she faced the her past.

Eric lived in a garage apartment on his brother's property a few miles from the next town. Rosemary hadn't been there too many times, and now she wondered if she'd been wise to come today. The place had been shut down while Eric was in prison. Now it looked forlorn and unkempt, lonely.

She parked and climbed the rickety steps leading to his front door, then took a deep breath and knocked twice. At first, no one answered. She was about to turn and leave, when the door slowly swung open.

Eric stood there in a pair of faded sweatpants and an unbuttoned cotton plaid shirt, the bandages from his bruised ribs clearly visible across the flat expanse of his midsection. He was a handsome man, in spite of the stubble on his jawline and the red-rimmed, sleep-laden darkness in his eyes. It was no wonder Melissa found him attractive.

"Rosemary," he said in a grainy voice. "What are you doing here?"

She hated the hope in his question, hated having to

do this, hated herself for being here. Remembering the warmth of Kirk's lips on her skin, the tenderness of his endearments, and her own need to show him she did indeed love him, she squared her shoulders and tried to smile at Eric. "I...I wanted to see how you're doing, and...we need to talk."

Eric stood back, then swept a hand out. "Come in."

Rosemary entered the tiny, cluttered apartment and felt the assault of a thousand memories. It was amazing how scent could bring back a multitude of feelings, how seeing a particular photograph could set her mind to reeling. The smell of his favorite aftershave warred with the smell of the musky, closed room. Sitting on a plastic shelf, along with his CDs and record collection, was a picture of them together back in college—a dance they had attended during football season.

"I...I never could bring myself to get rid of that picture," he stated bluntly, as if daring her to say something about it being there.

Rosemary didn't comment. Suddenly, she saw with clarity everything Melissa and Kirk had already seen. Eric still cared about her, maybe even still loved her. Looking around, she wondered how much he had suffered, sitting here in this dump of an apartment, and worse, sitting in a prison cell.

Well, whatever he'd suffered wasn't nearly enough to bring back her mother, she reminded herself. They should have given him ten years, but then, he'd had a crafty lawyer who'd tried to make it look as if her mother's driving had contributed to the accident. Not wanting to dwell on that particular memory, Rosemary lifted her head to face him. "Could I sit down?"

"Sure." He hobbled over to the gold plaid couch to shift magazines and newspapers off onto the ratty carpet. "Best seat in the house. You want something to drink? Strictly nonalcoholic, of course."

Not missing the sarcasm, she shot him a stern look, then quickly softened her features. "No, I'm fine."

Eric leaned back against the tiny dining table filled with dirty dishes, a grimace of pain twisting his features. "Okay, Rosemary, cut to the chase. Did you come here to see if I'd been on a drinking binge or were you hoping you'd find me dead from too much booze?"

"Why do you do that?" she asked, heat rising across her face. "Why do you assume that I'm here to condemn you?"

"Haven't you already done that?"

"Yes," she admitted with too much ease. "Yes, Eric, I did condemn you the night my mother died, and that's why I'm here. But not to do it again."

"Oh," he snorted, throwing up a hand, only to wince when his sore ribs protested. "You've decided I need a little pep talk, or maybe your sympathy." He pointed to the door. "Well, too little, too late, Rosemary. Get out."

"No," she replied, her throat dry, her hands clammy. "I want to talk to you and I'm not leaving until I say it all—everything that's on my mind."

"This oughta be fun." He rubbed a hand over his face, then looked down at her, temper lighting his eyes. "What do you want from me?"

Frustrated and beyond aggravation, she snapped, "I want you to feel some remorse. I want you to act like you care, Eric. I want you to show me that you truly are sorry for what you did to me, to my family. Do you even care that you destroyed all my hopes, my dreams, my life? Do you even care that my father detests me because of you? Don't you want to have a better life, a life free of alcohol, a life free of this guilt?''

"Are you finished?" he asked, his eyes blazing, his face red.

"Not nearly," she said simply, her breath hissing out in a rush. "You've come back into my life, unwanted and unwelcome, and everyone tells me I'm supposed to forgive you! I'm supposed to turn the other cheek and forget that you...you killed my mother! Well, I can't do that. I want to, I've prayed to be able to forgive you, but it just won't come. I can't get beyond what you did—"

"What I did," he shouted at her, pointing a finger in the air. "What I did, Rosemary," he said on a low growl, "was despicable, was beyond any of the low-life things I'd ever done before in my lousy life. What I did was unforgivable!" At her surprised look, he shouted again. "Yes, unforgivable. Lady, you talk about your need to forgive me—well, don't bother. I can't be forgiven. I'm beyond your worth, Rosemary. Can't you see that? Can't any of you see that I'm just not worth the effort?"

Rosemary started to speak, but he held out a hand to stop her. "I mean, I've been told that all my life. First by my old man before he drank himself to death, then by my brother before he booted me out of the house. Then by the law, by my teachers, by the bosses who couldn't tolerate me, then...then I got a scholarship to go to college. The only thing I had going for me was my ability to throw a football. I thought I had a chance, but...I liked to party too much. I was having such a high old time.

"Until...I met you." He stared down at her, his red-rimmed eyes widening in awe, his harsh expression changing to one of tenderness. "You, Rosemary. Such a sweet, *good* girl. You were like this beautiful flower that I wanted to touch, so fragile, so pretty. I had to be with you."

Rosemary caught a fist to her mouth, the tears rolling down her cheeks as she listened to him. Oh, how she had loved him once. She knew exactly how he'd felt back then. She'd felt the same way. And now, for the first time since her mother's death, she could actually acknowledge that feeling, and the anger that came each time she thought of his betrayal. Although she no longer loved Eric, she'd denied what she'd once felt for him, because of her own guilt. She hated him now because of what he'd done to her mother, but mostly because of what he'd done to her. It was a bitter realization.

Eric let out a long breath, then held his arms to his chest. "I could always get what I wanted, so I got you, through charm, through guts, through sheer determination. And from the beginning, I lied to you, but worse, I lied to myself." He shook his head, his eyes bright. "I actually thought I could pull it off. I tried, heaven knows, I tried so hard. But it was too late for me."

He looked down at her then, and Rosemary saw the torment in his eyes. She couldn't speak, couldn't move.

"It was just too late for us, Rosemary. The drinking took over…because I was so scared, you see. I was so afraid of losing you, so afraid I wouldn't meet your high standards, so afraid you'd see through my act."

She stood up, her worst fears hitting her full force in the face. She had to get out of here. She didn't want to cave in; she didn't want to *feel*, to feel anything for this man. But the feelings came, rushing at her, clawing at her with a vengeance, taking her breath away. Had she driven Eric to this?

Eric pushed her back down. "Oh no. You wanted to talk, so I'm talking. I was so scared the night of our party, Rosemary. After seeing all those people, all those good, Christian people, bringing gifts to…to me. Wishing me a wonderful life, wishing us a great future, and me knowing I didn't deserve it, I didn't deserve you. Then, a few nights later at your folks' house, it was the same thing all over again. Only maybe worse, with your mom so sweet, treating me like another son. And your father—well, we both know what he thought of me." He shook his head. "I just got so scared."

He whirled, turning away from her, turning away from the scene in both their minds. "So, yes, after I dropped you off that night, I stopped and got a fifth of whiskey. And I drank it, a lot of it. I was too drunk to be driving. I even pulled over a couple of times, but that just gave me a chance to think about us getting married, and what you and all those people expected of me. So I drank some more."

Rosemary moaned, then buried her face in her hands.

Eric pivoted back to give her a direct look now. "And then I took off down that winding road and…yes, Rosemary, I…" His voice cracked and the tears began to roll down his face. "I killed your mother." He gulped, trying to hold back his emotions. "I was so drunk, at first I just sat there in the truck, wondering what had happened. Then I saw the fire, heard the crackling…and I got out and I ran and ran—"

"Stop!" she cried, rising from the couch to skirt

around him, her stomach heaving, her throat filled with bile. "Stop, Eric. I can't listen to this."

"You wanted to know," he said, his voice weak. "You wanted me to show some remorse, well..." He slumped over, the tears racking his body. "I've paid, Rosemary. I've paid dearly for what I did. And you've never, ever known how much I regret it, because you never took the time to let me tell you."

Rosemary leaned her head into the door, her body so weak she thought she'd faint, the rush of emotions tearing through her too strong to fight. Then she heard a crashing sound, and turned to find the picture of her and Eric lying on the floor, its glass shattered, broken, mangled, over their smiles.

"Your life wasn't the only one that was splintered into a million pieces, Rosemary," he said. "I lost everything. I lost you."

His admission tore through her, making her realize what they'd both lost. She had loved him. Maybe part of her still did, but the main part, the good part of what they'd had, was gone forever. She'd never really accepted that, had never mourned that loss properly. Kirk had seen it, had warned her about it. But how, how did she go about healing this terrible, horrible rift?

She turned then, slowly, and with a hesitation that told of her own bitter pain and the revulsion she still felt, she reached out a hand to him. "Eric—"

"Don't," he said, backing away. "Just don't. I waited so long for you to do that, but now it's too late. I know that. I'm working toward accepting it." When she stepped forward, her hand still extended, he told her, "Go, Rosemary. Go back to him. He loves you, and...he'll be good to you. He's the kind of man you deserve."

Rosemary stood there, wishing a million different wishes, seeing the broken person Eric had always been, the person she had never really understood at all. Maybe she didn't deserve any absolution or happiness. Maybe she didn't deserve Kirk.

"I could have helped you," she said at last. "I didn't know, Eric. I didn't know about your life."

"I didn't want you to know. I was ashamed."

Rosemary turned to leave. He wouldn't let her help him now, not when she'd turned away from him just as everyone he'd ever cared about had turned away from him. What kind of Christian was she, to do that to a person?

She was about to tell him she was sorry, when the door burst open and Melissa rushed into the room.

"I saw your car," she said, her eyes focused on Rosemary's tear-streaked face. Then she glanced over at Eric, her own expression condemning and demanding. "You couldn't stay away, could you, Rosemary?"

Rosemary wiped her face. "Melissa, it's not what you think."

"You don't have to explain," the girl said. "I'm not stupid, you know. You rushed right over here after I poured my heart out to you." She went to Eric, her eyes bright, her words harsh. "She'll hurt you again. Can't you see that?"

"Melissa, stay out of this," Eric warned, his own face streaked and flushed. "Go on back home. Both of you, go on back and leave me alone." On a softer note, he told Rosemary, "I'll be okay. Really. I haven't had a drink for over a year, and right now, I want one bad. But I won't take it, I swear. I won't take it, Rosemary."

Rosemary looked at him, proud of him for the first time in a very long time, then turned to face Melissa.

"You're right. I did hurt him. And I'm sorry for that. I'm leaving, but...I think you should stay, Melissa. He needs you."

Relief washed over Melissa's features, but Eric's expression changed as rage colored his face. "Always the do-gooder, huh, Rosemary. Even now, you're still trying to make things so much better by giving Melissa and me your blessings."

Melissa sent Rosemary an understanding look. "We don't need her approval, Eric, but I do appreciate her giving it." Then she turned back to Eric. "We've got each other. We can forget about all the rest."

Unable to bear being there any longer, Rosemary rushed out the door and down to her car. But it was a long time before she could crank the automobile and actually drive away.

"Oh, Kirk," she whispered, her heart breaking with grief, "you were right. There's so much more to this, so much more to be resolved."

On the way home, Rosemary stopped her car at the lookout where the wreck had happened. The confrontation with Eric had been necessary, as painful as it had been. She could now accept what they'd had and lost. She could accept Eric as a human being with weaknesses and problems just like any other human being. She couldn't give him her love, but she could show him some compassion. At last.

As the sun set in the distance, a bloodred ball of fire, Rosemary stood there, shaken and broken, looking down on the spot where her mother had lost her life. And she asked God to help her to find her own again. She wanted peace; she wanted joy. She wanted to know love again. With Kirk. Only Kirk. Somehow she had to find the courage to acknowledge that love.

She still didn't know if she deserved it, though.

As she stood there, back from the edge of the ridge, her heart pounding with a new hope in spite of her ever-present vertigo, Rosemary also asked God to help Eric find his own peace.

After all, they had all suffered enough.

Chapter Fourteen

When Rosemary got home, she found Danny waiting on the front steps for her. He immediately jumped up, the dark frown on his face mirroring his black mood.

"What in the world is going on around here?" he barked, his hands on his hips, his eyes snapping open.

"Nothing that I'm aware of," Rosemary said, not ready to deal with her brother's questions after all the revelations she'd had today. "Why aren't you inside with Dad, anyway?"

Danny placed his hands on his hips, then rolled his eyes. "Because he's *not* inside. I found a note on the front door. He's gone to eat supper with Faye Lewis."

"What?" Rosemary was as stunned as her brother, but not nearly as upset as Danny by this bit of news. "Well, good. I'm too tired to cook, anyway."

"Can you believe that woman?" Danny said, following her up to the door. While Rosemary struggled with the key in the lock, Danny struggled with the image of his father with another woman other than his mother. "I mean, she's going after him with all the energy of a she-bear after honey. This is embarrassing, Rosemary. We've got to talk to him."

Rosemary threw her purse on the couch and went around turning on lights. "Danny, slow down. I've had a full day and I don't need this right now."

"Oh, fine," her brother said, folding his arms across his chest. "I make good on my promise to come by more often, and now I find Dad gone and you informing me you don't need this right now. I'm telling you, Rosemary, ever since your steeplejack came to town, things have been getting wackier and wackier around here."

Rosemary turned from pouring a glass of water from the tap, to stare at her confused brother. "So you want to blame this on Kirk! I can't believe you. Kirk has nothing to do with Faye and Daddy becoming close."

Danny threw his hands in the air. "You didn't start encouraging this until he came here. You're too busy chasing him around to even care about Dad."

"You're wrong there, brother," Rosemary said, her temper flaring, her patience shot. "You, of all people, should know, I care about our father. But I'm not going to discuss this with you right now. Now, do you want something to eat, or did you just come by to fuss at the rest of us?"

Danny looked humbled for a minute, then asked, "What do you have? I did get kind of hungry, waiting out there."

"Pound cake?" She turned to get him a slice, knowing it was his favorite. "But you can take it home with you. I'm just too tired to fight, Danny."

"What about Dad?"

"What about him? He's getting out more. He's found someone to spend time with. I'd say that's a good, healthy sign that he's coming to grips with Mama's death."

"You would say that." Danny took the large chunk of cake she'd wrapped in foil, then stood there with his head down. "I don't know. Somehow, it just doesn't seem right. I can't picture him with anyone else but Mom."

"He visited Mama's grave the other day, Danny," she said softly. "I think he's finally healing."

Danny stood silent for a minute, then braced a hand on the counter. "Wow. I never expected him to do that."

Rosemary patted her brother on the arm. "He'll be with Mama again one day. In the meantime, he needs a friend, if nothing else."

"Well, I don't have to like it," Danny replied before he sniffed the cake. "Did you bake this?"

"Afraid you might eat some of Faye's cooking by mistake?" Rosemary teased. At his guilty look, she added, "Yes, I baked it." Then, just to pester him further, she said, "How does Nancy feel about Dad dating Faye?"

"Don't call it dating," he warned. "And my sweet wife told me to mind my own business."

"A wise woman, that Nancy."

Danny held his cake in one hand, and raked his other hand through his thick hair. "How can I mind my own business when the whole town's talking about my sister and the steeplejack camping out together on the mountain, and now, my father flying off to be with another woman?"

Slapping him on the arm, Rosemary said, "I would hope you'd tell everyone else to *mind their own business*. Kirk and I got caught in a storm. And our father has a right to some happiness. Are you going to defend our honor, or whine about your good name being run through the mud?''

Danny frowned, then stood up straight. ''I'll sock the first person who says anything nasty about either of you, but that doesn't mean I don't have concerns myself.''

''Well, stop worrying,'' Rosemary said, so drained she just wanted to curl up and sleep. As she pushed her brother out the door, she told him, ''Danny, I went to see Eric today.''

Danny groaned, then stared at her as if she'd gone daft. ''One more thing for the rumor mill. You need to stay away from him, Rosemary.''

Rosemary looked out into the gathering dusk, quiet for a minute. ''I will from now on, but I'm glad I went today. We got some things off our minds, got things settled between us. Eric has had a hard life, harder than I ever realized—''

''Oh, don't tell me you're feeling sorry for the man!''

''No, I'm still struggling with what he did, but now, now I can at least accept that he's suffered, too. And I do believe that he's going to turn his life around.''

Danny snorted. ''How can you be so sure?''

Rosemary looked up at the first star of the evening. ''I've prayed for it,'' she replied softly.

Danny didn't have a retort for that, except to say, ''Then I guess I better go home and try to do the same thing, since I'm not accomplishing very much by trying to reason with you.''

Rosemary followed him out onto the back porch. At Danny's soft hiss, she looked up.

"Now I know why you're in such a hurry to get rid of me," he said.

Kirk was coming across the street, carrying what looked like a picnic basket.

"Didn't you say you were tired?" Danny whispered.

"I am," she said, even as her heart soared and tripped into a faster beat. Then to her brother, "Danny, go home and kiss your wife and your daughter."

"Good advice." With that, her brother got in his truck and drove away.

Kirk grinned as he waved to Danny. "Hope he didn't leave on my account."

Rosemary shook her head. "Danny's just confused. Things are changing, and he's never dealt with change too well."

Kirk set the basket down, then pulled her into his arms, his eyes searching her face. "And how about his lovely sister? Do you deal with changes better than your brother?"

She looked up at him, her eyes touching on his in the scented dusk, her pulse beating a warning tune against her throat. "I'm learning to."

Kirk rubbed a hand down her spine, then enjoyed the little moan of pleasure that escaped through her parted lips.

He tilted his head toward the basket. "I brought you dinner. I was restless, so I grilled burgers and I'm afraid I got carried away. I made too many." Then, "Did you see Eric?"

"I did." She stretched, leaning into the swirling massage of his fingers on her back, her whole body coming alive at his touch. For just a minute, she forgot all her troubles and her tired state of being.

"And?"

She didn't miss the hint of vulnerability in the one word. "And I think I've purged myself of him." Placing her arms around Kirk's neck, she told him the truth. "You were right. I did have feelings for Eric, strong, hidden feelings. I think I wanted to love him still, but the shame, the pain, was too great. I was so angry at him, not just because of the wreck, but because...he hurt me and betrayed me. But I didn't want to admit to it. So I simply buried everything away."

"What happened today?"

She stood silent for a minute, seeing the coiled tension in the tightening of Kirk's jaw. Then she told him the whole story, detailing the scene between Eric and her. "It all came rushing out. My anger...and his. Eric is really hurting."

At his questioning look, she raised a hand to his chest. "I can't feel any sympathy for Eric, but I do feel compassion. You know, the Bible tells us to pray for our enemies, and that's what I've tried to do. But until today, until I actually heard him telling me how sorry he was, how much he regretted what happened, I'd never felt any compassion when I prayed for him. Now I can."

Kirk stepped back, his expression guarded. "And do you feel anything else for him?"

Rosemary lifted her hands through his hair, wanting, needing, to touch him. "No. Only compassion, and a new understanding. I feel so sad, so empty. The bitterness is gone. All that's left is the acceptance, and this great sadness. But I can deal with that now."

"Are you sure?"

"Very. And I owe you a big thanks." To prove it, she lifted up to kiss him.

It would have been a chaste kiss, except that Kirk

needed more. All afternoon he'd waited, wondering what would happen when Rosemary finally confronted Eric. Would she cave in and tell Eric she still loved him? Would she run away, and become unable to really love anyone again? Or, would she find a certain peace and...come back.

"You came back to me," he said just before her lips grazed his. "You came back."

With that, he hauled her close and took her mouth against his, punishing her and rewarding her at the same time. This, this was more than a kiss. This was a dance, a ritual of timeless need, a meshing, a merging, of two souls that had paid the price for the love they couldn't deny.

Kirk burned with the fire of new hope, of renewed promises. He'd asked her to go to another man, neither of them knowing what the outcome would be. It had been a risk, but now it might pay off. He wouldn't let her get away again.

Rosemary sensed the change in him, in the way his mouth moved over her own, in the way he held her to him. She became lost, lost in the need to be with him, lost in the way he showed her his love, lost inside the sweet fantasy of a life with this man.

When he lifted his mouth from hers, his breath labored and hard, she took a minute to regain her own equilibrium. Then she stood back to stare up at Kirk, her love for him undeniable. "You sent me to him, not knowing what would happen, didn't you?" Amazed, she saw the answer in his tense expression, in the dark depths of his eyes. "You actually thought I might...I might go back to Eric, didn't you?"

Kirk closed his eyes in relief, letting his guard down at last. "Aye, that thought had crossed my mind."

"Why would you think that?"

"Because you loved the good in him once, and you're a nurturing soul, Rosemary."

She understood, and was touched and humbled by his unselfish gesture. "So you figured I might remember that good, since he's working toward dealing with his alcoholism, and you thought I might be tempted to try again with him. That's why you insisted I go to him. You wanted me to make a final choice."

He opened his eyes. "Yes."

Rosemary brought her hands up to cup his face. "I don't love Eric." Her heart thumped and thudded; her pulse raced. She had to take a deep, calming breath, and on that breath, she told Kirk her one last secret. "I love you. And...I love you in a different way from the way I once loved him."

Kirk's world shifted, broadened, expanded to include her and a future that would change everything. "Oh, and how is that?"

She brought her mouth close to his. "This is stronger, deeper. Kirk, I've never felt this way before. I feel so safe with you, so secure. I never felt that way with Eric. I was always nervous and cautious with him, trying to rationalize all of our problems away. I don't have to rationalize with you." She hushed to a soft whisper. "I've never loved anyone the way I love you. But...I was so afraid to tell you that."

Groaning, Kirk pushed her back against the porch wall, his lips meeting hers again and again. "And I...Rosemary, sweet Rosemary, I've never loved at all—until you. I want you with me, forever."

"Oh, Kirk, I wish, I pray for that, too. But I don't see how—"

"Come away with me," he said, his eyes holding hers. "Marry me."

She looked up at him, awestruck and still afraid. "What?"

"We can travel together," he said, giving her a tight hug. "I'll show you all the ancient cathedrals in Europe. I'll take you to Ireland to meet my relatives. We'll sleep under the stars, dance in the rain." He stopped, looking down at her with a clear, confident hope in his eyes. "I want you with me, wherever I go. I want to fall asleep with you in my arms every night, and wake up with you there beside me, no matter where I am. I want to take you to the edge, Rosemary."

Rosemary's heart pumped a fast-paced beat throughout her entire system. This was her dream. This was what she'd thought about over the last few weeks. She wanted to be with Kirk, to know his world, to love him, to have him. But...

"I can't, Kirk," she said at last, the finality of her statement ringing out over the still, settled night.

He lifted away to stare down at her, the hazy porch light illuminating his confused expression. "Why not?"

"You know why not," she said, already feeling the distance between them. "I can't leave Daddy yet. Not until I'm sure he's going to be okay."

Kirk tilted his head back, then faced her again. "He has Faye. And Danny's been more cooperative lately. You have to let go sometime, Rosemary."

Rosemary leaned back against the wall, fanning mosquitoes away as she tried to form her words. "Yes, but I have to be certain that he's going to be all right. I can't abandon him, not now, not yet."

Kirk backed up to the porch railing, slumping against

the white spindles as he stared over at her. "So all of your talk about loving me and feeling secure with me—what was that, Rosemary?"

"I do love you," she said. "And I want a life with you. I know that now, more than ever."

"So why are you denying what we both want?"

She swallowed, then lifted her head. "I guess I didn't expect things to happen so fast. I...I thought you'd come back for me, one day."

Kirk pulled a hand through his hair, then shook his head. "One day? And how long will one day be, Rosemary?" Pushing away from the railing, he stalked the confines of the small porch. "You know, you're running out of excuses. You're coming to terms with your mother's death, you've finally faced Eric, and your father is beginning to accept Faye as someone he can turn to—what's left for you to fix, anyway?"

His words hit a nerve, but he had a point. She was running out of excuses. But she wouldn't leave her father, not yet. "I have to know that he...I have to know that my father can forgive me, Kirk. I'd be heartbroken if I had to leave without his blessings."

Kirk nodded his head slowly, steadily. "So you're willing to throw away what we feel for each other, the happiness we can have, simply because you've been through this once before with your father?"

"Yes," she said, craning her head forward to glare at him. "Yes, I have been through this once before. I acted too hastily, I was too rash and it caused my entire family too much pain. I won't do that again."

Kirk stopped pacing to stare down at her. "I thought you were sure, after today, after talking to Eric."

"I'm sure that I love you," she replied. "But I'm just not so sure about taking off on this new life."

Wanting him to understand, she touched a hand to his arm. "You said you want to take me to the edge. Well, maybe that's the last excuse I have. Maybe that's the real reason I can't just pick up and go with you. Can't you see, if I do that, if I leave behind my life here, and everything and everyone I hold dear, it will be like stepping to the edge of a cliff. I don't know what's waiting for me out there. I don't have a net, or a rock to cling to. I'll be out there, free-falling. That's too risky, especially after what I've been through."

Kirk jerked away from her touch, but she came to him, both hands on his arms. "I'm only asking you to give me some time. You can go on to your next job and...we'll see how we feel then."

He frowned, then lowered his head to within an inch of hers, his eyes flashing fire. "I don't need to wait to know how I feel. Rosemary, I've bared my soul to you, I've changed my whole outlook on life because of how I feel, because of how you *make* me feel. That's all I need to know."

Taking her hands in his, he held her away, his expression dark and dangerous. "Can't you see, we didn't have a choice in this matter? From the moment I saw you, I knew. I *knew* that I wanted you, that I belonged with you. I didn't want to accept that, but I had no control over it. I won't let you walk away from something so good, so right—just so you can be a martyr."

"I'm not trying to be a martyr," she retorted, pulling away. "I just want to win back my father's love and respect."

"Aye, and what if he never changes? What if he continues to punish you by holding you here forever. Do you honestly believe that's the right way to do something—to sacrifice yourself, your own needs, to live out your life swallowed up by sorrow, because you happened to fall in love with the wrong man once?''

''I don't know,'' she said, her heart breaking with the weight of wanting to be with him. ''Please, Kirk, don't give up on us. Let me work through this, and...when you're finished with your next job, we'll find each other again.''

''No, Rosemary,'' he said, turning to place a hand on each of her shoulders. ''Listen to yourself. Listen to what you're asking. I'll be far away, and I'll call for you. And you'll have another excuse, another reason to keep you tied here. Your father, your brother, your job at the church.

''Maybe you're right. Maybe you do love me, but we come from different worlds. You're not willing to risk being a part of mine. And that, dear Rosemary, is the heart of the matter. For all your talk of a strong faith in God, you're not willing to turn things over to Him. You're not willing to take a leap of faith with me. All of this other, well, that's just a facade.''

Hurt, dazed, desperate, she said, ''And what about you, Kirk? Are you willing to settle down here in Alba with me?''

At his silence, she continued. ''No, of course not. We've both known that all along, and I've told you all along that I wasn't ready to take off into the wild blue yonder. But you've never once offered to stay.''

''Did you expect me to?'' he asked, temper flaring like lightning in his eyes. ''Is that what this is all about? You thought maybe I'd just hang around until you found the courage to let go and love me?''

Lifting her head, she faced him squarely. ''I told you I never expected anything from you, remember? I told you I'd settle for what little happiness I could find, and I guess that's exactly what I got.''

Kirk heard the finality in her words. ''So you're willing to end things right here, with just a few sweet memories between us? What about our prayers, Rosemary? What about our hopes, and our struggles? I fought against your father, I stood up to your brother, and I've had to deal with Eric. I threw all my so-called principles to the wind—just to be near you. And now you expect me to walk away—just walk away—because we can't seem to compromise?''

''You told me you never settle for second best,'' she reminded him, her voice shaking.

''And I also told you I was willing to meet you halfway.''

''Then do it. Give me some time.''

How could he explain to her? How could he make her see that he wasn't willing to let her slip away? ''I can't do that, Rosemary,'' he said flatly. ''If I leave, I won't be back. I won't give you time enough to start doubting all over again.''

''So it's now or never?''

He nodded, then turned to go down the steps. ''Aye, that's the way of it.''

Rosemary watched him go, her heart crying out in a loud, silent scream. She could go after him, tell him she'd follow him anywhere, but she stood there, frozen, numb, cold with grief. Then she wondered why it hurt so much, when all along, she'd known this time would come.

She couldn't go.

He couldn't stay.

That had been between them all along, only she had hoped, had prayed, that she could make him see they could have a long-distance relationship until they were sure.

Aren't you sure right now, this very minute? she asked herself.

Oh, how she wanted to be completely sure, how she wanted to trust in her faith, in her love. But she felt as if she were standing on top of Alba Mountain, looking down into the jagged rocks and dark, deep crevices. She was so afraid of taking that final step. So very afraid.

Needing to hide away, she turned to head into the house, then almost tripped over something by the door. Looking down, she saw the spilled contents of Kirk's forgotten picnic basket. She reached out then fell to her knees to gather the things back together. Then she saw the wrapped food he'd fixed for them, and a small handful of sweet-smelling lilies he'd taken from the garden by his trailer. And a small box.

Unable to stop herself, Rosemary lifted the square white box out of the basket and opened it.

Inside, lying against the soft, padded cotton was a ring. An unusual ring made from what looked like silver, knotted in an intricate weave that formed the wide band and came to a knotted crest that coiled and looped to form the ring's center.

"Three knots," Rosemary whispered. She turned the ring over and over in her hand. Then she saw by the yellow porch light that there was an inscription engraved across the smooth silver backing of the ring's center.

Without thinking, Rosemary held the ring close to the light, squinting to make out the inscription.

It read: A Union of Three, My Lord, My Love and Me.

Touched beyond words, and torn beyond grief, Rosemary carefully placed the ring back into its white box, tears blurring her vision. Kirk loved her, wanted to marry her, wanted theirs to be a union of love with God guiding them. Why couldn't she let go and follow her heart? Why was she holding back, when her heart was breaking by doing so? Was she waiting for forgiveness from her father? Or would she be forever unable to forgive herself?

Rising, she wiped her eyes and looked over to Kirk's small trailer. The faint light from inside flickered, then went out.

Rosemary felt as if that same light had just gone out inside her soul.

Chapter Fifteen

Easter morning.

Kirk stood underneath the oak tree he'd started thinking of as his own, sniffing the scent of the white Easter lilies lining the church steps in celebration of this sacred Christian day.

Easter. A new dawn lifted out from the east, its yellow sun plump and ready, set to shine on this brilliant Sunday morning. Set to shine on the steeple he was now through restoring.

He was leaving today.

He would go; but he'd be leaving behind so much this time. He'd be leaving his heart here in this rustic mountain village. Aunt Fitz had predicted it and she'd been so very right.

The mountain had captured Kirk. Because he'd been to the mountain with Rosemary. And he'd given her his heart. But not without a struggle; not without a fight to the finish.

Well, he'd lost. She wouldn't be coming with him.

Kirk had watched his Rosemary over the last few

days. They'd avoided each other, but it was impossible to avoid the multitude of feelings that surfaced each time she was near. Love had warred heavily with regret. Pride had won out over humility.

She'd left his picnic basket by the door of his trailer, along with the ring he had planned on giving her.

Was that her final answer?

Kirk sat there in his lawn chair, sipping the strong coffee Reverend Clancy had introduced him to. He watched as the churchgoers slowly started coming to their house of worship. And he wondered how a day could dawn so incredibly beautiful, how these people could show up here all decked out and smiling, when so many of them were hurting and hoping, still broken inside, still punishing themselves each and every day for simply being human.

Maybe that was why they entered those great open doors. Maybe that was why they couldn't stay away. They found their sanction, their solitude, their peace, inside the womb of their church. And today, some of them would enter that church for the first time in a year, hoping to find the resurrection within themselves through the timeless story of the Resurrection of Jesus Christ.

Today, they would hold a dedication ceremony in celebration of the renovations. Reverend Clancy invited him to stay and celebrate, but he wouldn't, couldn't do that. He didn't belong here, after all.

Earlier, much earlier, just before daylight, Kirk had gone inside the hushed sanctuary to study the stained-glass window depicting Christ. He'd stood in front of the altar, lifting his eyes and his heart to God, wondering and questioning, asking for some sort of miracle to bring Rosemary back to him.

Now, as he saw the sun cresting on this new day, he wished he had the courage and the right to go to her and ask her to be his. Courage, he could muster. But he didn't figure he had the right to ask something of her that she wasn't capable of giving.

So he sat there, the dweller by the church, and watched the fresh-faced children running around in their Easter finery, their mothers in spring hats and floral-print dresses chasing after them to straighten mussed clothes and bruised feelings.

And he wished. He wished he had a child to straighten out. He wished he had an Easter suit to don. He wished he had someone special to escort into that sanctuary.

Then he glanced up and saw her coming across the yard. Rosemary. His Rosemary, wearing a flowing creamy dress with a lacy collar and a hip-hugging sash. Rosemary, in her straw Easter bonnet, her chestnut curls as wild as ever, her eyes lifting up, her head turning until she saw what she was searching for.

Him.

She centered her gaze on him, stopping, her hand touching on the tousled hair of a child who'd come up to hug her, her chin lifted in pride, her eyes bright with regret.

The sun washed over her, illuminating her in a pale, ethereal morning light that took the breath straight out of his tired, aching body. Oh, he'd remember her just like this; he'd remember her as spring, and laughter, and sunshine and fire. His Rosemary.

Kirk told himself to get up and go to her. But his body wouldn't move. The weakness of his love held him down, the gravity of his own pride pulled him back. So he just sat there, watching as she moved toward the church, her eyes darting over the crowd, and always, back to him.

He'd be gone when she came out of there.

He'd be gone soon. Rosemary tried to accept this as she took one last look at the man who'd come to Alba to restore a church steeple, and had managed to change her life in the process, the man she loved with all her heart.

Kirk. Her steeplejack. Sitting there in his jeans and his button-down shirt. Sitting there in his foldable chair, by his mobile home, ready to move on. Ready, if not willing, to go.

Rosemary stood on the wide stone steps, listening to the comments about the newly renovated church.

"Why, it looks better than ever. See how that stained glass shines. And the steeple looks taller, somehow. Straighter. He really fixed it up right."

"Brand-new. I wish my great-granddaddy could be here to see this. You know, he had a part in the original building of this church."

"It's so beautiful. Kirk Lawrence has the touch. He has a way about him. I'd a never thought he could make it any prettier, but he sure did a mighty fine job."

"He poured his heart into it. That's his secret. He believes in his work. And he ain't afraid of climbing up there to get the job done."

"Someone told me he's leaving today. Is he coming to the dedication before he goes?"

"Let's ask Rosemary."

Somehow, Rosemary was swept along into the flow of finery and festivity. Somehow, she was inside the church before she could turn and run back out, before she could run to him and ask him not to go.

"Rosemary, is Kirk staying for the dedication after the service?"

Rosemary looked down to find Aunt Fitz watching her with those keen, clear eyes.

"No," she managed to say. "He has...another commitment."

"Are you sure about that, child?" the old woman asked quietly, patiently leaning her head to the side while a granddaughter adjusted the pink carnations and fuchsia orchids of her Easter corsage.

"Very sure," Rosemary said, taking the wrinkled hand Aunt Fitz offered. "Kirk has to move on."

"That's a shame. I liked that boy."

"I...I did too. So very much."

Aunt Fitz had to have noticed the tears glistening in her eyes, but thankfully, the old woman didn't push the issue. Instead, she said, "Come on in and sit down, Rosemary. The sermon today is all about forgiveness."

Kirk waited until a Sunday-morning hush fell over the church grounds and gardens, then he got up to put his chair away and gather the rest of his things. He wanted to be gone before those doors swung open and the whole town flowed out to honor him.

He didn't deserve their honor, nor did he want it. He'd come here to do a job, and having done it, he'd be moving on. Same as always.

As he turned to go back inside the trailer, he saw Rosemary's father standing out on the back porch, staring up at the church steeple, his stern features set as firmly in place as the stones of the building he watched.

Something snapped inside Kirk. Without thinking, without hesitation, he slammed the trailer door shut and stalked toward Clayton. There was one last thing he had to do before he left Alba Mountain.

Rosemary sat toward the back of the overflowing church, her nostrils flaring at the scent of Easter lilies wafting out from the hundreds of potted arrangements sitting on the altar in honor of loved ones, both dead and gone, and living.

One of those lilies was in honor of her mother.

Remembering the lilies Kirk had picked for her, Rosemary pushed back the sudden burst of tears she knew was coming. She wouldn't cry anymore.

Crying wouldn't bring back her mother. Crying wouldn't change how her father felt about her. Crying wouldn't keep Kirk from leaving her. No, she wouldn't cry anymore. She was done crying; done feeling sorry for herself.

Kirk told her she couldn't change those around her, and he was right. So she intended to change herself. She intended to rededicate herself to this church, to this town, to the children she loved to take care of, to God. Thanks to Kirk, the church had been restored, and...so had she.

She owed him for that. He'd shown her how to face her past and fight for her peace of mind. Although the latter might be a long time in coming, she intended to find it again, somehow.

It would be hard, so very hard, without him.

The choir sang the "Hallelujah Chorus," their voices lifting in praise and joy.

Rosemary looked around to see her brother there with Nancy and Emily. Mother and daughter wore matching chambray dresses and white straw hats. Emily giggled and pulled her hat off, her eyes full of mischief and delight.

A few rows over, Rosemary saw Eric sitting with Melissa. They held hands and whispered, but Eric's eyes touched on Rosemary briefly.

She should be angry that he was here. He didn't have any right showing up here as if nothing had happened. How could he smile and act normal, anyway? Rosemary searched deep to find the compassion she had stored up for him, but maybe because she knew her own happiness was about to take off down the road, she resented Eric's happiness with Melissa.

As the joys and concerns were announced, Rosemary thought about her father, still so firm in his refusal to come back to church. Was he changing? Or would he always be bitter and full of sadness? Would he even care if he knew she was giving up her dreams with Kirk, just to stay here and be near him? Would he ever forgive her?

Kirk stepped up onto the porch, a squeaking floorboard groaning in protest, a lazy lizard sunning on a nearby azalea bush scurrying off at the intrusion. Clayton stood with his hands in his belt loops. His hair was combed and he was wearing a clean blue cotton button-down shirt.

"You did a nice job," he said to Kirk by way of greeting.

Kirk took that as an invitation to come on up onto the porch. "So you approve, after all?"

Clayton kept right on looking at the shining steeple. "I still say it was a waste, but the thing does look better."

"I didn't change it," Kirk responded, his own gaze

sweeping over his handiwork. "I simply improved on its existing beauty."

"Is that what you're trying to do with my daughter?"

The question, as well as the glint in Clayton's eyes, took Kirk by surprise, but gave him the opportunity to fight for his lady.

"Rosemary needs no improvement, sir. I'm leaving today, but before I go, I just wanted you to know— I've fallen in love with your daughter. I asked her to marry me and come with me, but she reluctantly refused."

Clayton seemed dazed by Kirk's directness, but quickly recovered to glare down at him. "Did you do something to hurt my daughter?"

Kirk shook his head, one hand on his hip, the other braced on a porch column. "No, sir. My only mistake was in the loving of your daughter. You, sir, you've done the hurting. Rosemary loves me, and wants to be with me, but she refuses to do so, because she feels she has to stay here with you."

Clayton snorted to hide the sorrow cresting in his eyes. "I don't need her hovering over me."

"She hovers because she loves you and she wants you to love her in return. She's waiting for your forgiveness."

That got Clayton's attention. "You mean to tell me, she won't go with you because...because she thinks I need to forgive her first?"

"That's the way of it," Kirk said, his gaze level with Rosemary's father's. "And I'm here to tell you—I don't like it one bit. I'm here to ask you to please release your daughter from this punishment you've put upon her. Rosemary has been punished enough. It's time you let her go.''

''With you?''

''I'd like that, but I'm leaving in a few minutes. I can't force her to come. Whether or not she decides to come with me doesn't matter as much as whether or not you can find it in your heart to forgive her. If I can't have her, if I can't love her, then I'm asking you to give her back her worth, so she can find someone to share her life with.''

Clayton looked toward the church. ''I've never held my daughter back.''

''Ah, but you have, sir,'' Kirk retorted, his Irish temper flaring. ''She waits for a kind word from you, a gesture to tell her that you don't blame her for her mother's death. Can you give her that?''

Clayton's expression softened then and for the first time he looked Kirk in the eye. ''I loved my wife, son,'' he said, his voice so low Kirk had to strain to hear. ''It's been a hard year, getting over what happened.''

''But you need to get over it,'' Kirk said gently. ''Bitterness won't bring your wife back.''

''No,'' Clayton agreed, his eyes growing misty. ''If that were true, she'd certainly be standing right here.''

''Your daughter *has* been right here, all along,'' Kirk reminded him. ''And she's been patiently waiting for your forgiveness. Please offer it to her. My coming here to ask you—it's the only gift I can extend to Rosemary, as proof of my love. But I don't ask this for myself. I ask it for her.''

With that, he turned on his heel before he started begging, and headed to his waiting trailer. He couldn't stop. He couldn't look back. He'd done enough restoring on this old church. His work was finished.

The choir and congregation finished singing "On the Wings of a Snow-White Dove," and everyone settled in to listen to Reverend Clancy's sermon. Rosemary tried to focus on his words, tried to snap to attention when he lifted his voice during a strong declaration, but her mind kept going back to Kirk. Was he gone already?

She heard Reverend Clancy say something about forgiveness, then she looked over at Eric. She didn't think she'd ever be able to forgive him completely, but she would try very hard to accept things now.

Then the minister talked about how Jesus had died for our sins.

"You don't have to worry," he said. "You don't have to ask for others to forgive your transgressions. This is what Easter is all about. This is why we are here this morning. Not to mourn death. But to celebrate life. We celebrate the life of Jesus Christ, who died for us, and was resurrected for us, therefore giving us eternal grace in heaven.

"'We walk by faith, not by sight,'" the reverend quoted. "And by faith, we must learn to forgive. 'For the things which are seen are temporary, but the things which are not seen are eternal.'"

Rosemary wanted to celebrate life, wanted to see eternity, but she didn't think she had that right. Maybe she didn't deserve to celebrate. Maybe her faith wasn't strong enough, after all. She was afraid to follow something she couldn't see, she was afraid to let herself heal.

The reverend went on, talking still about forgiving offenders. "'...on the contrary, you ought rather to forgive and comfort him, lest perhaps such a one be swallowed up with too much sorrow.' This is what Paul told the Corinthians," the minister said, one hand lifted high, "and this is what I say to you today. Don't be swallowed up by sorrow on this Easter Day, don't be consumed by grief. Rejoice. Christ is risen. And He lives in each and every one of us, and it is by His grace that we can rejoice. It is by His grace that we are reborn."

The morning light shifted through the stained-glass windows of the sanctuary, casting out a pale net of warmth, a beacon of brilliance that shimmered across the altar and glistened off the stark white blossoms of the Easter lilies. Rosemary saw that light, felt its warmth from her spot in the back of the church.

And in that bright, comforting light, she at last saw her own redemption.

The minister preached on, his voice gentle now as he retold the story of Jesus dying on the cross. Her heart pumping, her palms sweating, Rosemary heard him loud and clear, as if a church bell had just tolled for her only. She remembered Kirk telling her she would spend her life swallowed in sorrow. Swallowed in sorrow. Drowning in pain. Sinking in a pit of gloom and despair. Letting her only chance for happiness drift away when she should be rejoicing in a second chance.

She looked over at Eric, tears streaming down her face. Eric stared at her, a soft pleading light in his eyes. She saw Danny, concern coloring his features as he watched her. Aunt Fitz's sweet face became a blur as Rosemary rose out of the pew to push her way into the aisle. She had to get out of here. She had to find Kirk before it was too late for her second chance.

She ran down the aisle toward the exit, her breath

cutting through her body. She didn't want to be swallowed by sorrow. She wanted to be healed. She wanted to rejoice in her love for Kirk.

And now she knew, now she saw with a crystal, shimmering clarity, what she had to do. *She* had to forgive in order to be healed. She'd been waiting for her father to offer her redemption, when she wasn't willing to offer it to herself. She'd held her own forgiveness away from Eric, sitting in judgment of both him and herself when it wasn't her place to judge at all.

She stumbled out into the narthex, then lifted her head to the tiny stone steps leading to the belfry. Suddenly, she wanted to go up there where Kirk had worked and sweated. She wanted to see her world from his viewpoint, to be near all the places he'd touched and transformed; she wanted to be closer to God. She wanted to find her redemption, not from her father, not because she could at last forgive Eric, but because she had been given redemption all along, from God.

Absolution was there. All she had to do was climb the steps to find it. She'd been searching, asking, praying for answers, and God had sent Kirk to her.

Yet she'd turned him away.

Forcing herself to a slow calm, Rosemary started up the steps to the tower, her heart pounding, her tears fresh and cleansing, her mind clear for the first time in a very long time. Gripping the heavy wooden railing, she took one slow step after another until she was past the point she'd always stopped at before, until she was past returning down the winding stairs. Slightly dizzy, but determined to make the climb, she lifted her sandaled feet one step at a time.

At last, winded and deathly afraid, but adamant and

resigned, she reached the opening to the belfry. A ray of white-hot sunlight streamed down to touch her clammy skin, its warmth like a signal from the hand of God. She felt Him there, knew He was guiding her. She took the last few steps on faith alone and found herself standing inside the belfry, the morning wind rushing over her damp face, the birds singing a song of joy that lifted out on the breeze. And then, she looked out over the world she'd always known, and felt the healing power of God's love.

The view was incredible. The same houses, the same trees and gardens, the same mountains—but different now. She could see it all so much more clearly.

Then her heart shattered as she saw a trailer-truck hauling another trailer, moving slowly down the street, moving away from the church, moving toward the interstate.

"Kirk!" she said, wanting with all her heart to bring him back. She needed to tell him she wasn't afraid anymore. She needed to tell him that she'd been wrong, so wrong.

All this time she'd been waiting to be *given* forgiveness, but she hadn't been willing to *accept* forgiveness. Yet it had been hers for the asking.

Just as it was Eric's for the asking. Melissa was right. He didn't need her permission or her acceptance to start a new life. He had God's love and grace. And because Reverend Clancy had known that, Eric had, for the first time in his life, someone who believed he could be forgiven.

It all made such perfect sense now.

But too late. Kirk was gone. Rosemary watched as his rig rounded the corner. How could she stop him, when she'd sent him away?

Then she heard another truck cranking up, and fascinated, watched as her father backed his vehicle out of the driveway and headed in the same direction as Kirk. Unaware that she was even doing so, Rosemary leaned toward the edge of the sturdy stone belfry wall to watch the two most important men in her life, both of them driving away.

Her father pulled his truck up behind Kirk's, then honked the horn to get Kirk's attention. Then he hopped out of the truck, leaving the door wide-open.

"What's going on?" she whispered, afraid her father had finally snapped.

But as she watched, horrified and fascinated at the same time, something amazing, something special happened between the two men.

Kirk got out of the truck to confront her father. They exchanged words, then to her amazement, Kirk grinned and clasped her father's hand. But even more amazing, Clayton returned the handshake, and...he actually smiled. Then he got in his truck, turned it around and headed home.

Kirk, too, turned his rig around and drove back, back toward the church. Back, Rosemary realized with a soaring heart, to her.

At about the same time Kirk switched off the engine and climbed down out of his rig, the church doors came open as the congregation poured out, laughing and chattering, happy.

Rosemary watched, and waited as Kirk lifted his face up to find her standing there in the tower, underneath the steeple he'd repaired. Without hesitation, she lifted a hand to wave down at him. Kirk smiled up at her, then took off running, pushing through the amazed crowd, past the startled, curious faces, to step inside the church, then take the steps two at a time until he'd reached her side.

"Rosemary?" he called, his breath coming hard and heavy as he took the last step up beside her.

"You came back," she said much with the same awe he'd held when she'd chosen him over Eric.

"Aye, I was just about to turn around and come drag you out of the church, when your father literally hauled me out of me truck and told me to get myself home to you right away."

"My father said that? Whatever made him have such a change of heart?"

Kirk shrugged and tugged her into his arms. "Only the good Lord can answer that." He kissed her, then said, "I'm back, that's a fact, Rosemary, my love. And I'm willing to stay—"

"You don't have to," she interrupted, her eyes shining with a new joy. "I'm willing to go with you. I want to be with you, Kirk. I...I want to take that leap of faith."

His dark eyes grew misty. "Are you sure?"

"Very sure," she said, one hand roaming through his tousled hair. "I realized something today. I was waiting for everyone else to forgive me, waiting for everyone involved in this to change, when I was the one needing to make a change, I only had to forgive myself. You tried to tell me, but...I'm stubborn about some things."

"I like that in my women," he said, relief washing over his features. "I do so love you, though."

"Enough to carry me away?"

"Aye, enough to marry you right here in this church." He gazed down at her, then said, "We'll build us a house on the mountain."

Amazed, she asked, "But what about your work?"

"I'll work, and...you can come with me when the mood strikes you. I could use a good office manager. I want you with me, but...I know how important your home is to you." He lifted her chin, his eyes shining and sincere. "I promise you this, Rosemary. I will always come home to you. And that's not a compromise. It's what I want. It's my life."

"Sounds more like a commitment," she said, grateful that he was willing to make one, thankful that it wasn't too late for them.

"A firm, grounded commitment."

She kissed him, then laughed when a round of applause exploded from the captivated audience below.

Then Danny shouted, "Well, go ahead and ring the bells. This is a celebration, remember?"

Rosemary laughed, her heart soaring as she saw Clayton standing in the crowd, with Faye by his side.

Kirk let her go to reach for the bell rope. Then he took her hand in his free one. "Are you ready to step to the edge, then?"

Rosemary looked down at her father, her one last hope shining clearly in her eyes. Clayton lifted a hand in greeting, his eyes telling her what his heart had felt all along. She had his blessings, and his love, always.

She was forgiven. She was healed.

Rosemary looked at Kirk and nodded. "I'm ready."

Kirk grinned, then held her steady as he rang the bell several times. The chimes lifted out in a sweet melody, heralding a new beginning, for the church, for Eric and Melissa, for Clayton and Faye, and...for Rosemary and Kirk.

Epilogue

A few weeks later, a wedding was held on Alba Mountain. Clayton gave his daughter away, without remorse or regret, without any bitterness left between them, in the church that they both loved. Then the entire town headed for the top of the mountain, and Rosemary then stood on the edge of the cliff, stating the rest of her vows to the man she loved.

When the ceremony was over, Aunt Fitz handed Rosemary her wedding quilt which had been lovingly stored. "I knowed you'd be needing this. Knowed it the day I set eyes on your steeplejack. I saw the signs."

"I saw them, too, Aunt Fitz," Rosemary replied as she gazed up with loving eyes at her handsome husband. "It took me a while, but I finally saw all of the signs, too."

"Thank goodness," Kirk said, bending to kiss his wife, his finger touching on the meshed ring he'd inherited from an artistic Celtic ancestor, the ring he'd placed on his bride's finger to forever seal his love.

"Thank God above," Kirk's mother replied, lifting

her hands toward the sky. "The boy was pining away something fierce."

Aunt Fitz, who'd taken an instant liking to Edana, laughed heartily. "Ain't love grand?"

A new season had begun. Rosemary's time to heal had come. Now, with Kirk, she would have her time to love. Kirk hadn't changed Rosemary; he'd only added to her existing beauty.

After all, that was his job.

And in heaven, one special soul watched over Rosemary and her new husband with eternal care and immeasurable pride, sending out blessings of hope as her daughter started a new life with the man who'd restored Rosemary's faith, in herself, and in love.

* * * * *

Dear Reader,

This book is based on the death of my sister, Glenda. She and her husband were coming home from a shopping trip when another car pulled out in front of them. They both received extensive injuries, but after a complicated surgery, my sister went into cardiac arrest and died. The person driving the other vehicle was drunk.

This wasn't the driver's first offense, nor would it be her last. Since then, I've become very active in MADD (Mothers Against Drunk Driving) as a means of coping with this horrible tragedy.

While this story is fiction, the emotions I and my entire family went through are mirrored within these pages. This was one of the hardest books I've ever written, because I felt drained with each scene. But it was also very cathartic, because in spite of all of Rosemary's very real pain, she found her happy ending through her faith and through Kirk's unconditional love. These two things have sustained my family, too.

On a lighter note, I decided to write about a steeplejack after reading an article in my local paper. A friend called right after I'd read the article, and I told her I'd just found an idea for another book. That was a few years ago. I never gave up on that story, and I'm thrilled that my steeplejack has become a character. I loved him from the minute he popped into my head. I truly hope we can all learn from his work.

Restoration is an important thing, for both steeples and for souls that need repair. We all need time to heal. Writing this book has helped, and I hope it helps you, too.

Until next time, may the angels watch over you while you sleep.

Lenora Worth

Beginning in January from
Love Inspired...

FAITH, HOPE & CHARITY

a new series by

LOIS RICHER

Meet Faith, Hope and Charity—three close friends who find joy in doing the Lord's work...and playing matchmaker to members of their families.

Delight in the wonderful romances that befall the unsuspecting townsfolk of this small North Dakota town.

Enjoy the surprise as these matchmaking ladies find romance is in store for each of them as well!

Don't miss any of the heartwarming and emotional stories.

FAITHFULLY YOURS
January '98

A HOPEFUL HEART
April '98

SWEET CHARITY
July '98

Love Inspired

IFHC1

The lives and loves of the residents of Duncan,
Oklahoma, continue to warm readers' hearts in
this series from *Love Inspired*...

*by
Arlene
James*

*Every day brings new challenges for young
Reverend Bolton Charles and his congregation.
But together they are sure to gain the strength to
overcome all obstacles—and find love along the way!*

You've enjoyed these wonderful stories:

THE PERFECT WEDDING
(September 1997)

AN OLD-FASHIONED LOVE
(November 1997)

Now Reverend Bolton Charles gets a second chance
at happiness in:

A WIFE WORTH WAITING FOR
(January 1998)

And a couple who marry for the sake of a child find
unexpected love in:

WITH BABY IN MIND
(March 1998)

Available in January from *Love Inspired*...

NIGHT MUSIC

**Don't miss this powerful tale
of suspense and renewed faith
by bestselling author**

SARA MITCHELL

Beautiful Rae Prescott is drawn into a world of
intrigue when she becomes Agent Caleb Myers's
prime suspect. But when Rae's life is endangered,
Caleb suddenly becomes *her* protector. Rae must
learn to put her trust in Caleb and rediscover her
faith in the Lord if she is to make it through this
adventure...with her life.

INM198

Dear Reader,

Thank you for reading this selection from the *Love Inspired* series. Please take a few moments to tell us your thoughts on this book. Your answers will help us in choosing future books for this series. When you have finished answering the survey, please mail it to the appropriate address listed below.

1. How would you rate this book?

1.1 ❑ Excellent   .4 ❑ Fair
.2 ❑ Very good   .5 ❑ Poor
.3 ❑ Satisfactory

2. What prompted you to buy this particular book?

_____
_____ 2,7

3. Will you purchase another book from the *Love Inspired* series in the future?

8.1 ❑ Yes—Why?_____
_____ 9,14

.2 ❑ No—Why not? _____
_____ 15,20

4. Did you find the spiritual/faith elements in this story to be:

21.1 ❑ Too strong? .2 ❑ Too weak? .3 ❑ Just right?

Comments _____
_____
_____ 22,27

5. Did you find the romance elements in this story to be:

28.1 ❑ Too strong? .2 ❑ Too weak? .3 ❑ Just right?

LIDEC3A

6. **What other types of inspirational stories would you like to read?**

   29 ❑ Mystery 30 ❑ Historical 31 ❑ Anthologies
   32 ❑ Humor 33 ❑ Nonfiction
   34 ❑ Other _____

7. **Where did you purchase this book? (choose one)**

   35.1 ❑ National chain bookstore (e.g. Waldenbooks)
   .2 ❑ Christian bookseller
   .3 ❑ Supermarket
   .4 ❑ General or discount merchandise store (e.g. K mart)
   .5 ❑ Secondhand bookstore
   .6 ❑ Other _____ 36,41

8. **Which of the following types of paperback books have you read in the past 12 months?**

   42 ❑ Contemporary popular women's fiction
      (e.g. Danielle Steel, Sandra Brown)
   43 ❑ Romance series books (e.g. Harlequin,
      Silhouette, Loveswept)
   44 ❑ Historical romance books
   45 ❑ Mystery
   46 ❑ Inspirational fiction
   47 ❑ Inspirational nonfiction
   48 ❑ Other _____ 52,57

   Inspirational Romance Fiction

   49 ❑ Heartsong 50 ❑ Palisades 51 ❑ Other _____ 58,63

9. **Please indicate your age range:**

   64.1 ❑ Under 18 years .4 ❑ 35 to 49 years
   .2 ❑ 18 to 24 years .5 ❑ 50 to 64 years
   .3 ❑ 25 to 34 years .6 ❑ 65 years or older

Mail To:
In U.S.: "Love Inspired", P.O. Box 1387,
       Buffalo, NY 14240-1387
In Canada: "Love Inspired", P.O. Box 609,
       Fort Erie, Ontario, L2A 5X3   LIDEC3B